THE ARTIST

Praise for Sheri Lewis Wohl

Drawing Down the Mist

"Vampires loving humans. Vampires hating vampires. Vampires killing humans. Vampires killing vampires. Good vampires. Evil vampires. Internet-savvy vampires. Lovers turning enemies. Nurturing revenge for a century. Kindness. Cruelty. Love. Action. Fights. Insta-love. This one has everything for a true drama." —*reviewer@large*

Cause of Death

"I really liked these characters, all of them, and wouldn't say no to a sequel, or more."—*Jude in the Stars*

"*CSI* meets *Ghost Whisperer*…The pace was brilliantly done, the suspense was just enough, and I'm not ashamed to admit that I had no idea who the serial killer was until almost the end."—*Words and Worlds*

"*Cause of Death* by Sheri Lewis Wohl is one creepy and well-written murder mystery. It is one of the best psychological thrillers I've read in a while."—*Rainbow Reflections*

"[A] light paranormal romance with a psycho killer and some great dogs."—*C-Spot Reviews*

"There's a ton of stuff in here that I enjoy very much, such as the light paranormal aspect of the book, and the relationship between our two leads is very nice if a bit of a slow burn. The case was engaging enough that I didn't really set this title down once I started it."—*Colleen Corgel, Librarian, Queens Public Library*

"Totally disturbing, and very, very awesome…The characters were amazing. The supernatural tint was never overdone, and even the stuff from the killer's point of view, while disturbing, was awesomely done as well. It was a great book and a fun (and intense) read."—*Danielle Kimerer, Librarian (Nevins Memorial Library, Massachusetts)*

"This thriller has spooky undertones that make it an intense page turner. You won't be able to put this book down."—*Istoria Lit*

She Wolf

"I really enjoyed this book—I couldn't put it down once I started it. The author's style of writing was very good and engaging. All characters, including the supporting characters, were multi-layered and interesting."—*Melina Bickard, Librarian, Waterloo Library (UK)*

The Talebearer

"As a crime story, it is a good read that had me turning pages quickly…The book is well-written and the characters are well-developed."—*Reviews by Amos Lassen*

Twisted Echoes

"A very unusual blend of lesbian romance and horror…[W]oven throughout this modern romance is a neatly plotted horror story from the past, which bleeds ever increasingly into the present of the two main characters. Lorna and Renee are well matched and face ever-increasing danger from spirits from the past. An unusual story that gets tenser and more interesting as it progresses." —*Pippa Wischer, Manager at Berkelouw Books, Armadale*

Twisted Screams

"[A] cast of well-developed characters leads you through a maze of complex emotions."—*Lunar Rainbow Reviewz*

Vermilion Justice

"[T]he characters are so dynamic and well-written that this becomes more than just another vampire story. It's probably impossible to read this book and not come across a character who reminds you of someone you actually know. Wohl takes something as fictional as vampires and makes them feel real. Highly recommended." —*GLBT Reviews: The ALA's GLBT Round Table*

By the Author

Crimson Vengeance

Burgundy Betrayal

Scarlet Revenge

Vermilion Justice

Twisted Echoes

Twisted Whispers

Twisted Screams

Necromantia

She Wolf

Walking Through Shadows

Drawing Down the Mist

The Talebearer

Cause of Death

Avenging Avery

All That Remains

The Artist

The Artist

by

Sheri Lewis Wohl

2022

THE ARTIST

ISBN 13: 978-1-63679-150-0

This Trade Paperback Original Is Published By
Bold Strokes Books, Inc.
P.O. Box 249
Valley Falls, NY 12185

First Edition: August 2022

Credits
Editor: Shelley Thrasher
Production Design: Stacia Seaman
Cover Design by Jeanine Henning

This book is dedicated to my grandmother, Ilah.
An artist in her own right,
she taught me to see a world full of color and shape and beauty.

Be not overcome of evil,
but overcome evil with good.
Romans 12:21 KJV

PROLOGUE

Mona Lisa threw the brush down and stared at the image starting to take form on the canvas. She longed to do more than simply throw away the brush. Tears pooled in her eyes. They didn't fall. No more tears. Not in front of her.

"Why have you stopped? This must be done, and you know it."

"I don't want to see the face."

The slap to the back of her head made her even more determined not to cry. It happened every time she said no, and she wouldn't give her the satisfaction. "Continue."

"No."

The next slap was harder, and it grew more difficult to hold back the tears. "You will finish this today. Arabelle is expecting a full series by Tuesday."

"I don't care." Her eyes never left the face that had begun to reveal itself beneath her brush. Her stomach hurt. It always hurt.

"This will be your biggest show yet. Buyers are coming from all over the world, so you better damn well care."

Tears burned behind her eyes. She would not cry in front of her, not that she would be granted even an ounce of comfort. By the time she'd turned six, she'd figured out the only comfort she'd ever get was from herself. No emotion was ever allowed, only the work produced at the tip of her expensive brushes.

"When will it be enough?"

"Never."

Again, not unexpected. She couldn't be sure of the exact balance in her trust fund, although the last time she'd sneaked a glimpse at a statement, the eight-figure amount stunned her. Of course, they would want to keep it high, because the higher the bottom line, the more they gleaned for their trustee fees. She'd been supporting their preferred lifestyle since her preschool days.

She brought up her chin and stared at her. The hard angles, the eyes so dark they were almost black, the thin lips always pressed together. His expression was as hard as hers. She'd never painted their faces, never wanted to because she'd spent every day of her life with them. The studio, this studio, for any other artist would be heaven. For her it represented a prison, and as her eighteenth birthday approached, she longed for release.

"I'm done." No more paintings. No more shows where they dressed her up in expensive gowns that made her look exotic and unique, where they paraded the wonder child they pretended to love and cherish. Or perhaps that wasn't quite fair. They loved her because of what she could do for them. For the *commissions* they siphoned from the sales of her work. She would give them credit for knowing how to make her money and, by extension, their money, grow.

The air changed as she started to step away, not fast enough, and the blow that struck her on the back of the head took her to her knees. Stars floated in front of her eyes, and a moment later, blackness enveloped her as she crumpled to the hardwood floor.

Her eyes fluttered open and then snapped shut again. She blew out a breath before making a second attempt to open her eyes. The reset helped, and the lightning bolts retreated. Bathed in shady light, the day outside the massive windows faded. Silence, blessed silence, wrapped around her, alone in her prison.

She sat up and ran her fingers through her long, silky hair. Her fingers came away wet from the gash that still oozed, and she stared down at red fingertips. A first, though not an unsurprising turn. The stakes rose with each progressive show, for them anyway. She cared for the money only for what it might provide her: freedom.

Her brush lay on the floor right where she'd thrown it several hours earlier when bright sunlight had poured through the windows. No doubt she'd been sprawled out on the floor, the door bolted from the outside, the whole time. It would be morning before it opened again, if she were lucky. It didn't require a big leap to figure out how they would react to her defiance. Not the first time they'd spilled her blood, even if this was the first time she'd experienced an injury to her head that resulted in an extended blackout. It wouldn't change the pattern. She'd resisted, and punishment would follow. They would withhold food, water, and freedom until she became compliant. Maybe she should have seen it coming. She'd gotten older and bigger, and the punishment more forceful in return.

Sighing, she pushed to her feet and stood for a few seconds, letting the dizziness pass. Stars floated in front of her eyes, and nausea wafted through her stomach. As it did, she had an overwhelming urge to pick up her brush. Rarely did she paint without the glorious light streaming through the windows. She swayed, and once more everything went black.

She blinked and stepped back, the room and the canvas coming into focus. A glance at the clock let her know more than an hour had passed. She didn't remember putting a new canvas on the easel. She didn't remember painting a woman's face. Beautiful, with green eyes and long auburn hair, her full lips were parted in a silent scream. What made her lean over and retch was the bullet hole painted in the center of the woman's head.

CHAPTER ONE

"You piece of shit." Casey stared at the remains of her garden fountain as her fingers danced over the handle of her gun. It shouldn't surprise her, and yet it did. Pissed her off too. The damage screamed a woman scorned.

Except she hadn't dumped Isla. Not technically anyway. In her opinion, it had been a breakup, plain and simple, and even that was a stretch. They were not right for each other, and Casey had figured it out pretty quickly. Not so for Isla. Somewhere along the line, she took their very brief dating experience as a full-on lasting relationship.

When Casey backed off and told her with kindness, and with complete honesty, that they weren't right for each other, things went south in a nanosecond. Isla had acted as though they'd been together for years, when in reality, they'd had only a couple of dates. A few kisses and nothing more. There had been fallout ever since, though this was a new low even for Isla. She blew out a long breath as she stared at the rubble that had been a beautiful flowing fountain when she left for work this morning. Isla had gone too far with this fit of temper, and she wondered why Casey called it quits early on?

Casey reached for her phone and then thought better of it. First things first. Any good detective would have their file complete before making a move. A quick glance at the camera on the eave of the house with the tiny green light glowing let her know it remained in working order. Just what she'd hoped for. Isla must not have caught on to the security measure Casey had installed earlier in the month. It just paid for itself.

Inside, she powered up her laptop and clicked on the security-program icon. It opened, and she rewound it to around the time she'd backed her car out of the driveway to leave for work. About fifteen minutes later, Isla appeared in the frame. As she watched the scene unfold on the screen, she shook her head. "Oh, Isla, you need a good doctor, and I can get you a list of names."

Two hours later, the techs left her house with the footage downloaded and a report on the damage. Property crimes tended to garner very little law-enforcement response these days, due to staffing issues, unless, of course, the homeowner happened to be a valued member of said law enforcement. Friends in high places and all that. Being a career public servant had some perks, a fact she felt compelled to remind her barely impressed family of every now and again. With a brother who was a doctor and a sister who had found her calling in higher education, a mere detective didn't rate very high on the pride scale in her family.

"You okay?"

She jumped and spun. "What the fuck, Stan? You almost gave me a heart attack." Good thing he possessed better-than-average CPR skills.

Her brother smiled. "Heard it on the scanner and thought I'd swing by on the way home."

She frowned before she remembered that the emergency-room docs at the local hospital kept a scanner in the break room. Kind of weird, in her opinion, but it had been in that room for decades and was part of a strange tradition. Rumor had it, the son of a doctor years ago kept getting himself in trouble with the law, and said doc brought in the scanner to keep tabs on him. It had never left, although several updated versions had replaced the original.

"You don't have to check up on me."

Still in his light blue scrubs, his curly dark hair flattened against his head after a day wearing a cap, he shrugged. "Of course I don't have to. Just my job, dude, just my job."

"In other words, if you don't come by and make sure I'm still alive, Mama will kick your ass."

He smiled and gave her a little salute. "You always were smart."

"Just not smart enough to fall in line and become a highly educated intellectual like you and Eleana."

He walked over and gave her a hug. "Don't let Mama get under your skin. You do know Sissy and I are jealous, right?"

She returned his hug before stepping back. "What the hell are you talking about?" What was there to be jealous about? They'd be paying off their houses long before she even got close to holding the deed in her hand.

"Seriously? You don't know?"

"Seriously, I have no fucking idea."

His laughter always made her smile. How this guy got through medical school and still remained the family bright light, she'd never know. The only time she ever saw him in a bad mood was when he lost a patient. Nobody could begrudge him that. "Dude, you are the only one with enough balls to do what you wanted to. You think being a doc was my idea?"

Dumb question. "Yeah. As a matter of fact, I did."

"Huh? I guess I'm a better actor than I thought. No, my brilliant sister. Being a doctor was what Mama and Papi wanted me to do. I had visions of becoming a screenwriter." He spoke with such emotion that she stopped and really looked at him.

"No shit?"

"I shit you not."

Memories of him writing and producing films as a teenager swarmed over her. He'd drafted all of his friends, as well as her and Eleana, as actors. She'd been terrible, but he never seemed to care. "I thought that was just a thing you did as a kid. I didn't realize it was anything beyond that."

A shadow crossed his face, wiping away the sunshine of a moment before. "Nobody did."

For the first time in years, she really studied her brother. She'd taken his journey to a medical degree as a given. He'd been brilliant as a child, graduated valedictorian at their high school and top of his medical-school class. His trek to becoming a doctor was just as magnificent as everything else he'd accomplished. It never occurred to her that he might have dreams beyond medicine.

"I didn't know."

He shrugged again. "I made a choice."

Had he made the right one? "Are you happy?"

"In a way, sure."

"But?"

A long beat before he answered. "But I long for more."

❖

"I'm not going to do it. I'm not going to do it. I. Am. Not. Going. To. Do. It." Tula Crane leaned both hands against the door of the large walk-in closet and waited for the urge to pass. She blew out a breath and stepped back. No worries. She was stronger than the push.

Or not. She opened the door.

For at least a full minute she stood and stared at her stash. Tears pricked at her eyes, and a familiar anger raced through her. Her hands trembled, and she took long, even breaths as she willed herself not to move. To step over the closet threshold would be to give in completely. She hadn't done that in years, and she wasn't going to do it today.

"Why now?" she whispered to no one, and no one answered.

Another series of long breaths and she stepped into the closet. Not temptation. Compulsion. She flicked the switch just inside the door, and the space filled with bright light. The shelves were long and white and tidy. Everything in its place, just as she'd left it after she'd moved in. It might have been better to toss it all and push on from that part of her life. Except to say it was only part of her life didn't ring true. She couldn't embrace the lie any more than articulate it. The contents of this closet defined her heart and soul, and that's why she could never bring herself to throw any of it away. Instead, she'd chosen to lock it up and then pretend it didn't exist. After a few years, she'd gotten pretty good at doing that. At a superficial level anyway.

The moment her fingers made contact with the easel, a thrill coursed through her whole body. No mystery how she'd feel when she picked up the handmade, hog-bristle brushes. Or the tubes of paint lined up in the boxes engraved with the letters ML. At least initially, joy would belong to her, and she'd treasure the good.

With the easel set up in front of the big windows that looked out over the lake, and with a blank canvas resting on it, all she needed was to retrieve her brushes and paints. The last part turned out to be more difficult than she would have thought, once she opened that door and stepped inside.

"Hey. I didn't know you painted too."

Tula screamed as she spun. "What in the hell?"

Diane Macy stood in the doorway to her studio with a big smile. Her thick, unnaturally red hair was pulled back into a ponytail, and, as usual, she wore jeans, a skin-tight spandex shirt, and bright Chucks. She definitely had a distinct style…and personality, both of which got on Tula's last good nerve.

"Sorry." She shrugged and grinned. "I knocked, you didn't answer, and the front door was unlocked. Knew you wouldn't mind if I came in and tracked you down."

Mental note: bolt the damn doors. And, yes, she minded a great deal. "What do you need?" Did that sound as bitchy as she felt? Definitely. Good. Diane made herself entirely too at home around Tula's house, and it pissed her off. Though they were next-door neighbors, she didn't have a hall pass to use whenever she felt like it. Didn't mean she actually liked the woman either, because that was iffy at best. She'd rubbed Tula wrong from the very first hello.

"Came to invite you over to have dinner with me and the bro. He's here from the East Coast for a couple of weeks, working on some stories, and I knew you'd want to meet him. I mean, we've been neighbors for a while now, and you two haven't gotten a chance to get to know each other. He's pretty good looking, as personable as *moi*, and his network job means he can get you awesome contacts for your work. He knows everybody everywhere. It could be a huge boost for you, and the two of you would look great together."

Oh, dear God! Nope and nope. "I appreciate the offer…"

"But you have other plans."

She nodded. "I do."

A frown replaced Diane's smile. "You always have other plans. Is it that you just don't like me? Or what?"

"I like you fine." Oh, now that was a lie. Diane was a giant pain in the ass, and Tula would move in a heartbeat if she didn't love her house on the lakeshore with the beautiful lawn and exceptional view. "I have a lot on my plate." That part wasn't a lie. She had contract deadlines to meet, copy to finish, logos to design. It didn't matter that she had plenty of time to get it all done.

"Come on. How much can a graphics artist have on her plate?"

Nothing too insulting about that, and she wasn't even going to bother to correct her on the difference between a graphics artist and what Tula really did as a graphics designer. Not worth the effort. "Quite a bit, but thank you for the invitation. And now if you don't mind, I have some work to finish."

Diane waved her hands in the air. "Yeah, yeah. I get it. I'll let myself out." A little snitty.

Like she let herself in, Tula didn't add. She did follow her to the front door and bolt it once Diane got halfway down the walk. Until she disappeared, Tula didn't move. Even after she thought it safe, she leaned against the door and stared. Like she didn't have enough on her mind at the moment, she had to also worry about a nosy neighbor invading her private space.

When she finally moved away from the door, she walked slowly back to the studio. The hope that the intrusion might weaken the compulsion that pushed her to crack the closet door faded the second she stepped into the room. Just as strong as earlier. Maybe even stronger or, perhaps, more urgent. The feelings from another time and place rushed in, and the tears she'd held back earlier now fell.

"I don't want to do this," she whispered and could swear the universe whispered back.

"You must."

❖

"I've got to help her." Angel stood at the water's edge and stared across the expanse of green lawn that flowed toward the tall windows of Tula's house.

"Yes, you do. It's starting, and that means you're on deck." He stood slightly behind her, mere inches from the lapping water, his hands in his pockets.

She looked away from the house and began to pace. "I know. I know. I know."

"Don't worry. You can figure this out. I have faith in you." The late-afternoon sun shone on his long, blond hair, his blue eyes intense.

"We've kept her safe for such a long time now. How could evil be drawn to her once more? I feel like I failed her. It shouldn't have to happen again."

"Not completely accurate. It could have been so much worse last time, if you hadn't helped her along. And remember, in the end, it not only stopped the killings, but it got her out of that situation. How can you consider that as failing?"

She stopped pacing and let her gaze wander once more toward Tula's house. "In a way, yes, she escaped. The life she's built in these last years has been good. Lonely, but at least she's been safe and free from harm. That didn't solve the bigger problem. It only paused it. Dark forces are closing in on her again, and it's not right. It's not fair. It should be over for her. All over. The universe owes her, not the other way around."

"You can't fix everything." Her gaze met his.

Of course, she knew that. Her transition hadn't wiped away the intelligence she'd been born with. She'd also been doing this long enough to have a feel for the way it worked. She could guide, and that was it. Some things, like free will, were out of her control. "Not everything."

He studied her face, his eyes bright. "You have an idea. See. I knew you'd figure it out."

She looked away and began to walk slowly along the shoreline, her mind whirling. The chatter of the ducks paddling near the shore was a peaceful sound. Nature had a way of soothing the soul. Blue walked behind her, not saying anything. Their close partnership meant that over the years, he'd come to know her well. He not only knew her, but he also shared her thoughts—most of the time. "I've already put it into motion," she finally admitted. She hated to do it, but what other choice did she have? Tula could make a difference, and that fact couldn't be ignored.

"You think that's wise?"

"It's the best choice, even if it hurts her heart. In the end, I have to believe she'll understand."

He smiled and shrugged. "She'll forgive you because she's a truly kind and loving woman. Like you."

"You always say that. My deeds would argue the point and prove you wrong."

"I only say what's true."

"Sometimes, we have a very different definition of truth."

Chapter Two

Stan took off, leaving Casey in the garden mulling over her brother's life-goal confession and her own failure to be open enough to fully see and appreciate him. She promised herself to do better and jumped when her phone buzzed.

At the name on the screen, she groaned. "Yeah, Mike. What's up?"

Her partner sounded as grumpy as she felt. "They found her."

"Her?"

"Cindy Homer." The irritation in his voice grew. Questions were his favorite. Not answering them, that is. He did love to ask them.

"Please tell me she's alive." With the chaos of the last couple of hours, the missing-woman case she and Mike had been working didn't immediately jump to mind. A little embarrassing, considering she'd been looking at a picture of her for the last two days. A first-grade teacher with bright green eyes and an infectious smile. A favorite educator who wholly embraced the leave-no-child-behind philosophy. Not the kind of woman who put herself in the path of danger.

"Negatory."

Why couldn't he talk like a normal person? "She's dead."

"Isn't that what I just said?"

She gave up. "You want to meet somewhere or pick me up?" Mike lived on the family farm between Moses Lake and Othello. She was located closer to town while still living on acreage. Nothing fancy, but she felt blessed to have her few acres complete with a large garden, grapevines, fruit trees, a big Maine coon cat, and even a couple of cows. Some might think it a lot for one person to take care of. She loved it, although with her unpredictable schedule, at times she had to rely on friends and family to cover the chores. There were advantages to having a relatively large family and lifelong friends.

"I'm already on the road. I'll pick you up in fifteen."

"Where did they find her?"

"Potholes."

"Narrows it right down." Given the Potholes Reservoir encompassed some 40,000 acres, that didn't tell her much. Mike had a habit of generalizing things while expecting her to magically know every detail about a case, a crime scene, or an arrest. She was good. She wasn't that good.

"Okay, okay. Not far off the Dune Ramble hike. Geez. You could just wait until I pick you up for the details instead of wasting time now." Given that he talked to her from the car, filling her in while he drove wasn't exactly a waste of time. She didn't point out that fact to him.

Her jaw tightened. *Relax, relax, relax.* Some of the tension released. "You can fill in the rest when you get here."

He didn't say good-bye, and she didn't expect him to. Some days she considered moving to Spokane or Seattle or Portland. Somewhere bigger with a much more diverse police force. Sure, she understood every agency had assholes, but at least in a bigger department, it would be easier to work around them. Here, she was stuck with jerks like Mike in her face, every single day, and frankly, it got pretty fucking old.

She rolled her shoulders and shook out her hands. No room for the *what-ifs* to occupy her thoughts. Plenty of time for that later. She walked to the end of her driveway and waited for Mike's dark, unmarked SUV to roll in and stop next to her. She sat in the passenger's seat.

"We don't have much time. It'll be dark soon."

Casey buckled her seatbelt. "Drive fast then."

"Whatever you say." He took her at her word, turning on the lights and racing toward the crime scene.

Despite his promise to share the details when they were together, they didn't talk on the way out to the Potholes. Just as well. Sometimes it helped to view a scene without any prior information. A clean look.

A uniformed deputy met them at the trailhead and walked them into the site located within the state-park portion of the area. Someone didn't put much effort into hiding their handiwork, which created far more work for the investigators currently at the scene. The responding officers had done a good job of protecting the perimeter by marking it off with crime-scene tape stretched between stakes pounded into the ground. Plenty of sagebrush and low bushes, very few trees. Even more protruding baseball-sized rocks that made the ground challenging to walk on. It required nice, strong ankles. Maybe that's why the killer didn't take the body farther in. A sprained ankle wasn't worth the risk.

"Damn." She uttered the oath softly because, for some reason, the quiet of this place required it. The woman lay on her back, her arms stretched out to her sides, her feet together. Her eyes were open and gazing sightless at the sky. Her clothing remained intact. Not deviant or sexualized, just dead, a bullet hole in the middle of her forehead. Someone intended to make a statement here. They would have to figure out what it was.

"Not a sex crime." Mike stood staring down at the body, his hands in his pockets.

Even though she agreed, she also preferred not to make any definitive conclusions at the scene. There were ways to do investigation and ways not to. "Let's wait to make that call until we get the results from the ME."

"Trust me. I know what I'm talking about."

His unsaid message for all to hear: she didn't. She'd been on the Moses Lake police force since she graduated with a degree in Criminal Justice from Washington State University. Had spent almost six years as a detective, and still he continued to treat her like she'd just come out of the academy. Some days she wanted to scream.

Instead, she said calmly, "And I know it's not our job to make that call out here." It might have been better strategy to let it go, but that wasn't really her style.

❖

For a long time after Diane left, Tula stood in the studio and stared at the easel. The paints remained in the closet. Finally, she closed her eyes and allowed her fingers to dance over the stretched canvas. A thrill went through her, and with it came tears. Once upon a time the mere touch of a canvas had brought her only pure excitement, a child's delight that made her want to spend all her time with paints and brushes and imagination. Bliss. Until it wasn't.

It wasn't joy that brought the tears now. Not a reunion with her happy place. Run away, her mind screamed at her. Run away!

Ten minutes later, she stood again in front of the blank canvas with a brush in her hand. The paints were now spread out on her table right next to the jar holding her favorite brushes of varying sizes and materials. She dipped the one in her hand into the paint waiting on her palette. "Here we go again," she murmured. Might as well give in. She'd tried to resist the pull twenty years ago and failed big-time. The compulsion came even more intensely now. She closed her eyes, and the world faded into blackness.

When she opened them again, an image had appeared beneath her brush as though a model had been sitting next to her. She tilted her head and studied the face. No one she'd ever seen before. Moses Lake wasn't a big metropolitan area, not like her hometown, though she didn't wonder why every face was a mystery. Tula wasn't very social. She kept to herself and had since she'd made this her home almost fifteen years ago.

The light had begun to fade by the time she opened her eyes. It didn't surprise her. It had always happened this way. One minute alert and aware, and the next, the passage of significant chunks of time she couldn't account for. Several decades and thousands of miles separated her from the person she'd been before, yet the proof that nothing had changed at all stared her in the face.

She dropped the brushes into the jar and set the palette down. Slowly she put the caps on her paints, though she left them scattered on the small table. In a way, to finally put paint to canvas again felt like coming home, like a piece of her soul had been returned.

Pain marched side by side with the peaceful feeling because she had no delusions about what the work meant. It wasn't a simple portrait of a beautiful woman, not at all, and now she had a dilemma on her hands. Or two, most likely.

The pounding on her front door cut her pondering short. If it turned out to be Diane again, she would lose it. After she peeked through the sidelight, she pulled the door open. No irritating next-door neighbor. "What's up?"

Angel stepped inside sans an invitation. "I need to place an order with you ASAP." She continued by Tula in the direction of the studio.

"I'm not really working today." She tried to cut Angel off at the pass. Nobody should be in her studio at the moment, and they sure didn't need to see what sat on her easel.

"It'll be fine. It's always fine, and it won't take more than ten minutes." Angel kept walking.

"Angel, really…" Too late. She'd let herself into Tula's studio.

"Okay, that's new." Hands on her hips, Angel stood studying the painting. "A little different than your normal work."

Her heart hammered and her mind whirled. Nothing came to her that might make sense if she tried to explain. "I haven't painted for a while. Thought I'd give it a run for a change. See if I can still do it." Lame.

Slowly, Angel turned to her. "You have talent. That's clear."

"A little." A little lie too. She knew exactly how much talent she possessed.

"This is somewhat freaky." Angel pointed at the face on her canvas.

Don't ask. "How so?"

Angel raised a single eyebrow. "Do you not ever check the news?"

She shook her head. The less she knew, the easier to maintain her equilibrium. "I try not to."

"Do me a favor. Pull up the local news channel on your phone."

"What?"

"Trust me. It'll make sense."

Weird request, but Angel was an interesting friend/client, who always marched to the beat of her own drummer. One of the reasons she really liked her. She picked up her phone, punched in the local news, and sighed when the lead story popped up. "Damn it."

"Damn it, indeed. She's been missing for several days."

"Not good."

"Not at all. Do you know her?" Angel inclined her head toward the canvas.

"No."

"So how did you paint her face, and more important, why does she have a bullet hole in the middle of her forehead?"

❖

The wind picked up as Angel walked away from Tula's house. Her face was cold, like the coldness that wrapped around her heart. She stopped a good distance away and stuffed her hands into her pockets. "It worked. She's been able to do it."

Blue nodded. "It's getting a pretty good toehold here, and you did what you had to. You couldn't protect her from this."

"She can help them. I know she can." Was she trying to convince him or herself?

He turned away and tipped his head to the sky. It grew dark as the stars began to shine. "Yes, she can."

"I don't disagree, but it hurts. She's been through so much already.

It feels wrong for her to have to relive it. I also don't want her to run from her beautiful home."

"She's stronger now. She was essentially a child before."

Angel remembered the first time she'd glimpsed her pretty little face and bright, shining eyes—so full of hope and life and promise. And it had all been taken from her. In the last twenty years, she'd gotten some bit of it back, and now, with this, it could be wiped away forever.

"At first, yes. She was able to be a child for such a short amount of time. They made her grow up too fast, pushed her when they shouldn't have."

"You know as well as I do how much is out of our control." Blue had a unique way with logic and the ability to consistently see the whole picture.

She often saw things quite differently. "Sometimes I wonder if it's us. Are we the beacon and she's the bait? I just don't know anymore."

"Does it really matter in the end?" Again, his logical and big-picture way of thinking.

"I suppose not." Chills raced down her arms at memories she didn't care for. "This job is so much harder than I ever believed possible. I'm incredibly tired."

He smiled, his eyes bright. "What living, breathing person, beautiful Angel, would have had any concept of what we were in for?"

He hit that nail on the head. "I keep wondering when it will end."

"It will end with the truth."

She tipped her head back and studied the night sky. "I don't know what the truth is."

"I think you do, and when the day comes that you embrace it, well, then I believe it will end. I only wish I could do more for you."

"Your hands are tied. I get that. It's soothing that you've always been at my side. I don't know how I'd have been able to persevere without you, even though we both know I don't deserve you."

"Come," he said. "We need to go."

She didn't ask where because she knew, and soon enough, they were standing among the sagebrush. For over an hour they watched law enforcement process the scene. At least ten officers, plenty of yellow crime-scene tape, techs, and a single body bag. With a shake of her head, she walked on into the night. As much as she hated what lay ahead, she couldn't avoid it either. She didn't ask for the journey she was on. She'd earned it just the same. No turning back. "We need to get to work. We're running out of time."

CHAPTER THREE

Every once in a while, Mike surprised her. Casey expected him to get pissed when she challenged him, and instead, he chuckled. Not loud. That would be unprofessional at a murder scene. Just enough to let her know that he'd heard her.

"I have to admit, Wilson, you've got some balls."

"After working with you for six years, I better. Self-protection."

"I might make a good detective out of you yet."

She thought better of correcting him this time. He wasn't making her anything. She was doing the work herself. Sometimes, however, silence was a much better option. Instead, she began to look around the area. The smallest thing could make a difference, and she didn't want to miss a single potential clue.

"Why here, do you think? This place presents a real challenge when it comes to hiking, and hiking with a body is crazy."

"You just said the operative word. Crazy. Don't try to rationalize the irrational, if you catch my drift." He took a toothpick out of his pocket and started chewing it.

Basic criminal theory. That's not what she meant. She didn't try to explain her thought process to Mike. He'd spin to whatever line of inquiry he happened to be working on. "Yeah. I catch your drift." She'd throw him a bone instead. Easier to work together that way, even if it meant she acquiesced to him more than she should have to. Some days were like that.

"You see anything?" His question caught her off guard. He'd changed lanes without signaling.

She did a full circle and narrowed her eyes. The wind picked up, a little cool and filled with the scents of the desert-like landscape. Under any other circumstances, she'd enjoy it because it smelled like home.

She'd run across this rocky landscape as a child, occasionally crashing and burning. Her knees had the scars to prove it. She wouldn't change her past for anything.

"Hard to see much in the dark." Even before it had grown dark, she hadn't noticed anything that screamed important to her. Whoever killed Cindy Homer had come here to dump her body, plain and simple. The rest of what drove him to kill her lurked far beyond the grounds of the Potholes.

Weirdly, though, she felt watched. It wasn't Mike, who did stare as she scanned the surrounding area. No, something else. Someone else. The killer, maybe, except it didn't seem that way. No casual observers showed up in a place like this, and it didn't seem that way either. Not a casual observer. Someone with intent and purpose.

She saw nothing. No watchers. No hikers. No one except those authorized to be here. It was also dark and getting darker. Still, she believed she'd see him, her, or them, if they were out there. She'd smell them on the night air. She kept her senses open to receive what information nature deemed to send her way. Nature offered her nothing.

She stopped her scan of the area and brought her gaze back to Mike. "My gut is telling me he dumped her here, and we're not going to find much of anything that will lead us back to him."

"Him? You don't think a woman could have killed her? Maybe someone who was jealous? Or maybe she stole someone's love interest? You know murder is a lot more equal-opportunity these days."

"All valid, I'll admit."

"But your gut says no."

She couldn't tell if he was minimizing her instincts or was interested in her opinion. "My gut says no, it's something else."

Mike did a full circle just as she had moments before. "Gotta say, Wilson, I agree with you. A man did this, and he's a sick son of a bitch."

"We'll find him."

"Damn straight."

❖

Tula didn't know how she got Angel out of the house, but it involved a lot of talking and pleading as she herded her back through the front door. After seeing the painting, whatever work Angel wanted Tula to do for her had been forgotten. Good. She didn't really like doing business with friends anyway. Too easy to cause an issue with the friendship if the end product didn't fit their vision and thus, didn't please them. With not a lot of friends, she'd prefer to keep the few she did have. Like Angel.

Finally alone, she paced the studio and fought the urge to light the canvas on fire. "This can't be happening again." She ran her hands through her hair as she walked from one corner to the other and back again. "What to do? What to do?" No one answered her question.

Maybe sending Angel on her way had been a mistake. She could use someone to bounce all of this off of, and Angel won the proximity award. Their friendship was pretty casual though. Sitting by the lake, chatting about the state of the world. Light and pleasant. Not the kind of friend she'd confide her deepest, darkest secrets to, and that's what she needed now.

She'd really like to call Matthew, the one person who knew all her secrets and had always had her back. In fact, he still did. She could talk to him about anything and everything, even murdered women. Especially murdered women.

From the locked desk drawer, she took out a brand-new SIM card. In less than a minute she swapped it out in her phone. She believed in being careful, even though after all this time, she hoped she'd be safe. Still, never hurt to be cautious. "Hey."

"Hey, beautiful."

The sound of Matthew's voice lifted her heart. It had been more than two years since she'd talked to him, yet his way of answering made her feel as though they'd spoken yesterday. Time didn't matter for them. They could pick up in a heartbeat. If things were different, she was pretty sure she'd have married him. Nobody could ask for a better partner. "I'm scared."

"I'm going to pour myself a brandy while you tell me."

Their conversations were free from names, locations, and details that might be used to track her. Easy to do, given their closeness. No in-depth explanations were required. "It's started again."

"Damn. How many?"

"One."

"So far."

"So far." How well he knew her. He'd been there before and was the keeper of her secrets.

"What do you need? Money? I can get you whatever you need first thing tomorrow. Too late to get anything moved tonight." He jumped right into rescue mode, just as he'd done on another long-ago night.

Without him, only God knew what would have happened to her. Every now and then, when she let herself think of the past, she wondered if she'd still be alive. She doubted it.

"No worries. I'm good for funds." Another of the magic tricks he kept in his back pocket. He'd known his path even when they were children and with that single-minded focus had set her up to flee and at the same time not starve. In the intervening years, he'd only gotten better, and every kernel of advice turned into gold.

"Then tell me. I'm with you if you need me. Just say the word, and I'm on a plane." When he said he'd hop on a plane, he meant it.

Tears started down her cheeks. "No. You stay put. I'm okay. I just needed to hear your voice."

"Little sister, anytime, anywhere. I'm as serious as a heart attack. You tell me where, and I'll be there."

"I know, and I love you for it."

For ten more minutes she talked, telling him about the painting and the fugue-like state that created it, about her fear and trepidation. He said very little, interrupting her exposition only long enough to ask a couple of clarifying questions. It's what she needed. Someone to truly listen. More specifically, for someone who knew her history to listen. Who knew her heart.

When the steam dissipated, she blew out a long breath. "That's about it. Bottom line—I'm scared."

He didn't even pause. "You got this. You did as a kid, and you'll figure out exactly what to do as a mature woman."

"I don't know about the mature part."

"Listen, beautiful, if anyone can puzzle this out, it's you. Remember, you're a survivor. Nobody else could have endured what you did and come out on the other side a well-adjusted, contributing adult. I've always been in awe of you."

"I love you."

"Back atcha."

When she pushed end and set the phone down, her tears were gone and her spirit refreshed. Though she wanted to take time to relish the feeling, she didn't. First things first. She popped out the SIM card and crushed it. Over the last twenty years, she'd learned a few things. Disappearing from a heavily monitored life and becoming someone else required a good deal of work. She'd been young when she'd taken it on and too desperate to care about little details. In the time since then, she'd lived and learned, and had gotten really good at the paying attention to the minutiae.

Talking to Matthew enabled her to come up with a course of action. Sitting here doing nothing didn't work for her. Not with the face on that canvas peering at her, expectation in the gaze. The woman might be a stranger, but that didn't mean Tula could turn away. She hadn't been wired that way even as a child. After ten minutes of pondering, she came up with an idea. Perhaps not the best idea, but hey. It was something.

With her phone, she took a picture of the painting and sent it to her wireless photo printer. Another precaution taken, she slipped on a pair of latex gloves before she pulled the photo off the printer and put it in a manila envelope. The address was easy enough to find, thank you, Google. Ten minutes later, she dropped it into the mail-deposit box outside the Five Corners Rite Aid.

❖

"It's a start." The weariness bore down on her more than she'd ever experienced before. "She'll get it."

He sat on the downed tree with his feet up on the trunk. A recent windstorm combined with damp, soft ground had dropped it near the edge of the lake, and so far, it had been left as nature had intended. She kind of liked it that way. Sometimes the human race interfered too much with nature.

"You'll get this," he reassured her, his head tipped back, his face to the night sky.

"I am so tired." She wished she could sit like Blue, relaxed and clear-headed. He never got anxious, never appeared conflicted. She always felt conflict, and after all this time, the intense emotion took a toll.

"I get it. It's been a long road. You're entitled to be weary."

"Do you think it's the end?" More and more that thought weighed on her mind.

His feet dropped to the ground, the sound a dull thud that didn't carry far. He stood and walked to the water's edge, where the moonlight sliced across the smooth surface. Very little wind tonight to ruffle the water. "I wonder…"

"If it is, it's even more important not to fail."

Her heart pounded. She didn't want to fail Tula. More than that, she wasn't sure she could leave her. For a very long time, she'd wished for nothing more than for it all to end. Her journey had been long and complicated. So different than what the robed masses had promised in all the sermons she listened to and the prayers she'd offered up. The reality didn't match the rhetoric.

She watched him and thought of the time they'd spent together, partners in a journey neither asked for nor imagined. Hard to think of not being side by side. Their pairing had become as natural to her as breathing. He was there for her in the beginning and continued to be there for her year in and year out. A piece of her heart.

In the sky, stars began to peek through, blinking in a way that made her think of beacons lighting the way home. Such an odd thought. Home, that is. It had been a lifetime or two since she'd thought about it. Would she even recognize it? The bigger question: would she care? A few good memories remained. The bad ones never faded. Her gaze dropped to her hands. Did she expect to see the blood still there?

She snapped her gaze back up to the sky. Her life, her memories, weren't worth wasting time on. More important issues stretched out before her, and no matter what had gone before, only this situation should concern her now. Redemption might or might not come her way. These days, she no longer cared. Somewhere along the line her reason for being here had become about something far bigger than herself. Bigger than him too.

"No failure." He turned and put his hands in his pockets, a familiar and reassuring posture.

She wished for the warmth of his touch and kept her own hands clasped together. She could reach out to him, but it wouldn't help. She would be content with the comfort that came more from the joining of their spirits in the mission presented to them than physical connection. "We won't fail," she echoed. They couldn't, for more reasons than one.

CHAPTER FOUR

What in the hell is this?" Mike held a photo in a blue-gloved hand.

Casey walked over and studied the eight-by-ten, full-color photograph. Odd, but then again, that term described a lot of what they saw. "It's a painting. Pretty good one too."

"Great work, Sherlock."

"Shut it, Watson." With only a few hours' sleep, her patience for his sarcasm wasn't exactly at an all-time high. She'd tossed and turned all night thinking about that poor teacher dumped in the sagebrush.

"Notice anything in particular?"

"Beyond the bullet hole in the middle of her forehead and the fact that the woman it depicts is currently on a stainless table in the coroner's office, not much. How about you?" Sarcasm was a second language for her as well. Or, rather, a third language, given she was fluent in both English and Spanish.

Mike dropped the picture into a bag. "Yeah. That pretty much sums up the obvious. Now, in my experience…"

Mike kept talking, and Casey zoned out the minute he used those three magic words: in my experience. While he blabbered on, her mind whirled, and questions raced through it. Who sent this? Who painted Cindy Homer's face with the same bullet hole she'd seen in the flesh last night? When? Where? And, of course, the biggie: why?

"We've got some wacko on our hands." Mike didn't appear to notice that her attention wandered from what he undoubtedly considered a sharing of his great wisdom with the poor female detective. He did love an audience of those he considered subordinate.

She caught the wacko part, and it made her flinch. She didn't call him on the PC slip but couldn't let it go entirely. "You're making it too simplistic."

It might be better for their relationship to let him ramble and believe he tutored her in the fine art of being a detective. Wasn't in her wheelhouse today. Not to say she discounted his experience, because she didn't. He had a solid twenty years under his belt and was good at his job. She faulted him only for his delivery and old-school mentality. In this day and age, it almost created a hostile workplace. Again, she'd confront that issue later, and while that might be a coward's way of dealing with him, she could live with it.

"Pray tell, *Detective*, enlighten me." The photo safe inside an evidence bag, he peeled off the blue gloves and tossed them into the trash can. One made it. One drifted to the floor. He left it there.

She shook her head as she stuffed her hands into her pockets. "Mike. Don't be an ass." Out of the corner of her eye she noticed Andy Andrews duck his head to hide his smile. She wasn't the only one who got tired of Mike's superior attitude. She was about the only one who would call him on it.

He blew out a breath and tilted his head her way. "Fine. Tell me what you're thinking."

At least he had moments when being reasonable was possible. She'd take whatever she could get from him. "It could be, probably is, the killer who sent that." She pointed to the bag holding the photograph. "And we can't rule out that he's not suffering from mental illness or some sort of personality disorder. We also can't rule out that whoever killed her did so in a clear-headed, well-planned way."

He picked up the evidence bag with the photo and shook it at her. "You think someone sane murdered that woman, left her body out at the Potholes, and then sent this to us all because, why?" He slapped it back down on his desk.

She ignored his theatrics. "Too calculated. Mental illness doesn't look and feel this organized." Basic 101 Psychology.

His eyes changed. She had him. Sometimes with Mike, it just took patience and rationality to get through. Put them together, catch his interest, and break-throughs happened. "Good point."

She wasn't done with her train of thought. "Or it could be someone witnessed what he did, and that's who sent the picture. An innocent bystander who doesn't want to get involved beyond letting us know what they saw."

"Okay. Now you're wandering off the logical path. If the woman was threatened and this pic might help to save her life, maybe. That's just not what happened here."

She didn't see it that way. It made sense that someone who saw something yet didn't want to get dragged into the official investigation would do this. Well, someone with serious artistic skill, that is. She didn't know many who could paint a portrait like this one. That talent would help pinpoint who to track down. Especially in a community of this size. "I don't follow you."

"Stay with me here. We were sent a picture of a painting, and for me, I'm not buying that our witness stood around looking at a body just to run home, make a painting, and then send us a picture of it. Does that really make sense to you?"

Casey blew out a breath. His point hit home. Damn it. "No."

"So we're back to wacko."

"Not politically correct, Mike."

"Political correctness aside, not far off track either."

"No."

He smiled. "Gotcha. Let's get this to the lab, and then we'll do some more, you know, real detective work."

"Asshole."

He laughed all the way to the lab.

Uneasiness made for a very restless night. Satisfied that sending the picture to the Moses Lake Police Department had been the right thing to do, Tula still spent hours second-guessing that decision. Living here had been pleasant. She'd found her niche and made a comfortable and successful low-key life. Very different from the first half of her life yet infinitely more freeing. A series of good decisions that kept her safe and somewhat happy.

Until she'd pulled that canvas and her paints out of the closet anyway. Then everything crashed down. Memories of her first eighteen years rushed back uninvited and most unwelcome. To pick up the phone and call Matthew again was a temptation she wanted to give in to. Maybe even take him up on the offer to fly out. She could use some real live face time. Good sense and self-preservation kept her from doing something that unwise. Always a risk, even with the precautions she took. She'd have to try to regain that feeling of empowerment without the sound of his voice and definitely without a visit.

College hadn't been an option for her. That didn't equate to being uneducated. When someone found herself faced with the critical need to hide in plain sight, she either learned really quick, or she crashed and burned. She hadn't crashed or burned. At least not yet. She didn't pick up her phone.

With a cup of dark coffee in hand, she walked into her studio and stood staring at the now-empty easel. The painted canvas had been covered up and tucked away where she didn't have to look at it. She'd done what she could and didn't need the reminder of how it turned out to have been a little too little, a little too late. The woman's murder was the lead story on the morning news on every single channel.

As she looked at the easel now, it occurred to her that it might be a good idea to stuff it back into the closet and bolt the door. Maybe even nail it shut. Put an end to the temptation to paint anything else. The way her fingers tingled and a whisper lingered in her mind, she worried that the worst might be yet to come. Like the death of the woman whose face she painted wasn't bad enough. Déjà vu didn't feel good.

She brushed her fingers over the wood. "No," she whispered. "Not again."

"Not what again?"

"Damn it," she screamed when hot coffee splashed over her hand. Shaking it off her skin, she watched drops of coffee hit the hardwood floor. So much for even thinking about painting. She'd be cleaning floors.

"Sorry."

She put the coffee cup on the desk and turned to Diane. "I swear to God, one of these days, I'm going to call the cops on you."

"For what?" Diane ran her fingers through her hair with its carefully casual look that she no doubt spent a great deal of time and money achieving. Her brother, whom Tula had finally caught on network television, wasn't the only one who went for the high-maintenance look. He didn't use the same hair-color, thank goodness. For the life of her, she couldn't figure out how Diane thought that color made for a good look.

"Breaking and entering."

She waved a hand dismissively. "The door was unlocked. Seems like an invitation to come on in to me."

Nice try. "Yes, the back door was unlocked. Locked or not, why would you think it's okay to just walk in? Why do you always think it's okay to walk in?"

"We're friends."

"No, we're not." Time for brutal honesty. Nothing else seemed to get through to her.

Diane laughed and waved a hand in the air. "Of course we are."

Right over her head. This woman drove her up the proverbial wall. She'd wondered more than once if her behavior would change even if she moved. Diane would probably move too. She seemed fixated on her, and that was the last thing Tula needed.

"What do you want?" If she got straight to the point, maybe the gods would smile on her, and Diane would leave her alone. She doubted it. Worth a try just the same.

A wide smile crossed her face. "Glad you asked. Dinner. Tonight. Seven."

"What?" She'd only been paying half attention. Often easier to space the woman out than to actually listen to her.

"Dinner with my brother is at seven tonight. Dante drove into Spokane this morning for some background work on a story and will be back here late this afternoon. I've got grass-fed steaks and gorgeous bakers. Oh, and a nice bottle of 14 Hands Red Blend."

She did appreciate the wines from the Central Washington winery, just not enough to want to share a bottle with Diane and meet her brother. Nope. Even good wine didn't help that out. "I can't."

Diane waved her hands in the air. "Baloney. You're here, Dante is expecting to meet you, and I've got dinner for three set up. I'm not taking no for an answer, and I'll sit right here until you agree to come." She plopped down in the tall chair in front of Tula's drafting table, spinning around and around.

"Diane, come on. I've already told you I can't."

"La la la la la." She kept spinning.

"I can't." Third time might be the charm. She hoped. The thought of spending the evening with Diane and even one of her family gave her chills.

"You can."

"Oh, for Pete's sake." Her last good nerve twanged dangerously.

"You will."

"Fine, but I'm leaving as soon as we're done eating. I have a lot to do before the day is over." She hated herself for giving in.

Diane jumped up and clapped, triumph rolling off her. "See you at seven."

❖

Angel walked around Tula's empty studio and frowned. The energy in the room had taken on an ominous tone. Not particularly surprising. For months now the darkness had crept closer until it finally wrapped around the lovely home on the water. Reminded her of another place and another time when she would watch the sun set over a different body of water and listen to the waves as they pounded against the shoreline when the winds kicked up and storms rolled in. There, too, the light had been replaced by a creeping darkness that ultimately smothered her. At the time, she hadn't noticed. She'd learned to pay more attention since then.

A tear slid down her cheek. Not often these days when she strolled down memory lane. She'd gotten over that luxury eons ago and looked only one direction: forward. The mission defined her life, and that suited her just fine. A hero's journey of sorts, and right now that meant keeping Tula safe. She'd do her best, although no one who had an inkling of Angel's history would ever equate her with a hero. No. It would be a comparison of a quite different nature.

Hard not to worry about Tula. Many important elements were out of her control, and her powers were limited. She could influence only so much, and she could only pray it would be enough. Had to be. She'd discovered that lesson all on her own. Her path had been made crystal clear to her: help those who needed protection, like Tula. Guide her to the light. Keep her safe. Easy-peasy. Right? Not quite. Not so easy, not so peasy.

With an assist from earthly angels like Tula's friend Matthew, things fell into place. She'd guided Tula before anything else could happen to jeopardize her well-being. She'd watched over her for the better part of two decades and kept her safe from harm. Now this? She didn't know if it meant yet another test for her or that evil refused to relinquish its hold on Tula. An innocent as a child. No less an innocent as an adult.

She leaned against the wall and decided it was a wash either way. Whether it came directed at her or Tula, the goal remained the same. Keep her safe from the forces of darkness.

The sun began to dip below the mountains to the west. She liked this time of the day, the colors of the sunset as beautiful as the art that lived inside of Tula. Most here knew nothing about the master inside her heart and soul, and that made her sad. So much talent restrained in the shadows and screaming for release. Certainly, the path Tula had forged here gave her a creative outlet of sorts. Her success as a graphics designer attested to that truth. It didn't change the magnitude of the tragedy. Her true brilliance lay hidden, suppressed by necessity, and for that Angel would always be angry. She'd wanted to do more, yet even with everything at her disposal, that had been far out of her reach. A personal failure on her part that Tula was forced to keep her brilliance hidden from the world.

She stood in the closet doorway and smiled. The artist could be taken out of the studio, but the art could never be taken out of the artist. The paints, the brushes, the canvases all still rested on the shelves, locked away from curious eyes and kept regardless of what had come before. Tula's locks, while effective for everyone else, couldn't keep Angel out.

Time to do what little she could before Tula returned. She stepped into the closet and laid her hands on the box of paints. Whatever she had, she'd use. Her head tilted, her eyes closed, she said, "Heavenly Father, hear my plea. Bring her the sight, bring her the vision, bring her the light. Let her see what others try to hide. Let her bring it all into the daylight. I ask this in your name."

CHAPTER FIVE

Casey flexed her fingers again and again. Why did it take so long to get anything worthwhile out of the lab? Yeah. She got that they could do only so much with what they had. They were a small county with a limited budget, but still, it was the twenty-first goddamn century. Things should get done a whole lot faster.

"I've got a little news." Letia Hernandez was her second cousin and a pretty freaking good forensic tech. In all honesty, she could easily make the cut at the state forensics lab, except she preferred to stay closer to home. Casey didn't get it. If she got an offer from a larger force in Seattle, Olympia, or Spokane, she would accept in two-three seconds. Of course, big words from someone who'd never applied to work anywhere else.

"What have you got?" She focused on the papers Letia held.

"First, I dusted the pics for prints."

"And?"

"Nada. That thing was clean as a baby's butt." It wasn't just because they were related that Letia talked this way. She talked to everyone the same.

"Shit." She'd been hoping for a print or three. It would be nice if something went her way, and quickly. That a killer was in her town grated on her. Gang violence they dealt with more than they should have to around here. The thing was, they were all dialed into it. A murder like this, no, and she didn't like it. She also hoped it was something she'd never have to dial into.

"No worries. You know I have skills. Some, I haven't even used yet." Letia snapped her fingers in the air. "A master."

Casey smiled. Letia had a way of taking down the level of tension. "Yeah. Auntie Sophia always says that about you."

Letia winked. "Different set of skills."

Now she laughed. It was nice to have someone like Letia around. She would miss her if the Washington State Patrol ever did snag her for the crime lab. "So tell me what you've got."

"CCTV, my sista. CCTV."

"Seriously?" That sounded too good to be real. It also made her want to slap herself on the forehead for not thinking of that line of inquiry herself. Geez. She would make sure Mike didn't catch on to that slip. If he did, she'd hear about it for the next ten years.

"Seriously. It took only a few calls, and we hit pay dirt. We have a beautiful white girl dropping a lovely manila envelope into the mailbox right outside of the Rite Aid."

"We can't be sure it's our picture." Even with video, she had to question reliability. A good investigator always questioned every angle.

"Naw. Nothing's a hundred percent, but don't get stuck on the percentages. What I'm looking at is probability, and it's telling me that we found our sender."

"I think I love you."

Letia laughed and patted her hand. "You gotta love me. I'm familia."

"I love you because you're fucking brilliant."

Letia winked. "I am fucking brilliant."

"Humble too."

"You look at what I've got, and then you tell me if I'm wrong."

Casey pulled a chair up next to her and sat as she brought up a file. Soon images were flashing across the extra-large monitor. The familiar Rite Aid at Five Corners appeared. At about ten seconds in, an attractive woman with long silver hair walked straight to the mailbox and dropped in a manila envelope, one the same size that held a color photograph of a painting. No attempt to hide her face and Casey wondered if she even realized cameras were in place. "How the hell did you find that?"

"Skill, baby, skill."

"Really?"

Letia laughed. "Okay. I'll admit I got lucky. Second CCTV I tried pulled up this gem. Five Corners seemed like a good place for someone who hoped to stay under the radar with all the traffic and activity there. I'm guessing she didn't think it through, because if she had, she'd have figured out all the major stores have cameras these days. Before you ask, I did check all the others too, to cover the bases. Nothing else jumped out. This remains the big winner."

"Now to find out who she is."

"Give me a little time to work my magic."

As happy as she was that Letia found the footage this quickly, she worried they might not have time to uncover her identity. The woman could be long gone by now. "Call me the second you find anything."

"Copy that."

❖

To leave her house and walk over to Diane's with rock-hard shoulders and a stiff neck brought on physical pain. She did not want to do this and resented that she'd been pushed into it. More accurately, she was pissed at herself for not having the balls to stand her ground and refuse. In her defense, the thing with Diane's obsessive personality meant if she didn't get it over with now, she'd be back at her door again and again and again until Tula finally folded. At least this way, she'd be done with it and be able to enjoy peace and quiet afterward. It was a pattern she'd come to understand after Diane moved in a couple of years earlier.

"Thought you'd stand me up." Diane smiled as she opened the front door wide. "I'm pleasantly surprised."

"I told you I'd be here." Tula worked to keep the snap out of her voice. Diane's grin said she'd accomplished that goal. Either that or she was excited enough about the dinner that she didn't care.

"That you did. Come on. I've got the wine breathing, and my bro will be here any minute. He called me a little over an hour ago as he was heading out of Spokane. I'm dying to try this red blend. It's won a bunch of awards. Can't beat Central Washington for good wine."

Not that she wanted to be rude, but Tula didn't like her senses dulled at any level. At least not when she was in the company of others. Too many years of being on hyper-alert to become comfortable with the side effects of alcohol. Drugs never ever even entered into the equation. Not in her world anyway. She hadn't even seen a doctor since she'd moved here. Or ever. Her fingers strayed to her head.

If she sat alone in her house watching the moon rise and the stars come up, well, that was a different story. Then she'd enjoy a glass, as in a single glass, of wine. Or perhaps a splash of brandy in a cup of coffee on a cool night. This wasn't even close to sitting outside by herself enjoying her home and a moonlit night.

Diane handed her a glass with a healthy pour of the deep-red wine.

No way she'd even get close to emptying it. She did take a tiny sip, and, as promised, it was good. Just because she chose not to imbibe didn't mean she couldn't appreciate a tasty vintage.

"This is nice." She held up the glass. Hopefully, Diane wouldn't notice how little she drank if she made a good show out of it.

Diane smiled. Points scored. Good. If Diane felt appreciated, it would be easier to get the hell out of here. "You know, people underestimate this region. We have some killer wineries in some out-of-the-way places. I mean, 14 Hands is up in Prosser. Who would think to swing in there for this? I might not have been born around here, but I have to say, I like that this region is kicking ass in the wine department."

Though she resented being pushed into this dinner, it did smell pretty great in here. It was surprising that hunger gnawed at her, given she'd been fixated on the painting all day and whether it'd been delivered to the police department. To travel down the same path that sent her fleeing from her birthplace didn't sit well with her. After all the years of living here, the hiding bit of it aside, she'd thought that part of her past. Reliving it in any way unsettled her.

"Feed me!" A deep male voice came from the hallway. A few seconds later, the booming voice was followed by tall, dark, and handsome. Yeah, not hard to figure out why he worked in media. Diane's brother was the whole package and better looking in person than the glimpse she'd gotten of him on the television last night. She could see why he enjoyed success. She bet he had no trouble getting people to talk to him.

Diane laughed and her eyes sparkled. A little weird to be that excited about her brother, but what did she know? She'd been an only child. "About time you got here. Poor Tula is close to fainting from starvation."

She shook her head. "I'm fine. Your sister exaggerates."

Diane waved a hand in the air. "You're just being polite. You have to understand that my dear brother here doesn't believe in schedules. He'll be late for his own funeral."

Tall, dark, and handsome stepped close and held out his hand. "Dante Macy at your service. You must be the elusive Tula. I really am sorry to have kept you waiting. The story I'm working on took a little longer than I expected."

She took his hand, shocked by the sensation that rushed up her arm. It wasn't a pleasant one. With effort she managed what she hoped came across as a welcoming smile while she extricated her hand at the same time. "Nice to meet you. Your sister has been singing your praises."

"Oh, dear. I'm so sorry." His expression telegraphed more amusement than apology. She had the sense Dante liked to be talked about anywhere, anytime.

She changed the subject as she took a step back from him. "What brings you to Moses Lake? A visit with your sister?"

"Well, that's always a good excuse. In case you've never had the pleasure, big sis is one hell of a cook. I'm actually here in Washington on assignment. Just a nice coincidence that Diane lives here, and that means no hotel for me this time around. I do get tired of hotel rooms and restaurant food. It smells good in here, by the way."

Diane beamed.

"Assignment?" The only biggie she could think of was the murdered teacher, and given that had broken less than twenty-four hours ago, she wondered what story he'd be on.

"Murder is always a good gig."

"You're talking about the woman at the Potholes?" The dots were not connecting.

"Not initially. I'm working on a murder out of Spokane, but with the body dumped out at the Potholes, I now have two assignments. A pretty heavy lift, but I'm used to it. My producers and my audience expect it of me, and I never disappoint."

Uneasiness made her want to run home. Not just his words but his facial expression. Pure thrill. The revulsion she had already experienced because of the image that came at the tip of her brush intensified in the presence of this man who seemed to feel nothing about the loss of life except the opportunity for a good story. He appeared to want nothing but to get his face on national TV and make a buck or two on someone else's misfortune. Combine that with the chills she experienced when their hands touched, and she really wanted to bolt for the door. Ugh.

Diane frowned at her brother. "Enough shop talk, Dante. We don't need some poor woman's murder to take over a pleasant dinner. I wanted you to meet Tula, not gross her out with the morbid details of your job."

For a change, she actually agreed with Diane.

He shrugged. "My apologies. Let's talk about something lighter and brighter."

Diane nodded, and the big smile returned. "Exactly my point.

Nothing dark. I say we let Tula tell us all about the paintings she tries to hide from everyone. I for one am *très* curious."

She wanted to scream no! Instead, she politely said, "I say let's not."

Diane poured a glass of wine for Dante and also topped off her own, again. Tula shook her head when she tilted the bottle in her direction. "You know I won't give up until you tell. I'll share my secrets if you'll share yours."

Tula shook her head again and held her wineglass tight for fear Diane would still try to pour more for her despite her declining. "Not going to happen." She turned her attention to Dante. "Tell me more about your job *sans* the murders." Her bait-and-switch worked. Dante lit up at the invitation. Thank the good Lord for self-centered windbags who liked to talk about themselves. By the time he finished pontificating, dinner was over, and she took the opportunity to run for the door. Not literally, but in her head, she was sprinting like Jesse Owens.

❖

"What are we going to do about him?" Angel had earlier watched the handsome man sneak around to the back of Tula's house and let himself in. Clearly it wasn't his first break-and-enter endeavor because he was able to get the back door open in under five minutes. Pretty comfortable about it too. Breaching personal barriers always bothered her.

Blue frowned. "He's a complication you don't need."

An understatement. Enough evil swirled around without the man adding to the mix. "Not at all. I don't like the feel of him. Something's off about that pretty boy. I mean, something off besides the felony."

"Big time." He leaned against the trunk of a tree, looking casual and relaxed despite agreeing with her about the creep.

She wished she could feel even a fraction of what Blue presented. Her thoughts dwelled on the man and how he'd checked out the kitchen, opened drawers in Tula's bedroom, and, worst of all, invaded her studio, including her treasured closet. The way he'd been able to get the lock open didn't sit well with her. Too practiced. Inside the closet, he'd touched the stored canvases, the boxes with her paints, and every single one of the beautiful brushes. In short, he violated her inner sanctum in a very unacceptable way, if violation even had an acceptable way.

"I don't understand this guy. Why would he take the risk?" Blue turned his beautiful eyes on her. The concern in them matched the concern that flitted through her. He might look relaxed, but he wasn't.

"Reporter, and not a very moral one at that." She'd seen others like him. Hadn't cared for a single one of them. Honest, true, and kind worked a lot better for her. Like Tula.

"Hoping for an Emmy or some kind of award for outstanding journalism. That would be my vote."

Definitely the type who'd do whatever he could to win an award just to show the world how much better he was than everyone else. "Hoping for sure. I just can't figure out for what. The man is up to something, and I'm betting it's something bad."

"Indeed."

Angel paced back and forth, her fingers laced behind her head. "What if we get stuck this time? What if we can't figure it out? With complications like this man, we're fighting more than one war. I don't have the time or the energy for the guy. I have to be able to focus on Tula."

As each hour passed, sand slipped through the invisible hour glass with frightening speed. This was the first time she'd experienced the sensation of speeding time, and it wasn't at all pleasant. To keep the very special Tula safe was a sacred duty and one for which she simply could not stumble. Once before, she'd managed to help her to escape the path of evil before it took her life. To have darkness reappear here, and with an intensity that far surpassed that of several decades earlier, was disheartening. She could use a break about now. Tula could use a break. When the final grain of sand fell, she wanted to know Tula would be safe.

Blue, the perpetual optimistic, had a way with keeping her off a discouraging path. "Don't think about it that way. We have powerful forces on our side, after all. Good will triumph again."

"At what cost? You saw that man, how he invaded her space searching for any little secret that he might be able to use against her. I don't understand people like that. I never have. They turn my stomach. I hate bullies." One of them had gotten her into this situation to begin with. A bully, and her own propensity to leap into action before her brain fully engaged. Act first, think later. She still worked on that one. She still had a long way to go.

He shook his head, and the moonlight caught the shine of his long golden hair. "You'd think evolution would have brought men forward more than what we saw in that one."

"One would hope, yet he is no better than Judas Iscariot."

He held up both hands in a gesture that was so Blue. If she'd seen him do it once, she'd seen it a thousand times. "We have seen many like Judas in our time. They exist in every generation, in every culture. Men and woman with no moral compass. We can't get rid of them, so we have to work around them."

She sighed. "Very true, which is why it doesn't make sense that this man bothers me so. The thing is, he makes my skin crawl, and that's new. In the past, I found a way to sidestep guys like him. We're going to have to head straight at this one."

"Sometimes we need the bad to appreciate the good. We need to face an occasional Judas to remind us that good prevails more often than not. Perhaps he is our reminder. No matter what he is, we will figure it out together, as we always have. Tula will stay safe."

"You promise?" How she wished she could embrace the same sort of optimism that Blue did. They'd always had a different way of coming at things, which, of course, was the very reason why they were where they were at the moment. If she'd been more like Blue, things would have turned out quite different.

He gave her the smile that had made her heart flip for so very long. "Have I ever lied to you?"

No need to respond. They both knew the answer.

CHAPTER SIX

Casey paced the house. She'd wanted to stay in Letia's office until she got a name to go with the face the camera had caught. Like most CCTV, the video wasn't exactly crystal clear but enough that she could catch the long, wavy silver hair and slim build. No clue as to eye color or age, although she'd guess mid to late thirties. Pretty sure she was right.

Letia finally made her leave after she spent an hour staring at her. Told her that she'd be in her way and she would get a lot more done, a lot faster, if Casey beat it, quote unquote. As much as she wanted to argue, she didn't. If someone wanted to hang in her office while she worked, she'd tell them the same thing. Get the hell out.

First, she'd headed back to her own office to meet up with Mike and compare notes and thoughts. That accomplished, she'd grabbed her coat and headed out. All the way home she ran their thoughts and theories over and over in her head. For a change, Mike had been pretty darn collaborative. For a few seconds, it almost felt like they were an honest-to-God team. No doubt tomorrow, he'd say or do something infuriating and ruin it. She'd worry about that later. For the moment, she'd just be grateful.

For probably the tenth time since she'd gotten home, she picked up her phone and stared at the display, willing it to ring. She needed to know the identity of that woman sooner rather than later. Though the quality of the video left a lot to be desired, something had come across that captured her interest. More than simply the woman putting the envelope in the repository. She didn't like to use the term aura, but there it was anyway. The woman in the video had some kind of freaky aura.

Her gut told her the woman had answers. It also told her the woman wasn't their killer. If she mentioned any of this to Mike, he'd laugh in her face and tell her to go back to school. If one of the guys said it, he'd tell them they were losing their edge. He didn't think she had an edge.

She liked to give him the benefit of the doubt. In her heart of hearts she knew he wasn't a bad cop. In fact, if pushed, she'd admit he was a pretty good one. An asshole, but a good detective in spite of it. His biggest problem came in the blinders he refused to take off. Still on the old-school side, he didn't particularly care for women detectives doing a "man's" job or, though more subtle, the fact she was of Mexican heritage. Neither worked in the lane he liked to drive in. He did, off and on, make an effort to come into line with the twenty-first century, and she hoped he'd get there one day. That he was making it a really slow trip didn't fill her with optimism for the completion of that particular journey.

Thus, sharing any type of intuition with him would be futile. He'd shoot down her thoughts and theories in a second. Not worth the time or effort to go there. Better to keep her thoughts to herself for the time being and work it in her own quiet way until it yielded results. Once she had something concrete, she'd approach him and lay it all out. Things worked smoother with Mike when she could show something to him in black and white. A consistent show-don't-tell kind of guy.

When Letia finally called, her heart raced as she grabbed the phone. Game time. "Yeah."

"Hello to you too."

"Yeah, yeah, yeah. Hello. Tell me you have something concrete."

"A name do it for you?"

"You're a wizard."

Letia laughed. "As much as I agree with you, I can't actually take credit for this one."

"What do you mean?"

"One of those unexpected instances of right place, right time."

Letia loved to tell stories in a dramatic fashion. She wanted the facts. Quickly. "And?"

"And our mystery woman is none other than Tula Crane."

The name meant nothing to her. Not someone who came into contact with law enforcement and no one in her personal circle. "Facial recognition?" Some amazing tools were becoming available these days. Not that their little lab had much of a budget for the latest and greatest toys.

"Oh, hell, no. Not even close. Using that kind of software isn't exactly the magic people think it is. Takes forever and gives only a range of suspects. It doesn't narrow down to one individual like all the television shows make it seem. Not to mention the big elephant in the room. We can't afford that shit in this county. Hell, I'm not even sure Spokane can afford it, and they have a few hundred thousand more folks living there than we do."

"Okay. So how did you get to this Crane woman?" Dragging it out of Letia was trying her patience. Enough with the stories. Spit. It. Out.

"Happenstance. Her face was up on my screen when Jake from the PR office walked by and asked why it was there. Bingo! He knew her because she's done some graphics work for the nonprofit he volunteers with. Jake for the win."

"Dumb luck."

"You got it. Like I said, right place, right time, and I'll take a W any way I can get it."

Boy, didn't she relate. "I'll take it too."

"Figured you would. I mean, I do get cred for finding the video at the speed of light and having the right people around me to work it out, so it's all good."

"You're always good. Appreciate you getting this so quickly."

"Always happy to help, especially for something like this. We have to find the bastard who killed the teacher. I'm counting on you to do that. You know, she taught my neighbor's kid, and I hear she was amazing. You take him down."

"I'm on it."

"I know you are. Now, I'm going to jet out of here and pick up some dinner on the way home. The teenagers at my house are getting restless."

With three sons in their teens, she had Casey's sympathy. "Get those boys fed, and Letia, I owe you a really nice dinner." She owed her a lot more than that.

"Bring over a big bag of burgers and a bucket of fries for the boys, and we'll be even."

"Once this case is solved, consider it done."

Casey put her phone down and logged onto her laptop. Energy roared through her, as though she'd just awakened from a perfect night's sleep. "Okay, Tula Crane. Show me your secrets."

❖

Tula walked through the front door and stopped. With her eyes closed she took several deep breaths. "No and no."

For a long time she'd lived here in peace, and now it had evaporated. The breach revealed itself in the air that swirled around unseen yet heavy. Someone had walked through the rooms where she'd built a comfortable life.

In her studio, the heaviness grew. Even here, where she held her secrets close, the touch of a stranger sang through the air. Anger more than despair coursed through her. Years ago, fear would have sent her packing. The passing of time had done a great deal in terms of building strength. Where once she'd seen only one path, now she saw options. She could run, and without question, that would be the easiest. It wouldn't be the first time she'd rebuilt, and she could do it again if she had to. The thing was, she didn't want to run, didn't want to rebuild.

She liked it here in this out-of-the-way place far different from where she'd come from. Diverse and grounded, it offered much. Most people zipped by Moses Lake at seventy miles per hour, veering away from I-90 only long enough to grab coffee at the Starbucks right off Exit 179. They ignored the lake, the fields, and the giant planes that took off and landed at the old Air Force base turned pilot training facility. All of that combined had captured her interest as she'd driven across the country searching for a place to hide. That same Exit 179 had beckoned to her for more than good coffee, and she'd pulled off the freeway, stopped, and never looked back. The life she'd created here still sang to her, and she wasn't ready to give it up.

Now the world tilted again, complicated by an intrusion of her inner sanctum. She suspected she knew the identity of the intruder and gazed toward her neighbor's house. As pushy as Diane was, it wouldn't be a stretch to think her brother Dante embodied the same no-boundaries philosophy. The more she thought about it, the more convinced she became that Dante had been her uninvited guest. But why? Did he sense that a story hid within the walls of her house? Or was it simple curiosity? People in his line of business seemed to believe they had the right to know everything about everybody. At least some of his counterparts worked that way. Not fair to lump them all together.

It didn't feel like an answer would be forthcoming any time in the immediate future. Sometimes if she allowed a thought to percolate, something important came to her. It especially proved true in her work. With painting, creativity had never been a problem. Images simply formed in her mind. With the graphics she created for a living these days, not so much. They required conscious effort and great thought. The right direction always showed up sooner or later. Sometimes, it was a lot later.

She reached for the closet-door handle and then changed her mind. Maybe running wasn't the right route at the moment. It didn't mean she shouldn't be ready. Better to put plans into place than be surprised. Turning, she went to her desk and opened the locked drawer. The SIM-card swap took only a few seconds. She always kept a few on hand. Just in case.

"You change your mind?" Matthew didn't even sound tired, even though he was hours ahead of her.

"In a way, yes."

"How much?"

"Twenty-five thousand."

"Is that enough?"

Given she had no clue what might happen, hard to say. "It will do." With that kind of money, she could put quite a distance between herself and Moses Lake.

"How quickly?"

"You can send me the money as soon as possible. As for leaving here, I don't know yet. I just want to be ready." She read off the account numbers for him. Once he made the transfer, she'd pull the funds and close the account. End of that particular trail.

"Got it. What else can I do for you?"

"You've already done plenty."

"You're the only sister I have."

She could hear the smile in his voice, and it brought tears to her eyes. "You're the only family I've ever had. Who said blood matters above all else?"

"Nobody with a clue. I love you."

"I love you more."

❖

"I can't just ignore that the jerk invaded her space. I don't like that man. I feel like I need to do something about him. Just can't figure out what." She'd been fussing about his intrusion since it happened. She couldn't shake the uneasiness it left her with.

Blue looked at her and nodded. "I'm with you. He radiates bad waves. It's like we talked about earlier. We've seen his type before.

They're always around somewhere, and wiping them all off the face of the earth is a task no one can undertake."

"We could try."

"Maybe. Maybe not. The old good-and-evil thing never goes away. Also have to consider that someone being a bad person doesn't necessarily make him dangerous. We can hope he's a minor complication and not one of the dangerous variety."

"I don't argue that point. He's more than minor though. Don't you sense there's more to that one than a handsome face? It's like he's wearing a mask, and whatever is underneath it is ugly."

Blue nodded. "A little too smooth, if you catch my drift."

Angel did, indeed, and she got why it bothered Blue. His ability to read people was a thing of legend. The majority of people, anyway. He'd sort of misread her and was still paying for that one. In this instance, she wanted to believe he was spot-on with this guy.

That she couldn't tap into the interloper like she could with most people made her nervous. Mistakes brought on by blindness could have no place here. She had to stay focused on Tula and uncovering the identity of the killer before anyone else lost their life. No time for a distraction of the snoopy, breaking-and-entering type.

"He's bad." She needed to let it go and couldn't.

Blue tapped his fingers against his leg. "Most definitely. We must figure out exactly how bad and, if we need to, pay closer attention to him."

She held out her hands. "I can't reach him. Nothing. A big blank."

This time Blue turned and looked at her. His grim expression matched her mood. "That's not like you."

"No, and I don't like it. It scares me."

"Damn."

She cocked her head and studied him. "I would say more accurately, he's damned." If that were true, then it made less sense. The damned should be able to reach the damned. Right? She wouldn't run that one by Blue because he'd argue. Some things they didn't agree on, particularly when it came to the state of her soul.

"Well, if he isn't yet, I lay odds he will be."

"Too late for prayers."

"Not too late to save her."

"What about the others?"

"How many?"

She resisted the urge to close her eyes and see the future. Some people thought so-called psychic abilities were a blessing they'd give anything to possess. Not so for her. This thing she could do might be necessary for the job she'd been given, but never once had she considered it a blessing. The urge pushed at her until she could no longer resist. It always happened this way. It wouldn't be denied, and so she closed her eyes and let the images flow. Tears rolled down her cheeks. "Possibly four, maybe up to five."

"Damn. And so far there's only been one."

"That we know of." She opened her eyes and met his dark gaze.

"We'd know." He sat and leaned his chin in his hands. How she remembered the first time she'd seen him. Back then she'd been taken aback by his beauty. Still was. More than his physical gifts made him special. Strong and smart and noble. Everything a person could ever want in a partner. He could have been a conceited ass. He wasn't now and never had been. The beauty on the outside matched the beauty on the inside.

She nodded slowly. "I suspect you're right."

"It's more than that. You know I'm right."

"I do." Because he wasn't wrong. She would know if others perished nearby. When this thing happened, that's what she could see. Not the face of the killer but that of the victim. She became an unwilling witness. If the universe would allow her to see his face, things would be different. Instead, she was forced to find a way to facilitate the discovery of the killer's identity through others, like Tula.

Blue stood up and stretched his arms over his head. When he dropped his arms back down again, he met her gaze. "Let's figure this out. We can stop him before he harms anyone else. One is one too many."

She opened her mouth to agree and, instead, screamed.

Chapter Seven

Stop!" Casey reached over and slapped her cell phone. Didn't work. It kept screaming at her. Granted, she'd chosen the obnoxious alarm tone to make certain she never slept through it. That didn't mean she appreciated it. The groan she let out scared Diego Rivera or, as she liked to call him, D—her six-year-old six-year-old cat—and he jumped off the bed. For a roly-poly cat, a trait that had a big hand in the selection of his name, he could move surprisingly fast and was light on his paws.

"Sorry, D." He didn't care. He was long gone. "Dude, you need to be tougher." Now, she laughed as she grabbed the phone, stopped the annoying screech of the alarm, and then swung her legs over the side of the bed. Her arms stretched over her head, she rolled her head from side to side. Probably would have been a good idea to have given up on her search effort a little earlier last night. She'd had to sleep fast and was feeling it now.

What she'd managed to find still rattled around in her mind. Pretty damned interesting, considering the woman who'd dropped the picture in the mailbox outside of Rite Aid didn't seem to have a history before about twenty years ago. Her spidey senses had gone on high alert. People didn't appear out of nowhere unless they needed a change in scenery or, more likely, had a history they wanted to hide. They also didn't buy pricey lakeside homes without money coming from somewhere. As in dirty money that needed to be cleaned. A nice home would be a perfect wash. The lady with the envelope possessed a story, and she wanted to know exactly what it was.

She'd have to share with Mike what she'd found, although she figured she could keep it close for a little while longer. Give herself time to process before he interjected his preconceived ideas about who killed the teacher. If he could stay neutral and really sort through what she found, she'd love to have his input. The man had some serious experience, and when he wasn't being a jerk, she learned from him. At the same time, she didn't appreciate the quick dismissal that typically came when she tried to posit something outside of his train of inquiry. Once he got on a particular path, he worked it until it either gave him what he wanted or he drove it six feet under. Right now, she wanted possibilities, not preconception.

Thus, she planned to avoid Mike for the day and see what she could come up with on her own. Give her instincts a little time to grow and mature. Her abuelita would very much approve. Unlike her very grounded mother, her abuelita embraced the spiritual world and had always encouraged Casey to pay attention to everything, whether seen or felt. Not that she should point fingers at her mother. She didn't exactly put a lot of weight on the otherworldly theories either. She supposed she fell somewhere between her mother and her abuelita when it came to these things, with a decided tilt toward her mother.

For now, she wanted to percolate. Tomorrow would be soon enough to compare notes with Mike. She wasn't asking too much. Was she? If he knew she had something and didn't bring it to him immediately, he'd consider it a breach of partnership trust. At least on her part. If he was working a lead, he wouldn't think twice about leaving her out in the cold until he followed it through. Turnabout and all that.

Sleep had eluded her for the most part because she couldn't turn her mind off. Every time she rolled over in bed, she'd looked at the clock, hoping enough time had passed that she could get up and go meet the mysterious Tula. A list of serious questions formed in her head for the woman who, by virtue of the information available, should be all of about twenty years old. The face in the video was not that of someone who'd spent only two decades on Earth. In fact, the face could belong to someone in her own graduating class and on her way to a twenty-year reunion. She'd point to the long, silver hair as well, except the trend of younger women dyeing their hair silver made it an unreliable measure of age.

By the time the alarm went off she'd managed about five hours of sleep. Not great. Not bad either. She could function pretty well on that amount. In the shower, the hot water rolled off her. Amazing what it could do for tense shoulders and a stiff neck. When she stepped out, all the weariness had vanished.

Once dressed, she shot Mike a text. Though old school in a lot of ways, the guy really liked his phone, for a couple of reasons. First, he bragged about his highly developed skills in using it, because many others his age resisted the technology. Feeling superior worked in all aspects of his life. Secondly, he really liked being able to reach and touch whomever he wanted to at any given moment. Keeping a finger on the pulse of the department wasn't his job. He took it on anyway, and everyone humored him. Easier that way. Because he was as happy with a text as a call, she didn't have to talk to him and risk having something he said piss her off and ruin her morning. Or that he'd push for more about why she was laying low. His return text was one letter: *k*.

Well, that had turned out to be easy. Maybe too easy. Or not. Could be he intended to work on a thread he'd come across, or something more interesting might have hit his desk already. Sounded unreasonable, given that murder wasn't exactly a low priority. Mike just had his own way of looking at things and lining up his own ducks. Whatever he had going gave her space to do some investigation on her own. She'd take the gift and run with it.

❖

"Oh, son of a bitch."

The paintbrush dropped to the floor, and Tula ignored the bit of paint that splattered onto her bare foot. She blew out a long breath and stepped back from the wet canvas. Tears began to flow down her cheeks, and she didn't try to stop them.

She sank into a chair and stared. A beautiful face stared back at her. This woman was younger than the last one, with dark eyes, long black hair, and a hint of a smile that spoke of a good soul. A bit of color to her skin hinted at the possibility of Hispanic heritage. Promise shone clear in her eyes. Tula cried harder.

"I'm sorry," she whispered. "I'm so sorry."

With the palms of her hands, she finally wiped away the tears. They weren't going to help the woman, and they weren't helping her. Slowly, she got up and headed to the bathroom, with no idea how long she'd been in the studio creating that painting. The last thing she remembered was finishing a cup of herbal tea, turning out the light, and then drifting off to sleep. She'd hoped for a decent stretch of rest, although given the events of the previous day and the wholly uncomfortable evening at Diane's, it hadn't appeared to be a promising prospect when she pulled up the covers. Still, she'd drifted off nicely, only to wake up to find herself in front of a fully completed painting. She could scream all the denials she wanted, and it wouldn't make a difference. The proof was right there. It was starting again. Maybe she should be grateful she'd had two decades of peace. She wasn't.

The shower helped, and the scented lotion she rubbed on her skin smelled like fresh flowers. The tears dried up. No more left to cry anyway, only some thoughts on where to go from here. First thing, she'd have to send this picture to the police too. One woman was already dead, and if history, in fact, repeated itself, another would be too. If she wasn't already. Ice slipped down her back.

The doorbell rang as she pushed the brew button on her coffee machine. Better not be Diane, or, swear to God, she'd pinch that woman's head off. She marched to the front door with solid steps. It wasn't Diane. Good news. A stranger stood on the porch, and the badge she held up to the peephole was the only reason she opened the door.

"Tula Crane?" Black jeans, a white shirt, and a black jacket all said business. Not a social call.

"Yes. Who's asking?" Tula straightened as she looked up into dark eyes. Tula wasn't short, but this woman had to be at least six feet tall.

The badge remained where Tula could see it clearly as she said, "I'm Detective Casey Wilson of the Moses Lake Police Department."

Damn. That didn't take long. She'd figured she'd have a little more time before they discovered who sent the picture. She'd underestimated the efficiency of the local police department. They could give the NYPD a run. So far this morning she appeared to be batting a thousand on everything. "Come on in." She held the door open wide.

"You don't want to know why I'm here?" Dark eyes narrowed as they studied her face.

Tula didn't look away. "I know why." No sense pretending. They didn't have that kind of time to waste.

It had all clicked into place for her the second she saw the badge through the peephole, and since then she'd been silently berating herself for being stupid enough not to stay anonymous. In her rush to try to do something to help, she'd decided to mail the picture and didn't think her action all the way through. At the time, it had made sense to do it from a public box. Yet it hit her as she'd peered through the peephole: the ubiquitous security cameras. Or could her choice have been something a little more Freudian? Didn't matter. The die had been cast, and now a detective stood on her doorstep.

"Coffee?" She kept her voice calm. Quite different from how she felt inside.

Detective Wilson looked confused, and really, who could blame her? Most would freak out when they opened the door bright and early to see police on their doorstep. To be faced with someone calm and collected likely had her wondering. But most hadn't walked a mile in her shoes. Same dance, different city.

"No thank you. I'd like to talk." All business.

In the kitchen, she poured herself a cup. The detective might not want one. She needed one. "About the photo."

She nodded. Like the woman she'd painted overnight, Detective Wilson had dark hair, held back in a clip, and intelligent eyes. "Yes, about the photo you mailed us."

"You're sure you don't want a cup of coffee? This conversation could take a while." So far, so good. She managed to keep her voice even.

"All right, fine. Black, please." Most likely she agreed to get Tula to stop asking.

Tula pulled a second mug from the cupboard, filled it, and handed it to her. She picked her mug back up and then said, "Follow me."

As much as she dreaded the conversation they were about to have, she dreaded the revelations even more. Kind of like pulling a bandage off, she decided to get it over with quickly. They'd probably want to commit her, and that was fine. Maybe that's what she'd really needed all along. She ran her free hand over her head, lightly touching the scar beneath her hair.

The air in her studio stilled as they stepped inside. She waved toward the small sofa. "You might as well sit because this explanation is long, and in fair warning, you're not going to believe me."

Silence met her comment. Tula turned to the detective, who stared at the canvas that remained on the easel. Her facial expression was hard to describe except to say it telegraphed shock. "What?" she asked when the silence dragged on.

Detective Wilson set her coffee mug on the table and let her hand drift to her holster. Tula jumped at the sound of the strap release. She took a step away, her hot coffee spilling over her hand to drip on the floor.

"What?" she asked for the second time.

"Why do you have a painting of my cousin on your easel?"

When Tula's mug hit the floor, hot coffee splattered everywhere.

❖

Angel sat and cried, her shoulders shaking. "I couldn't stop it."

He stood looking out over the lake. "I don't think any of us can. Our time is coming to an end, and the power to influence has begun to wane. Do you feel it?"

She nodded. "I feel powerless, and I hate it with every fiber of my being. It's never been like this before. It makes me want to scream."

"From the beginning, we knew the day would arrive."

She remembered, except it had been so long ago she'd managed to put it out of her mind. Selective memory. "She's the most special one we've ever helped, and I can't leave her until I know she's safe. Loved. I can't let it end like this. It's not fair to her."

"You're not God."

Blue didn't need to remind her. She knew all too well how godlike she wasn't. Sin was her middle name. That didn't change the facts. She'd been put here to protect those in danger and had been watching over Tula since those long-ago days when she crossed the threshold from life to death and back again. "I can do more."

He turned to gaze at her, his expression full of the same sadness that rolled over her. His usual optimism was missing, and she hated the look in his eyes. "We can only do what we can do."

For a change, she traveled the high road, because she had to. "If this is it, then I'm not letting it end with a colossal failure. That's a whole different kind of hell, and I refuse to go there. She will get through this, I will save her and, through her, as many others as possible. Period. End of story."

This time he smiled, and the light she loved came back into his eyes. That alone filled her with promise. "You've always had a good heart, and I've said prayers of thanks all these many years that we were put on this path together. I love you and always have."

That he could say that to her made the tears come again. If the roles were reversed, she wasn't sure she'd have the same strength of character to both forgive and to love. He had always been a much bigger person than she. "Do you ever wonder what would have occurred if things had happened differently?"

His head tilted and he studied her face. "Every day."

"And?"

"And we'd have grown old together with our children and our grandchildren. We'd have loved and laughed and rested together for eternity."

Now she smiled. "I'll settle for eternity."

"As will I."

They sat on opposite ends of the fallen tree, his favorite, and watched in silence as the sun moved over the mountains to the east, filling the sky with bright light. It reminded her of home and another downed tree. They'd sat together on that one too, only in those days they'd talked of dreams and ambitions, of what forever would look like. She dropped her head and studied the sand, remembering. She'd had a clear picture in her mind back then. It hadn't looked anything like this.

Angel raised her head and glanced over at Blue. He was gone.

CHAPTER EIGHT

Casey tapped her gun with her fingers. What a fool she'd been for coming here alone. Stupid on a whole lot of fronts, and she was smarter than that. Or at least she liked to believe she was. This faux pas made her wonder.

When Tula first opened the door, she'd been taken aback. The video they'd used to determine her identity didn't begin to capture her true loveliness. She radiated something that Casey couldn't quite define but found compelling at the same time. The long, silver hair of this slim, delicate woman framed her face and flattered her skin tone. Not many people pulled off that hair color like she did. Casey found it—her—quite appealing. Damn it anyway. Not very professional, and she prided herself on her professionalism.

All that disappeared when she stepped into the studio at the rear of the house, where large windows let natural light pour into the space, and the lake beyond provided a stunning backdrop. As per her standard operating procedures, she scanned the room, taking in every corner, cobweb, or lack thereof. Tula Crane evidently worked in this room. An impressive worktable filled with commercial designs in various stages of completion took up one wall.

As she shifted her gaze from the windows to a painting sitting on a tall easel, the urge to cuff the beautiful artist overwhelmed her. She managed to refrain from rushing into judgment, even if her hand moved to her gun, almost without conscious thought. Bullet holes had a way of sending her straight into custody mode. The act-first, ask-questions-later sort of action.

"What do you mean, your cousin?"

The confusion she heard in Tula's voice was enough to move her hand away from her gun. "That," she pointed to the painting, "is my cousin, Rita."

The color drained from Tula's face, and tears welled in her eyes. Not exactly the reaction Casey expected, particularly if she stood in the room with a killer. "Your cousin?"

"Yes, my cousin." She thought she'd made that pretty clear. It wasn't like she'd been speaking Spanish. Nope. The question had been asked in concise English.

Tula wiped at her eyes and then breathed in deeply. "Oh, dear Lord. This is worse than I feared. You better sit down, and I'll explain as best I can. As fast as I can."

"Maybe we should take this downtown." No maybe about it. The upcoming conversation belonged in an interview room with witnesses and a recording.

Tula shook her head. "Please, can we talk here first, and if you still believe I should go in for a formal interview, I will. You have my word." She sounded sincere.

Against her better judgment, Casey nodded. Mike would kill her, yet instinct told her to give Tula a chance. She'd make a call on it after she heard what the woman had to say. It better be good too, because a portrait of Rita with a bullet hole in the middle of her forehead required one impressive explanation. She didn't like threats against anyone, especially against one of her own family, period.

❖

Well, the arrival of the police had just turned from not good to disastrous. The moment Tula had returned to consciousness earlier this morning and saw what she'd painted, despair crashed down on her. History proved to her that the woman was in danger of dying, if she hadn't already been killed. What happened beneath the tip of her custom brushes didn't result from the natural creativity she'd been born with. It came unbidden and organic, as if the unseen evil forces in the universe guided her hand. As if they taunted her.

Twenty years wasn't long enough to erase the memories of how it had gone down before. Again, her hand strayed to her head, and she rubbed her scalp as if that simple gesture could make it all go away. Erase the raised and ragged skin, and make it as smooth as it had once been.

"You're going to think I'm crazy, and I won't blame you if you decide to cuff me and throw me into a cell. I won't fight you if that's what you feel you need to do. Just let me start by saying that I've hurt no one. Never have and never would."

"I hear a giant *but* in there."

She sighed. Smart lady. Explained the special badge. "Huge."

Detective Wilson's dark eyes were focused on Tula's face. A little unnerving. "Just tell me, and don't get caught up on the buts. Spit it out, and we'll go from there."

This time Tula nodded. "Most important and most immediate issue—if this woman is your cousin, you need to know she's in danger."

The cop's hand strayed once more to the gun, and her words held an edge. "What did you do to her?"

"You don't understand. I didn't do anything, and you can take that to the bank. But whenever this happens"—she pointed to the canvas—"the person whose face appears is a targeted victim. If we don't find them soon enough, they die. If we don't find *her* now, she has a very real chance of losing her life."

"You kill them."

"NO! You're not listening to me." She rubbed her hands over her face. "I'm sorry, I'm sorry. I didn't mean to yell. As I told you before, I've never hurt anyone, let alone killed someone." She couldn't help the catch in her voice. This was harder than she thought.

The hand moved off the gun, and the detective's voice softened, a little. "All right. I'll try to chill. Tell me everything, and don't leave out a single detail. I'll know if you do."

Tula believed her. Not that she'd planned to lie. She brought her eyes up to meet the officer's gaze, and something there relaxed her. "Please sit. This is a long story."

The detective sat, although Tula wouldn't have called it a relaxed posture. Not that she blamed her. She'd be shaken too if her cousin's face had appeared on the canvas. It didn't matter that she had no cousins; she could still relate. Her heart hurt, and she didn't even know the woman.

With a deep breath, she began. "It started when I was a child. After an untreated head injury."

"You suffered a TBI?"

"Yes." At the time, she hadn't known about traumatic brain injury. It had just been another painful reminder of the consequences of defiance. She knew now how lucky she'd been to recover without medical help, even if her recovery came with a freaky kind of psychic ability.

"What did the doctors say?"

"No doctors."

"Are you telling me your parents didn't get you treatment? For a TBI?" Something close to horror sounded in her voice.

She closed her eyes and tried not to go back there. Some memories hurt more than others. "No, they didn't, but that's not important to the story. What's critical is what began to happen afterward. This—" She pointed to the canvas.

"Painting women's faces."

"Painting the faces of murdered, or soon-to-be-murdered, women."

"It's here."

Blue stood up and stretched out his arms in a casual motion that for most people signified a simple move. For Blue it was more about touching unseen energy and drawing it in. It made him glow brighter. At least it had always in the past. Lately, the light had dimmed. "I feel it."

"We are too late."

"You tried."

"Not hard enough." Another death. Another failure. Too many in her life and she hated it. The reality made her wonder why she was even still here. What was the point if she couldn't change anything? Why keep her here?

"You sent her what she needed."

She'd hoped for more. "I don't believe it was enough, and if it had been, that woman would still be alive. I'm beginning to believe that no one can stop this evil. He's too strong this time."

"You are helping her to stop him. You just don't see it."

Not true. Her vision remained clear, and she could see it all crumbling. "I'm guiding her, but that's not real help. I've got to do more. It crushes me to be powerless as we watch people die over and over again. It's tearing me apart."

"Go to her," he suggested. "Let her see you."

"For what reason? And to say what? Hey, you have to stop a killer? It's all up to you?"

"Yes." His calming words didn't have the same soothing effect on her. Easy for him to throw out scenarios he'd never have to act on. A lot harder for her.

"That's not the way it works, and you know it." He'd been with her this whole journey. He knew the truth as well as she did.

"What have you been saying lately? That our time is growing short, right? What have you—what have *we* got to lose? I'll be at your side no matter what happens. You can't give up now, when we're this close. You both still have much to do—both for you and for her—and you've never quit before. Do not quit now."

The wind had picked up today, and waves crested bubbly and white on the water. The work to mold her into a better person had ended on a night filled with darkness and bad decisions, despite his constant reminders that she wasn't a lost cause. He preferred to see the upside to everything and everyone. Unlike Blue, she focused on reality, and the reality here was quite simple. Tula could be saved. *She* couldn't. She'd given up that right a long time ago.

"I have nothing to lose. She has everything. I'm not giving up on her." She took a last look at the choppy water and turned to Blue. "Let's go."

CHAPTER NINE

Casey wasn't sure how long she sat there in silence after Tula finished talking. Two minutes? Five minutes? Half the day? She was rarely speechless, yet the story she'd just heard shut her up big-time. It took her a while to formulate a response. While her mind whirled, sunshine washed the room in bright light, a distinct contrast to the dark mood inside the same room.

"Say something." Tula's eyes glistened.

Many criminal interviews through the years included tears, manufactured in the mistaken belief Casey would consider them real. Not the case here. Everything about Tula screamed genuine. Or, mostly everything. The threatened tears, yes. The emotion behind her words, absolutely. But she hadn't shared the entire story. She had intentionally left out something, and omission, in Casey's book, equated to lying.

Her thoughts lining up, she said, "So, let me get this straight. You're an artist who doesn't paint, because when you do, it's in a fugue state, and you create the images of murder victims. Did I get that right?"

"In a nutshell, yes."

She started to call bullshit on the story filled with references to paranormal influences. Then she thought of her abuelita once again. She would scold Casey for closing her mind to the possibilities of the universe. In good conscience, Casey wouldn't dismiss the wisdom of her elders, and rather than jump immediately to the bullshit, she paused to let it all settle. Let her heart and soul weigh in, as well as her analytical mind.

She'd get right to the pertinent point. "What aren't you telling me?" She didn't intend to allow Tula's omission to go unchallenged.

"That's pretty much everything." Tula looked away.

Well, wasn't that telling? Another basic in interview psychology: that slide away of the gaze. "Pretty much isn't everything."

Tula met her eyes again. "Anything else is trivial detail that has nothing to do with this. I want to help, and I'm trying."

"Why do you want to do that for people you profess not to know?" How many well-meaning citizens showed up to help, only to slow down an investigation? That's not what she needed here, and whatever Tula Crane failed to disclose could also slow the search for the killer.

Tula paused and turned her head toward the windows. "I don't understand why this happens to me, and I don't know why me at all. The first time it happened, I had no way of even knowing what I'd done. Afterward, I was scared. In the long run, once we figured out that it sometimes came with time to alter the course of events, it made a difference. I'd hoped it wouldn't happen again, but it has, and I can't ignore it, knowing what I do. That's why I sent that picture to you. I thought it could help you get to her in time. I was wrong."

"This has really happened before?" The overall story rang strange enough that even trying to channel her abuelita made it a stretch for her to buy into the fugue-state portrait painting. Lord knows, they'd had plenty of so-called psychics want to help in their investigations, kind of like the well-meaning citizens. This was the first time she'd come up against an artist reaching out with a hauntingly accurate representation of a victim. It was so bizarre, she had to roll the situation over in her mind again and again, trying to make even a tiny bit of it believable. Wasn't working very well. Still sounded like a grade-B horror movie, and she hated those things.

Her gaze strayed to the picture of Rita, and her stomach flipped. If there was any truth to what Tula had been telling her, then time was clicking away. If she gave this woman the benefit of the doubt, she might save Rita from the same fate as the teacher. If she ignored her as a quack and it turned out to be true, she might sentence her cousin to death. Damned if she did. Damned if she didn't.

This time tears did slide down Tula's cheeks, and in her eyes, she saw pain. "I'm afraid so. I was eighteen the last time I picked up a paintbrush."

"You really paint the faces of dead people?"

Tula shook her head. "No, not exactly like that. You have to understand that I started painting before I could talk. It was literally my life, and I was good, really good. I still am. The painting of the murder victims started after the head injury and ended when…"

Tula fell suddenly quiet.

"When what?"

"When I ran away and locked up my paints and canvases."

❖

"She's got company." Angel bit her lip and shifted from foot to foot.

"Well, that's an interesting twist." Blue walked along the shoreline, his hands behind his back. The wind picked up his hair and blew it around his face. He didn't seem to notice.

"You remember how it started the first time?"

"Of course. I have absolute recall."

"It wasn't really a question." Despite what he might think, she remembered everything, every little painful detail, just as well as he did.

"I know. Kicking things back to you is more entertainment than anything else."

She stopped, put her hands on her hips, and narrowed her eyes. "Really? You think now is the time to be flippant?"

He stopped as well, then turned and tilted his head as he studied her face. "In my experience, it gets you out of your head."

"I don't get into my head."

Blue said nothing, just continued to stare at her.

God, how she hated the fact that he was always right. "Fine. Maybe I do a little."

"A little?" He raised both eyebrows, and one corner of his mouth curved up.

She turned away from his smirk and returned her attention to the house down the lake a fair distance. "I can't go in with someone else there."

"No. It wouldn't be wise to even try it. Too many complications."

"Why do I feel like I'm abandoning her?" Her heart hurt. She wanted so badly to rush in and throw everything she had at Tula. To stop the madness right now. Today.

"Because you care, and that's one of the things that has always made you special."

She didn't buy into the special part of what he said, if he meant special in a good way. "Hard not to care about her. I wish her every good thing possible after what she's had to endure."

"You've always had a good heart and stood up for those less fortunate, those who have been hurt when they deserved nothing but love. You are"—he held up a hand to stop her protest—"special and deserving of love and forgiveness. Now, come on. She'll handle this just like she did before, with your help."

"She was awfully young before."

"And she handled it," he repeated. "Now she's mature and wise and capable. All powerful things. More ammunition to work with. We'll still have her back, but when we have to go, she'll be ready. I feel it." He put a hand to his heart. "Here."

"I don't know if I'm ready." The thought of leaving Tula alone, of leaving the journey she and Blue had long traveled together, made her want to run and hide. Silly, really, considering she'd been longing for release the entire time. The road had been too long. It had tested her faith and her resolve. She'd never understood why she had been chosen, and she supposed it wasn't important. If God had wanted her to understand, he'd have let her. As it was, she focused less on herself and more on those she came to help. It made it easier, even if, like now, it hurt to fail. She had to find the faith to believe everything would be all right.

Angel sighed and closed her eyes. In silence, she said a quick prayer and hoped it would be enough.

Chapter Ten

"Well, that was pretty fucking weird, and you're a fucking nut job for not taking her into custody." Casey talked to herself as she sat alone in her car, resting her forehead against the steering wheel. She'd left Tula inside her house with the warning that she'd be back and not to leave town, all in her sternest cop voice. Far from the proper protocol, yet she'd walked out the door alone because she believed the woman and the crazy-ass story she'd told.

It wasn't the pretty face that pulled her in. She'd been in this game long enough to know better than to believe the cover on the book. Evil came in all kinds of packages, and that included very attractive ones with soft eyes and full lips. It would be nice if malevolence did present itself as cracked and ugly, and sometimes it did. More often, it looked more like the next-door neighbor invited in to share a cup of coffee. Just ask the folks over in Spokane about the serial killer who had buried one of his victims in a flowerbed at his lovely, middle-class home in an upscale neighborhood. Nobody saw that one coming when bodies were discovered all over the city and the trail led back to that nice home.

Now, she had a bigger problem on her hands than the pretty woman with so-called psychic abilities. Making sure her cousin was safe and sound took priority over everything. So far, though, Rita hadn't answered either her calls or her texts. She twisted around and looked at Tula Crane's latest painting that now rested in the back seat of her unmarked car. Tula hadn't balked when she'd told her that she intended to take it, and she could have. With no warrant and, at the moment, no probable cause, she could have told her no, and that would have been that. Once again gut instinct drove her. That, and the fact that the face it portrayed happened to be family.

As tempting as it was, she resisted calling her tía. Her aunt wasn't exactly what she'd call the strongest branch of the family tree. She was a whole lot overprotective of all her children and, in fact, all her family. If Casey called to say she couldn't get ahold of her daughter, it would set her off like a five-alarm fire. Despite the way her own nerves tingled at her inability to connect with Rita, nobody needed her aunt's trademark hysterics at this particular point in time.

She opted to call her brother instead. Mike didn't figure into any of the scenarios that entered her mind. She didn't need his kind of help at the moment. Later, yes. Not now. Her brother could be far more useful.

The phone rang three times before he picked up. "Stan, I know you're busy, but I need you to help me find Rita." She rattled all that off before he could even say hello.

"What?"

"I need to get ahold of Rita, like right now."

"Casey, come on. I've got a full caseload today. Tracking people down is your forte. I fix them, not find them."

Sometimes getting him out of his doctor head took work. "In this case it's important and more efficient for you to do than it would be for me." Rita, a nurse, worked at Samaritan Hospital, and given that Stan practiced there, it would be quicker and easier for him to find out if she was working today. He was a smart guy. She shouldn't have to explain that fact to him.

"Fine. At least tell me why."

"I can't."

"Really? You want me to push back care of my patients to do this for you, and you won't tell me why? I call bull on that. We both know you could if you wanted to."

"It's not that I don't want to. I promise I'll explain it to you in detail when I see you, or as much as I can anyway. Right now, please just trust me and track her down. Have her call me the second you find her. Please, Stan. I really need your help."

While their professions might be light years apart, their ethics were not. He wouldn't share his patient information with her, and she couldn't divulge case information to him, despite the comment about not wanting to share. Splitting hairs, she supposed, given that Rita wasn't actually a case at this point. Unless, of course, she believed everything the artist told her. If it turned out to be true, it would bring heartbreak to her family and stoke the fire in the hunt for a killer.

While she waited for Stan to find Rita, she decided that more information on the lovely Tula Crane would be a good thing to tackle. It would help if she knew someone in the New York City Police Department, because that could speed up her search. She didn't know anyone there, although the way she figured it, if she asked around, someone in her circle might. Worth a try without taking up a ton of time.

At her desk, she hit paydirt in less than five minutes. She got a name and a number from a recent transfer from Spokane. Usually, they left the MLPD to go to Spokane. In this instance, he'd made the opposite transfer because he'd wanted to come home. As he told it, he'd worked a case with a detective out of the NYPD and got her the number in nothing flat. Even better, the NYPD contact happened to be at his desk when she put in the call. Sometimes the gods smiled on her.

"Sonofabitch," she said under her breath. She hadn't been wrong to give Tula the benefit of the doubt because, as it turned out, she hadn't been telling her a tall tale at all. It had been the truth, except for the part about the name of the artist. The big lie there. Technically speaking, Tula Crane hadn't been the one to paint the faces of murder victims in New York. A young lady with the rather pretentious name of Mona Lisa and a prominent artist known all over the world had been the painter. Who the hell named their kid Mona Lisa?

A bit more digging and she discovered that this particular artist had started life as Candice, and upon discovering that their child was a prodigy, her parents legally changed her name to Mona Lisa. She'd been only three years old at the time, and Casey wondered if she knew her birth name. Talk about exploiting a child. It didn't take a lot of brain power to figure out that Mona Lisa and Tula were one and the same, particularly after reading the stories about the artist who vanished at the age of eighteen, along with the bulk of her sizeable trust fund. She'd done a credible job of thwarting the exploitive parents. Went to the point about her being quite intelligent as well as talented.

"Wow. That's quite the situation," she said to Detective Marc Dane of the NYPD.

"If I hadn't been there to see it, I wouldn't have believed it. First and only time in my career I've seen legit psychic abilities. We've had some cases in the years since she disappeared that I'd have asked for her help if she hadn't gotten into the wind."

"Really?" She never heard something like that from another cop. Psychics soothed families. They got in a cop's way.

"Really. She's that good and that real. If your artist is our Mona Lisa, tell her hello for me. She did some good things here, and I, for one, have always been grateful, even if her parents are a couple of assholes."

"That bad?"

"Let's just say none of us working the cases at the time were surprised when Mona Lisa grabbed the money and disappeared. Every one of us hoped she'd gotten away but also wondered if the parents had done something to her. I'm quite glad to find out she's alive and well. Good for her."

❖

Tula's urge to run almost pushed her into defying Detective Wilson's warning not to leave Moses Lake. She didn't want to go through this again. Not fair to her on any front. She'd never done anything to anyone to deserve this, and what she'd done before should have been enough to grant her a reprieve from this thing that happened in her head. It pissed her off that it didn't.

She bit out a wry laugh. What a selfish and immature thing to even think. If she'd learned anything, it was that life just happened. Good and bad both existed side by side and sometimes in the same space. Being good and kind didn't guarantee that nothing bad would happen. How she'd learned that lesson. It could have warped her view of the world and made her a sour, bitter woman who hated life. Unhappy and angry didn't work for her. Fascination at the world around her remained intact, though a wariness of people's motivations did keep her circle very, very small. All things considered, she figured that a pretty good result in the face of an unconventional upbringing. It could have been much worse.

Still, she wished those canvases had stayed in the back of her closet. Certainly, she missed painting. The most alive she ever felt was when she let her creativity soar at the end of a brush. The universe opened to her in rainbows of color and light. It spoke to her soul, and while using her talents in the graphic-arts arena gave her an artistic outlet, it wasn't even close to her true calling. Those early days of painting for nothing more than the pure pleasure of it had been such a joy. Even as young as she'd been, she still remembered how it filled her. What they did to her should have stripped away the joy, yet it didn't. She could escape the real world the second she put paint on a palette. Only after the faces started to appear did things change. Only then did her brushes bring as much fear as happiness.

Back in the old days, she'd been scared once the meaning behind the paintings became clear. The people who came to talk to her were kind, though, not attempting to disguise their disbelief. Disheartening to her at the time because she desperately wanted someone to believe her. One detective, Frances Aldon, a gruff woman with dark, gray-streaked hair and green eyes, broke through the fear and became her confidant. She'd been the one to believe in her nearly from the beginning. She'd been the one to stop not one, but two different killers, ending the nights of painting the faces of dead women.

She'd also subtly encouraged Tula to make a change. Frances had been smart enough to see beyond the façade that was her life. Through her words and her example, Frances filled her with courage, and that's what it took to break free. Tula's only regret was that two years after she'd run from her old life, she'd found out that Frances had died. The big C. She never knew that Tula had made it. That she lived far away, free and happy.

As she thought about her earlier visitor, she wondered if Casey Wilson might have the same heart as Frances. She'd been understandably skeptical if not outright angry. Who wouldn't be when seeing a family member's face on one of her canvases? Tula had revealed enough of her history that it wouldn't be a heavy lift to discover the truth behind it all. The detective would figure out at least some of her secrets before the sun set. Not that she liked it. Not that she had a choice.

Well, that wasn't quite correct. Choices always existed. They just weren't always great ones. Exactly the situation she found herself in now. How in good conscience could she run with the knowledge that at least one woman lay dead and another one would die if she did nothing? All she had to do was help stop this killer, and then she could be on her way. She'd made a new life here all those years ago, and she could make another one somewhere else. The last run had given her twenty years of peace, and perhaps running again might give her another twenty. Worth a shot.

She walked out to the backyard and sat in one of the patio chairs. The lake was serene this afternoon, the sun warm on her face. The ducks that liked to waddle along the beach were paddling on the water as though they were having an afternoon tea party. The grass beneath her feet gave her the sensation of being grounded. It all helped to soothe the soul and calm the mind.

"Hey."

She jerked and turned toward the voice. Then she smiled and motioned toward the empty patio chair. "Hey."

Angel dropped to the other chair and kicked off her flip-flops. Her toes curled into the thick grass just like Tula's. She wondered if it made her feel grounded too.

"So, tell me what's going on." Angel tilted her face to the afternoon sun.

"I don't know what you mean." It always amazed her how intuitive Angel could be. This client-turned-friend had a way of showing up when she needed someone to talk to.

"Bull. You gave me the bum's rush out of here when I asked about that bizarre painting, and I want to know why. That's not the kind of thing anyone would paint for fun, especially someone with your gentle nature."

She didn't look at Angel because she'd see the truth on her face. One thing she'd learned about her quirky friend was that she could almost see into her soul. Special that way and most of the time she appreciated it. Not so much right at the moment. She'd prefer to be a mystery from everyone, Angel included.

"You'd never believe me if I told you."

Angel turned to stare at her. "Try me."

She met her eyes and figured what the hell. Given that the chances were better than average she'd end up leaving this place, not a lot to lose.

"I paint the faces of murdered women."

❖

"Progress, my friend, progress." Angel walked with Blue along the shoreline. The sun had gone down, and the lights in the homes that sat along the massive lake glittered like diamonds. Very pretty, and in many ways, it reminded her of home. More and more lately, she found herself making these comparisons.

She didn't care to think of home or what had brought her into the life she'd lived since then. Nothing had turned out the way she'd imagined as a young woman who'd felt like a world of opportunity stretched out before her if she had the chance to make the right changes. All of that had been wiped away in minutes.

Her hand strayed to her hair. Once it would have hung down her back in long, golden braids. She'd been so proud of her silken hair. Not many boasted of the pale color and the deep-blue eyes that set her apart from the others. If only she'd known then what she did now. That misplaced pride changed everything.

Her gaze strayed to Blue, and she smiled. Without him at her side she didn't know how she'd have made it. She'd have still done the job given to her because it was the right thing to do and, despite her many stumbles, made her feel as though she had managed to make amends in some small way. Yet he brought her more than partnership; he also brought her a measure of joy. Some blessings were simple and immense all at the same time. She didn't deserve blessings. She'd take them anyway.

"I can't believe she told you. That's important."

"Surprised me as well. Not much prodding involved either. She's changing."

"We all change, given enough time. It's a beautiful thing, if you let it be."

She ignored the last comment, directed right at her. "I wish it didn't take evil to make this happen."

"It takes what it takes."

She rolled her eyes. "That's your great wisdom after eons of learning?"

Blue shrugged. "Sometimes it is that easy."

Leave it to Blue to break it down to the simplest explanation. He did have a way of uncomplicating things, while her strength fell into making everything more difficult. She stopped and leaned against a tree, her head tipped back. The sky was dark, the moon nearly full. She closed her eyes and breathed in the cool night air. "It didn't feel the same there this time."

"Explain."

Again, simple and to the point. "The air around her was off, as though evil had walked through, shedding its darkness as it went."

For probably a full minute, Blue said nothing. "The interloper."

"I believe so."

"If it's him, we have to watch her even closer."

She nodded and didn't disagree. While she couldn't pick up on the voices that filtered through the universe unheard by most, she could sense changes brought about by them. Some of the voices were good. Some were not. Blue had a way of distinguishing between them. "I'm with you there."

"Could you tell if she sensed it too?"

Angel thought about her conversation with Tula, about the faraway look in her eyes as she talked. "I think she did."

CHAPTER ELEVEN

"Oh, sister, don't you have some secrets." Casey leaned back in her chair and reread the email. The file Marc sent her from the NYPD added a lot more detail to what he'd shared with her earlier. A fascinating read that seemed to imply that Tula, aka Mona Lisa, had been some kind of savant. Judging by everything else she read, including the estimate of the funds transferred out of the trust fund, savant might have been an understatement.

"Who has secrets?"

Crap. She hadn't heard Mike come up behind her. Wrapped up in what she'd been researching while at the same time worrying about Rita had her oblivious to everything else. Not good. She didn't like being startled and, in particular, not by Mike. "Everybody. You included."

He made a clicking noise out of the side of his mouth. "True story there. What have you come up with on our dead girl? You follow up with the chick who sent us the pic?"

While she'd stayed out of touch with Mike all day, he'd still been provided the same information from the crime-lab folks that she'd gotten. Letia might be family, but she played by the book. Part of what made her great at her job.

When Mike had sent her a text after talking with Letia, she'd told him she'd follow up with Tula. Kind of surprised her when he'd agreed to let her do it without him. The unexpected move worked for her, and she'd run with it rather than question it.

"I did." She wasn't about to tell him about the painting yet. Still in processing mode with that one, and she didn't need his input until she figured out how to deal with it. Later, sure, but not right now.

"And..."

"And she'd done a painting of our victim and wanted to get it to us. She thought it was important."

"Let me get this straight. She told you that she painted it before our unfortunate teacher got herself killed? With a bullet hole in her head? And she's not the killer. Am I hearing you right?"

If she understood the story from Tula correctly, strictly speaking the answer was yes. She went with that. "Yes."

"You find out why she added the bullet hole then?"

"Of course."

"And…" The irritation in his voice would be impossible to miss, and he had to be catching on that she was being deliberately obtuse.

"She said she didn't know why she'd painted that feature."

"Get real, Wilson. She's playing you. The whole thing sounds fishy to me. I knew I should have handled this."

"I don't disagree with you that she's playing us on that score. I'm telling you though, nothing else was out of place."

He stood over her as she sat at her desk. "You should have brought her in."

She resisted the urge to stand up to put them eye to eye. "We need to give her a bit of rope. I made that call and advised her to stay put while I came back here to do some additional investigation, which I've done."

"I'm not sure I agree completely with that move, but given I've got some leads of my own to follow up on too, we'll roll with it for now. You know, a couple of our frequent flyers who might be good for this. Better candidates than some hippie artist."

Hippie artist? Really? What decade was he living in? She did understand where he was going with his frequent-flyer leads. Everyone knew he had a hard-on for a few of the local residents who had managed to get under his skin. He was perpetually on the lookout for anything that would get them behind bars for as long as possible. He'd been dogging a couple of these guys since his uniform days, and he'd been plainclothes for years. Talk about not letting things go.

The thing about it? She didn't see any of his favorites as having the kind of bent it would take for the level of violence visited on that poor teacher. Still, if he wanted to go down that road, it would give her some free time to pursue her own avenues of inquiry. It would keep him off Tula's back while she figured out what to do with her.

"You following up with your leads?"

He picked up his jacket from the back of his chair. "You know it.

I'm going to get these sons of bitches if it's the last thing I do. You keep working your chick, and I'll work these bastards. One way or the other, we'll get the responsible party and throw their ass in prison until hell freezes over."

"Sounds solid." The intent anyway. His vendetta against his chosen few would be a dead end, as much as he might wish it otherwise.

"You need anything from me?"

Ever the helpful mentor, as long as it was his kind of help, and that she didn't need. "I'm good, but I'll let you know if I hit a brick wall."

He waved and walked away. "Good. I'm heading to the Ponderosa for dinner with my lady before I come back here and hit it. Later, gator."

She started to get up and do the same. Way past time to go home to feed the animals and herself. As she walked toward the door, her phone rang, and she glanced at the display. Stan. Finally. "Did you get ahold of Rita?" A call earlier would have been appreciated, and she'd left him three messages conveying the same. She also recognized that the man had a demanding career and people's lives took priority over helping his sister track down one of their relatives. Her own inquiries had yielded nothing.

"Tía tracked her cell phone."

"Great. You found her." Relief made her sit back down. At the same time, Mike came back into the office, frowning. He looked at her and jerked his thumb toward the door in a gesture she recognized as "let's go." Something had happened.

Her brother's voice caught. "She's dead."

❖

Tula felt it. Not even like a sixth-sense kind of thing. A great deal more like a full-on punch to the stomach. Nobody had to tell her what it meant. Even with all her efforts, even after baring her soul to the hot detective, none of it mattered. Another life ended.

The worst part came in knowing the lost was someone said hot detective loved. Every other face painted had been that of a stranger with no ties back to her. Not that this was actually a tie to her, but in that six-degrees-of-separation kind of way, it felt personal. Whatever way it might be, it hurt more than the others.

As she'd done earlier, she went outside and sat in a patio chair that she pulled onto the lawn. The patio itself was lovely and a key selling point for the house. Spanning the length of the house, it gave her a perfect view of the lake. A couple of years back, she had a gas firepit installed, and a retractable patio cover allowed her to sit outside even on rainy days. A perfect setting for romantic evenings on the lake. If one were to have romance, that is. She'd dismissed any chance of that happening years ago. An occasional one-night stand remained the safest thing for her. While far from providing an emotional tie, it did at least fill a momentary physical need. She had become quite good at ignoring the loneliness that regularly crept into her heart.

She opted not to sit on the built-for-romance patio and instead chose the grass, where she could feel the earth beneath her feet. That physical connection did amazing things for her. She might not have much in terms of connections with other humans, but she did have a solid kinship with the physical world. When the rest of her life tilted and forces unseen tapped at her psyche, the earth offered her a firm base. It gifted back to her the stability she lacked in life.

With her head tilted to the dark sky, she closed her eyes. The tension in her shoulders started to ease as she curled her toes into the cool grass. It always helped to simply relax and clear her mind, think of nothing, and let peace flow in.

"Whatcha doing?"

She yelped and sprang out of her chair. Whirling, she stopped the incoming flight response. Then she got a good look at the intruder, and the fight response kicked in. "What are you doing here?" Diane's brother, Dante, stood in a circle of the patio light, smiling and cover-model ready.

"I saw you sitting out here in the dark and thought you might want company."

GO AWAY. The scream stayed silent. She didn't want anyone out here with her, least of all a guy who made the fine hairs on the back of her neck stand up. He ruined her serenity. "I'm fine. Just enjoying some quiet time. By myself." Rudeness wasn't typically her style. Sometimes, and some people, called for it. Diane and her brother fell into that category. Intrusive and obnoxious must be a family thing.

"Well, you know, I was up and about, and since you were too…" He shrugged.

"You were watching me?"

"No. Not like that at all. Sneaking out for a smoke, and there you were, and now here I am." He held his arms out.

Liar. "I appreciate the neighborly gesture, but I was just about to go inside." She'd retreat from her communion with nature if that's what it took to get rid of him.

Her hand on the back of her chair, she picked it up and carried it onto the patio again. If Dante was anything like Diane, the only way to get rid of him would be to run inside and close and bolt all the doors. Not fair that she'd be forced to become a prisoner in her own home again.

He glanced up toward the sky. "If you're sure? It's a nice night to enjoy the moon and stars. I haven't spent a lot of time in Moses Lake, but it's growing on me. Interesting people, a beautiful lake, and tons of places to explore. I can see why my sister picked this place. Nice to spend some extended time here."

The thought of him hanging around made her throw up in her mouth just a little. "I'm sure. I have a lot of work to do tomorrow and need to get some rest. I suspect you do as well." He'd made a point of bragging about his big assignments. He needed to back up the big mouth.

His smile wasn't particularly warm or friendly. Perhaps it was a trick of the moonlight that made it look creepy. "I got a lot done tonight, so I'll be all over sleeping in. But, hey, you have a good night. Maybe we'll see each other tomorrow. Do coffee or something."

"Maybe." *When hell freezes over*. She forced herself to walk, not run, into her house. Seconds after she turned the deadbolt and leaned against the door with a sigh, her phone rang.

"Hello."

"She's dead, but you knew that already, didn't you?" The bitterness in Casey's voice wasn't lost on Tula. She couldn't blame her.

"I could lie to you."

"Don't." The word had a menacing edge.

The unspoken threat wasn't what took her to the truth. She didn't intend to lie. Casey was too sharp, and besides, she didn't want to. "I knew. I felt it."

"I'm on the way over. Don't you move an inch."

❖

"They've found her," Blue said as he leaned over the bridge railing and stared down at the water. The confirmation wasn't necessary, given hours ago the air blew cold and foreboding. Nobody had to explain to her what it meant. Death turned the very molecules heavy, making it feel as though a truckload of bricks had dropped down on her shoulders. Talk about yet another epic failure.

"I had hoped we could save her."

"This is not on you. Never has been."

"Easy to say. Not so easy to believe. I should have found a way, but I didn't. I was too slow. Too inept. I'm not right for this job."

"Not true. You know as well as I do that, despite everything, much remains out of her control and ours. We can guide, and that's it. Free will can trump even the best intentions. Evil forces can often stomp on good intentions. Many things are beyond our reach."

"That's messed up." She'd railed against those things out of her control during her whole existence.

"Indeed. True nonetheless. You know better than to fight it. Find a way to work with it."

Tears started trickling down her cheeks. "I've got to change things. I can't deal with any of this. Not anymore. It's not fair. We've done so much good. How can God send us out here to help and then leave us to flounder? You tell me, how is that fair? How is that right regardless of what I've done?"

His eyes softened as he studied her face. "My darling girl, whoever said any of this was fair?"

"It should be."

"Should is a very dangerous word."

"I hate when you're all philosophical."

"It is but one of my redeeming qualities."

She couldn't help the small smile. "You have a lot of redeeming qualities. That isn't one of them."

"Au contraire. I am at my most charming when I delve deep into philosophy."

"Au contraire, you are at your most irritating. But…"

He raised a single eyebrow. "But?"

"But I love you when you're irritating or happy or wise, and would be lost without you. I couldn't have made it all this time if you hadn't been here with me."

"I always have your back."

She wiped away the tears with the back of her hand. "I know."

"Now." He smiled. "How do we help her? You can do this. I have faith in you."

Her heart lightened. It always did when Blue buoyed her. One of his gifts. “This is just beginning.”

He nodded. “It is.”

“So, the best thing I can do is channel sight to her.”

“She is on the radar of the detective.”

“They will have to work together.”

“They will.”

She met his eyes. “I can give her the vision, and together they can stop him.”

He looked to the sky. “Thy will be done.”

CHAPTER TWELVE

You need to explain what the fuck happened to my cousin." Casey's voice caught, and she took a second to steady herself. If a time ever existed to restrain extreme emotion, this would be it. She stood once again in Tula's studio and curled her fingers into her palms to stop the trembling. "How did you know she'd been killed? What did you do to her?"

At first, she thought Tula would refuse to talk at all, because she turned her back on Casey, and the silence grew deep. Then she heard a sound that, for a second, confused her. Then it clicked. Tula was crying. "Did you research me?"

Who the hell cared about her right now? "We're not talking about you." If Tula thought the poor-me routine would work, she was mistaken. Regardless of what the NYPD had told her, there was more to the story, and by God, she would get it out of Tula one way or the other.

"Of course we are. Your cousin's life has been stolen from her, and you think I had something to do with her death. Am I getting that about right?"

"You know something you're not telling me, so yeah. I think you played a part in it."

"Did you look me up? The real me?" Tula turned back to face her, the tears wiped from her cheeks though still glistening in her eyes. She appeared distressed. Could be she was nothing more than a very good actor. Though she'd refuse to admit it out loud, she didn't believe it was the latter.

Damn the woman. Casey didn't want to be swayed by base emotion. She also didn't want to believe anything she'd heard or read. Too out-of-this-world for murders that were real and close to home. "Yes. I looked you up. I tracked you down."

"Then you know I didn't have anything to do with harming her. I see only what I see. I don't know where it comes from, and I don't know why it comes to me."

Something about her last statement didn't ring completely true to Casey. A note in her voice maybe, or perhaps something as simple as her cop's instincts. Combine that with living under a false identity, and Tula Crane had a lot more explaining to do.

"You're connected to a lot of murder. I don't care that you were a kid when this started, and I sure don't care that the NYPD thinks you were an innocent pulled into something evil."

"What do you care about then? Nothing has changed in the last twenty years. I had nothing to do with the deaths of those women in New York, and I have nothing to do with the women killed here, your cousin included."

"You painted her face with a fucking bullet hole on it." The obvious couldn't be ignored. Rita's face had been right there on the now-empty easel.

"Yes, I did. That doesn't mean I killed her."

"It doesn't mean you didn't."

"I came here to start over. To make it stop. You think for one minute that I like starting all over again? Look me in the eyes and tell me you really believe I'm a killer."

The mild-mannered artist morphed into someone with intense emotion. Did it surprise her? Not so much. She would expect that from a person with something to hide. "I touch a nerve?" Maybe they'd get to it now.

Tula sighed and shook her head. The fire left her, and she sounded tired. "You have no idea what I've lived through. You with your family and a town you've never been forced to leave. You can't even begin to understand. Truth is, I tried to help when it started again, and look how that's turning out. I should have packed up and left this place. You think this benefits me in any way whatsoever?"

Something in Tula's voice took the wind out of her, an underlying truth she couldn't ignore. "You're making a leap about me, my family, and this town, given you don't know me, but point taken. Here's where I'm coming from. You're smart enough to know that I'd be a damned poor detective if I didn't look closely at you."

Her eyes closed and she took a deep breath. "Fair enough, and yes, I understand. Believe it or not, I also respect you for it. I'm asking you to suspend suspicion of me and, at least for a few moments, open your mind. I truly have no idea why this happens. I'd like to suggest that rather than looking at me as your killer, use me to help find the real one."

❖

Tula couldn't believe she'd let the words cross her lips. Casey clearly thought her responsible for the two murders, so to suggest she help in the investigation was, on the surface, pretty bizarre. A hail Mary because she didn't know how else to get through to her.

"What the fuck are you talking about?"

She caught Casey's gaze and held it. In her eyes she glimpsed anger, despair, and the expected disbelief. In most ways, she got it. Any rational person would question Tula's sanity, even in the face of the evidence her real history could provide, and she was certain Casey had done enough digging since she left her earlier to be fully versed. Now something flashed in those beautiful eyes, and it gave her hope.

"I wanted to stop the killing. This thing I can do really disrupted my life and my art. Back then, I didn't know who to turn to, and at first no one believed me because I was a child. If not for a couple of detectives who decided to take a chance, I would have been written off as a crazy kid stuck away in a room without friends or a family that loved her. It's no different now. Once more I'm faced with the skepticism of traditional law enforcement, and don't get me wrong. I understand why. All I'm asking is that you open your mind and hear what the universe is trying to tell us."

The pain of losing a loved one to violence covered Casey's face. She wanted someone to be held accountable, and Tula didn't blame her. But accusing her didn't help. Somehow, she had to find a way to redirect Casey, make her realize she was wasting precious time by focusing on her and not on the one responsible.

"And how am I supposed to do that?"

Her next idea wouldn't go down well. If she could think of something better, she would. Unfortunately, nothing else came to her on the fly, and she didn't have time to do anything but blurt out her thoughts. Nothing ventured, nothing gained. "Stay here with me."

"Excuse me."

"Hear me out. The thing is, I don't know when it will hit me. Hell, I don't even know when I'm in it. But I do know that he's still out there, and he's going to do it again. I can feel it in my bones. When he does, I'm betting I will do another painting. If you're here, you'll be a witness. Then you'll understand that I'm not part of it."

For at least a full minute, Casey stared at her. Her expression said that she believed Tula had lost her ever-loving mind. Might not be too far off the mark either.

She waved her hands. "I can't do that. It's completely outside of protocol."

Tula might have been a kid when it started all those years ago, but she'd been aware of how things worked. A bright child back then, she was an intelligent woman now. "You're not an investigator on this case any longer, are you?"

The "oh shit" look crossed Casey's face. Direct hit. "No one has officially linked the teacher and Rita yet."

"My question remains the same. Are you on the case, either case?"

"No." The single word dripped with pain.

"Doesn't take a rocket scientist to figure out you'd get taken off a case that involved a family member, and the two murders are too close together to not be considered linked."

"That's the current unofficial logic."

Now that it was out in the open, she pressed on. "So, here's my thought process. It wouldn't be a conflict if you stayed here. Besides, you can't help but wonder if I'm involved. How better to figure it out one way or the other than to see with your own eyes how the paintings come to me. The proof is right here in this house. With me."

Casey shook her head, her expression dark. "It's way outside standard operating procedure."

No argument there. She still wasn't giving up. "But technically, it's not wrong."

Casey opened her mouth and then closed it. Yes! She had her. "I don't know."

Tula went to the closet and pulled out a blank canvas. She set it on the easel and turned back to Casey. "Yes, you do."

"Fine." She sounded like a child who'd been sent to her room.

"You'll stay?" Tula sounded like a child who hoped for a giant piece of chocolate cake.

"I'll stay."

Chocolate cake won.

❖

Angel heard the last of the conversation. Tears rolled down her cheeks. She'd come here hoping for some kind of miracle, and it appeared in the form of one lady detective. She tried hard to put all the pieces into place, yet she could do only so much. Tula had taken a leap that could make all the difference.

"What's going on?"

"She talked Casey into staying with her."

"You won't be able to visit with her at the house."

"True, but it's a good thing. They need each other."

"How so? That woman's a cop, one with a very suspicious mind. I don't think she's open enough to the universe to really capture what Tula can do. Is that the kind of help she needs?"

Angel had a good feeling about this, the right kind of feeling, like the pieces were starting to come together. "Tula can bring her around. We're going to need her too. The only way to stop this once and for all is to put the right people together at the right time. This Casey is one of them. We're not going to be strong enough to do it without outside help."

"Are you sure?" Blue didn't often question her. Where had his trademark optimism scampered off to?

"Did I bring her the right people in New York?"

He nodded and smiled. "You did."

"Did they stop it by working together?"

"They did."

"And did Tula get to safety?"

"Again, my dear, you are right. Tula found a safe haven. Only one thing."

Angel studied his face. The smile was gone. "What?"

"It's never going to end for her. Not really. She'll never be free even after we're gone."

"I made a choice back then."

"You did, and I respect what you did. I'm just saying…"

"That if I'd have allowed her to die from the head injury, she'd be free."

"Well, yes."

She brought her eyes up to meet his. "I made the right choice. She was a child, an abused and neglected child. She deserved to live, and that awful woman had no right to harm her."

"No, she did not."

"I couldn't help what came back with her. If I could take the visions away, I would, but I can't. All I can do is try to direct them. I did the best I could then, and I'm doing the best I can right now."

"We're running low on time."

She closed her eyes and listened. A gentle swishing sound echoed in her head—a bit like the sound of sand falling through an hourglass. That damn hourglass. "She's going to need Casey. She's the one who will get her through this."

"I don't know."

Angel did. She opened her eyes and looked at Blue. "She has to."

CHAPTER THIRTEEN

What in the actual fuck had possessed her to say that? It was all kinds of wrong to agree to stay at the house of a person of interest, and Casey knew it. She'd aced her ethics classes. True enough that Tula hadn't been formally listed as a suspect or a person of interest. Minor detail. Mike took lead on the case, and he'd connect the dots soon enough. Shit would hit the fan if he found out she'd stayed here.

On the other hand—screw Mike. This wasn't just any case. Her family would never forgive her if she played it safe. In her own mind, this wasn't the time for that either. Balls to the wall, as her brother would say, when their mother couldn't hear, of course. Abuelita would tell her to stand tall and do whatever needed to be done. Right now, that meant staying here with the artist and seeing if the story she'd shared would hold water.

"You're sure?" Tula didn't seem all that certain she'd heard Casey right.

She nodded. "I'm not going to say that I trust you because, chica, I don't. I'm also not sure I disbelieve you. I'm walking a fine line, and at the moment, I don't have a clue which side I'll come down on."

Tula let out a long breath. "Thank you."

"Don't thank me yet. If for one second I think you're conning me, I'll slap cuffs on you so fast you won't know what happened. I'll put your ass in jail until we figure out what the hell is going on around here, and depending on what we find, you may or may not get out."

"I understand probable cause."

"I don't know that you really do, or you wouldn't have sent that picture to us. You put yourself right in the center of the target. This is a tight-knit community, and the murder of two well-loved women won't sit well with folks. If a certain element gets wind of those paintings, well, I think you can guess how that would go down."

"And you don't believe I thought about that long and hard before I did it? I knew the potential existed, and I did it anyway."

Tula surprised her. She was born in a city home to millions. Easy to disappear in a place that size. Here, a very different story. Not a small town. Not a big city. That special place in between. Everyone didn't quite know everyone's business, yet disappearing wasn't easy either. "Why?"

Tula didn't hesitate. "Because it was the right thing to do, just like asking you to be here, to be a witness, is the right thing to do. I don't want anyone else to die. I feel the evil right here." She tapped her chest. "It's all around us and growing stronger. The only way I can think to make it stop is to help you. I have one weapon to do that with, and I need you, or what does it matter what I can do?" She picked up a paintbrush and held it out toward Casey.

Truth rang in her words, deep and heartfelt. Hard even for a skeptic to miss. Her abuelita would admonish her for her cynicism. She'd tell Casey to let her heart feel what her eyes couldn't see. "This is for you, Abuelita," she murmured.

"What?"

Oops. She hadn't meant to say that out loud. "Nothing. Talking to myself. Here's the deal. I'm going to my house to grab a few things, and then I'll be back. Don't run away while I'm gone. I mean it. Stay here."

Tula nodded. "I'll be right here. You have my word, and besides, I have nowhere to go."

All the way to her house, Casey wondered if she'd lost her freaking mind. She'd worked like a crazy woman to earn her shield, and now she'd jeopardized everything by agreeing to stay with someone whose sanity she questioned. Regardless of a family history steeped in an embrace of spirituality, she took a more grounded stand. She believed in the physical, the real that she could see and touch.

Like a portrait of her murdered cousin, a beautiful young woman with a face forever destroyed by the path of a bullet. That was physical. That was real. Not the heebie-jeebie stuff that Tula seemed intent on getting her to buy into. Well, they'd see about that, now wouldn't they?

Before she could leave the house with a small bag and her laptop, her phone rang. Her mother. "Mama, I don't have time right now."

"You should always have time for your family."

No point in arguing. Mama could make even the most persistent look like an amateur. "What?" Diego rubbed against her legs as she talked. He'd enjoy his moment of attention and then disappear.

"You have to make this right."

"I'm off the case."

"Get back on it."

"I can't, and you know it."

"She's family."

"And that's why I have to step away. I can't put the investigation at risk. We could lose everything that way."

"Find a way."

"Mama, I'll do what I can, but I can't make you promises I won't be able to keep."

"Do the right thing. That's all that matters."

She ended the call and slipped the phone into her pocket. Do the right thing. Such a simple statement and so damn hard to follow. Going to Tula's felt like the absolute wrong thing. It also felt like the only thing. To top it off, she had to stay out of Mike's way, or she'd compromise the investigation. She wouldn't risk that possibility. The stakes were too high. Doing nothing wasn't an option either. No matter how she came at it, she couldn't win. At least at Tula's, the potential for peace of mind existed. One way or the other, she'd figure out if the beautiful woman was full of shit or the real deal.

At the car, she tossed her bag into the back seat. In for a penny, in for a pound. She flipped on her lights and drove back to Tula's, not bothering with speed limits.

❖

Tula hurried around the house and tidied everything from the kitchen to the bathrooms. While growing up, she'd inhabited a minute world, one easy to keep in order, which had been important to her. An illusion of control. The same compulsion followed her into adulthood, and most of the time she didn't think much about it. Just a part of her life, a comforting part and, given she lived alone, never a big deal.

Now, the thought of someone sharing her space sent her racing around with a dust cloth and the vacuum cleaner. Not that much dust had the nerve to remain on her furniture or dirt on the floors. A tidy ship, she liked to say. Any good psychologist would tell her she needed therapy, and she wouldn't disagree. Maybe someday, if she got the chance to step out into the light, she'd give it a go. Clear out the cobwebs, as it were. She really didn't know if that day would ever arrive. The way things were going, the odds of ever stepping out into the light fell somewhere between not now and never.

By the time the doorbell rang, not a speck of dust anywhere. In particular, her studio sparkled under the overhead lights. Her painting supplies remained in a controlled jumble on the table. No point in putting them in the closet. Whatever would hit, would hit. She'd tried to hide from it as a child and shoved all her paints into the hallway. Her mother, of course, promptly put them back. Her little meal ticket would paint whether she wanted to or not—whether she painted magnificent landscapes or the faces of murdered women.

The adult in her had a better handle on things, even if said things presented from a realm that couldn't exactly be defined. Instead of fighting, she gave in to the compulsion. A bright new canvas rested on her easel. Tubes of paint lay on the table right next to the container of brushes. The sight gave her a little thrill. Her fingers tingled, and a small smile turned up the corners of her lips. The artist inside her, decades denied, screamed to be allowed free access. Creativity pressed upon her soul like the weight of the world.

The only problem for Tula? She really, really didn't want to paint the faces of murder victims. What she wanted, regardless of how heartfelt, didn't mean squat. She'd learned that lesson as a mere child. Whatever debt she owed the universe, it continued to take its pound of flesh.

She shouldn't whine. If she really thought things through, she could see where, as hated as her ability might be, it might also help stop another killer and save at least some lives. It had happened that way before, and it could again. Her own sense of right and wrong kept her from stepping out of the equation. Not a possibility.

She could be a witness of sorts. Her parents had regarded her gift not as something that could help others but as an opportunity for exceptional press. As witnesses, they were useless. In fact, after her parents discovered the significance of the first painting, they withheld the others until the deaths were confirmed for the sole purpose of making them more newsworthy. If not for Frances, they'd have played that game longer in order to reap the notoriety. They didn't acknowledge or embrace boundaries.

Now, with Casey as her partner, she could make a difference. Tula had a good feeling about her, even if Casey made it crystal clear she didn't trust her. Not unreasonable, and she could live with that. She only hoped that if Casey could see her in action, it would serve as the catalyst to bring them together. If that happened, as a team, they could end this nightmare. Certainly a risk, but one worth taking.

"Come in." Tula's fingers danced on the doorknob as she opened the door for Casey, who held a bag in one hand and a laptop in the other. The intensity she'd noticed about her when they'd first met had amped up and made her look competent and darned attractive, a powerful combination.

"I still think this is wrong." Casey hesitated at the door. Second thoughts?

She opened the door wider. "I appreciate your taking a leap of faith regardless of why. Please, come on in."

"Leap of crazy."

"You're off the case, so what's to lose?"

Casey's brow furrowed. "You're not serious? I have everything to lose. No way you can be anything but a person of interest, yet here I am, all packed up and ready to sleep with the enemy."

The last comment made Tula narrow her eyes. "I don't believe that was ever on the table." She was just as intrigued by an attractive cop as the next person, but jumping into bed at the speed of a grasshopper? Definitely not her style.

Casey shrugged. "I didn't mean it literally."

"Okay. Just so we're both on the same page. I need you to understand what I can do and how to use it to help. That's it. No other agenda."

Casey saluted her. "Gotcha. Now, where's my room, or shall I sleep on the sofa in your studio?"

That stopped her. "I have a room ready for you, but you might have a point about the studio. I need you to see it for yourself, and what if you don't hear me?"

"You can wake me up."

She shook her head. "It doesn't work like that. The thing is, I don't even know I'm doing it until it's completed. That's why I need you as a witness—to see it in real time, to be an unbiased witness. That's the only way you're going to believe me."

❖

"All right." Angel stood on the sidewalk and watched as Casey disappeared inside Tula's house. "She's there."

"I'm still not so sure about this."

"Nothing to lose and everything to gain. Isn't that the kind of thing you'd tell me? We take the magic where we can find it."

"If you say so."

"I can't believe you don't feel it?"

"What? The evil surrounding the bastard killing these women? Without a doubt. He's so bad, it almost smells rancid on the air."

Angel shook her head. "No. That's not what I mean."

Blue closed his eyes. "Oh, that."

"Yes, that. Do you feel it?"

"I want to say no."

"You can't."

"I can't."

"We have to hurry."

"We do."

Angel walked away from Tula's house, the moon rising in the night sky. If she kept going, she'd reach the Columbia River at Vantage, where soaring cliffs once served as the range for herds of wild horses. Magnificent and breathtaking, the sheer magnitude of the landscape reminded everyone of the power of nature. Sometimes she needed that reminder.

"He's stalking another right now."

"He is."

"Help me."

Blue stood close as she stopped on the lakeshore and closed her eyes. His energy wrapped around her, warm and comforting. It's what she needed. With her hands clasped, she began to pray from the book of Matthew. "Give to him that asketh thee, and from him that would borrow of thee turn not thou away."

CHAPTER FOURTEEN

Totally, totally fucked up, and if Casey were wise, she'd turn around and haul ass out of this house. Seemed pretty clear she wasn't wise, because here she stood in Tula's entry with a death grip on her stuff and without even a hint of retreat in her heart. Some days she was a total dumbass.

Faith. She needed to keep that one word rolling through her mind to remain steadfast in a course of action that might result in the implosion of her career—the "might" part being generous. Nonetheless, she held tight to the belief that, in this instance, the potential reward would turn out to be worth the risk. Her family depended on her.

She followed Tula past the guest room and to the back of the house to the studio, where she'd first seen the horrible portrait of Rita. Setting her bag on the floor, she let her gaze sweep the room. Easy to see why Tula bought the house. This room alone would do it. The windows took up most of one wall, giving her an unobstructed view of the lake, where, at the moment, moonlight lit up the water. During the day, it would also allow an abundance of natural light to flow in. Perfect for an artist. Hell, she wasn't even an artist, and she'd love a room like this.

On one wall, a large standing desk held numerous projects in various stages of completion. The day job. The last time she'd been in here, she'd only glanced at the work. Now, she paid a lot more notice and recognized at least a couple of the projects, having seen the logos and copy in local print and television advertisements. The quality of the work was undeniable. No mystery how she captured clients with deep pockets. Also accounted for the lovely lakeside home that had to have come with a hefty price tag, even if she'd purchased it some years ago. Like many cities and towns in Washington, real-estate prices, particularly waterfront real-estate prices, had been soaring skyward over at least the last decade.

"I'll get you some bedding. I apologize that it's far from as comfortable as the guest-room bed, but I think you hit on something about being in here if—when—my compulsion strikes. You won't miss anything this way."

Casey inclined her head in the direction of the sofa. "It'll be fine. Not like I'm moving in. This is temporary and short, I hope. A blanket and a pillow will suffice."

Snarky, and that's not exactly how she meant to come across. Her normal firm and confident manner would be more appropriate. Objectivity and, yes, Abuelita, an open mind would be all she'd need to follow this unconventional lead to its conclusion. Keep it easy and professional.

Tula nodded before she turned toward the door. "I hold the same hope. This monster has to be stopped, and soon. I don't want anyone else to be harmed, and if I can help, I must."

One thing she'd say about Tula, she didn't come across as a killer. Honesty echoed in her voice, and when she studied her face, the one thought echoing in her mind was "open." She'd been around plenty of ethically challenged individuals and could recognize deception at a hundred yards. Of course, she wasn't naive enough to believe she couldn't also be fooled. Everyone could on occasion. Not often in her case, thank goodness. Recognizing deception might be her super power. Very few ever pulled anything over on her, and she didn't believe Tula was capable of being one of them.

Before she could respond, Tula disappeared out the door. She returned a few minutes later with sheets, a pillow, and a comforter that she laid on the end of the sofa. "If you get cold, I've got more blankets."

"Thanks, I'll be fine. Why don't you sit. Let's chat."

With a nod, Tula sat on the stool in front of her desk. Casey opted to stand, given that the only other seats in the room would drop her below Tula. She wanted to keep at least a level gaze between them. She'd gotten an A in that class.

"What do you want to know?"

Loaded question, considering everything she'd discovered in her research thus far. "Let's start with one of the biggies."

"Ask away. At this point, I'm an open book."

"An open book?"

"The way I see it, telling you what I can do pretty much proves it."

She had a different take on that statement. "Well, open book, then tell my why you've been living under an assumed identity for years."

❖

Tula didn't even twitch. It had been a foregone conclusion that Casey would find out her true identity. Any investigator with a modicum of ability would, and she'd make a hefty bet that her houseguest possessed an impressive amount of skill. She'd disappeared and made a new life, and Casey knew it. Good enough that her parents hadn't, to date, tracked her down. To get away from them had always been her end goal. That said, with everything she'd given Casey, it wouldn't be a hard story to unearth.

"May I ask you a question first? I promise then I'll explain, but I need to establish some context before I get to the heart of it."

Casey's eyes narrowed, and Tula thought she'd balk. Then her expression cleared. "Okay. What's your question?"

"How does your family treat you?"

Her eyes narrowed. "What?"

"Please. It will make sense. I promise."

Casey held up a hand. "It better."

"Your family?"

She hesitated before answering. "They treat me fine."

Too simple an answer. More context was needed. "I mean, do they support you in a loving, nurturing way?"

The irritation of a moment earlier fled from Casey's face, replaced by confusion. "Yes. My family has always been loving and nurturing. They have supported me in everything I've wanted to do."

"In other words, a normal, healthy family."

"Basically, yes."

Tula stood and started to pace. She didn't usually talk about her family. No, that wasn't right. She never talked about her family. Hard to get the words to pass her lips. "Mine wasn't."

"Healthy and normal?"

"Not healthy, normal, loving, or nurturing. Cold and calculated might be words that better describe my parents. Horrible would be another."

"I'm sorry. No brothers or sisters?"

"You read my history, so you already know I'm an only child."

"A prodigy."

"So they loved to scream for all the world to hear. I made my first million by the time I was seven years old."

"That's insane."

"On the contrary, that's actually the sane part of the story. The insane part is earning obscene amounts of money while locked in the beautiful apartment studio that doubled as my bedroom. That's not even correct. It was my studio, my bedroom, my prison cell, my entire universe. The only time I left that room was to attend the obligatory art shows, where I was dressed up and paraded for all the world to see."

"That's straight-up abuse."

"I'd call that part the mild abuse. The punishments when I defied them, particularly my mother, now that would most assuredly be classified as physical abuse." Her hand strayed to her head.

"I'm starting to get the gist of your answer to the identity question."

"I ran as far and as fast as I could. Eighteen years old and aided by my only true friend, who also happened to be brilliant, I escaped. Forced to become someone else, I let dear, sweet Matthew help me do it. I got out of New York with the bulk of my trust released to me and tucked away where they couldn't get to it."

"Why didn't you just stand up to them?"

"Ah, the million-dollar question. Sounds simple and it wasn't. The paperwork my mother had in the safe threatened everything. She loved to show it to me, dangle it in my face. If I defied them in any way, they'd petition to have me committed for my own safety. Unstable, you know. Only with their fine care was I able to function. Or so said paperwork declared."

"They couldn't just do that. There's a process that involves evaluations and doctors."

"Let's just say they had friends."

"Dear God."

"This thing I do. It started when I refused to paint one day. I was barely a teenager, all raging hormones and attitude, and I wanted to be free. My mother struck me harder than ever before, and I fell and hit my head on the radiator. When I woke up many hours later with dried blood sticking my hair together in a large mat, things changed forever."

❖

Blue didn't look quite right, which divided Angel's focus. She needed to concentrate on Tula, yet as she studied his pale face, she couldn't resist the pull toward him. They both knew from the beginning it wouldn't last forever. Longer than they deserved, yet with an expiration date nonetheless.

That knowledge didn't make it any easier. She couldn't describe the depth of her feelings toward Blue even to herself. They'd become as one over the years, and the thought of being without him shattered her. *To everything there is a season, and a time to every purpose under the heaven.* Right now, she really hated Ecclesiastes.

She turned away from Blue and forced herself to concentrate. "I feel him. Do you?"

Blue shook his head slowly. "Not really. Perhaps a small twinge."

"You should stay here. Rest while I check on Tula."

"I'll go with you."

This time she shook her head. "No. I'll do this alone. You rest, I'll be back soon." In a perfect world, she'd love to have him at her side every second. Their world had never been perfect, and now it tilted once again. Their time together was drawing to a close, and she might as well start to learn how to be alone.

"I don't trust him."

He wasn't wrong on that count. "Nobody should. This one is bad. There's something deeper and meaner about this killer. He's got to be stopped."

"Which is why you need me."

She took a few steps and then looked back at him. "I always need you. Don't ever doubt that. This time, I'll do this on my own. It will be fine. I promise."

He didn't argue anymore, and that struck a chord with her. The Blue she'd known since childhood would have argued until she gave in. It was his way. Always by her side. Support. Clarification. Love.

That difference stuck with her as she made her way along the shoreline, stopping only when she saw Tula's house. At least for a little while, she pushed her worries about Blue to the back of her mind.

The lights behind the windows let her see both Tula and Casey. It pleased her that Tula managed to persuade the detective to stay with her. In the past, she'd been safe in her house overlooking the lake. Angel had done her job by keeping watch on Tula, just as she'd done before she'd fled the city and become someone else. The help she'd been provided on the other side of the country had also been unknown and more difficult, given her very unsavory parents. She hated those people and wished she'd possessed enough power to do something about them. Bullies, regardless of where or when, made her blood boil. Never her mission to hold the parents accountable. Rather, her job had and always would be to help Tula. The rest, whether it be assistance or justice, would have to fall to someone else. One thing she'd come to learn during her journey: karma did exist, and it came to all sooner or later. Those horrible people would get theirs someday.

She focused on the house and the two women she could see in the light of the studio. She didn't need to hear their words to figure out the substance of their conversation—revelations that had to be made. If she could help ease that burden for Tula, she would. She didn't possess that power. Everything had limits, even for someone like her.

Folding her hands, she closed her eyes and tilted her head to the sky. She said a silent prayer and then brought the image of Tula's face into her mind. The energy she sent to her would have to be enough.

For another five minutes, she stood and breathed in and out. Finally, she walked away. Nothing more she could do. It wasn't near enough. The hair standing up on the back of her neck told her so.

CHAPTER FIFTEEN

Casey didn't think she'd be able to fall asleep. Everything felt surreal, and talk about off-the-charts anxiety. She questioned her own sanity repeatedly as she lay on the sofa staring at shadows as they danced across the ceiling. The very real possibility of throwing away a hard-earned career pressed on her. Possibly putting her own life in danger. How in the world did she get so off track? Oh, yeah, a cousin getting murdered and a very attractive artist painting a picture of said murdered cousin. A mother demanding she do anything and everything to find the killer. That's how she got so far off track.

No excuse. She knew better. Damn it, she'd worked three times as hard as any of the men who also held detective badges. To jeopardize that accomplishment now was plain old stupid, and that just wasn't her.

Except for that gut-instinct thing. That abuelita-whispering-in-her-ear thing. As much as she wanted to ignore both, she couldn't. The strange and beautiful woman down the hall, who made her tea and brought her pillows and bedding, drew her in like hummingbirds to sugar water. Impossible to run away. Damn her anyway.

Her abuelita didn't help either. She had a way of worming into her thoughts at times when she wanted to concentrate on the tangible. She'd remind Casey of her bruja blanca roots and tell her to be open and receptive to things not seen yet felt. Abuelita's version of gut instinct. As much as she wished she could pass it off as the outdated beliefs of a spiritual woman, she'd never been truly able to.

The sound that brought her upright came to her through the cobwebs of the sleep she didn't think she'd get. Slapping her hand over her mouth, she managed to stifle her scream just in time. The studio remained shrouded in darkness, broken only by moonlight coming in through the large, unshuttered windows. Buttery rays streamed over

Tula as she stood in front of the blank canvas she'd placed on the easel earlier.

Her movements were not those of someone alert and cognizant. Though darkness muted everything, Casey could tell that she moved through the fog of sleepwalking. Or something like sleepwalking anyway. Casey dropped her hand away from her mouth and stayed on the sofa, trying to be as silent as the rest of the night, afraid to move or even breathe for fear of disturbing what unfolded before her.

For over an hour, Casey stayed on her makeshift sofa bed, still and watching in silence, because that's how long it took Tula to fill her palette with paint, pick up a brush, and turn the blank canvas into a chilling portrait. No relative this time, only a pretty face of a woman who looked to be no more than twenty-five. Long reddish hair, sparkling green eyes, full lips, and, as with the other two paintings, a black hole marring the smooth flesh of her forehead.

When the palette and the brush crashed to the floor, the noise caught her off guard, and this time she did jump and gasp. Tula spun toward her, and her eyes blinked rapidly. In a flash, awareness flooded into them, and then she threw up.

❖

Tula might have just proved to Casey that her claims were real. Didn't mean she took any satisfaction in it. The proof of being right splashed all over the floor of her studio. A detail she'd neglected to share with Casey earlier. She'd wanted her to witness the reality of her otherworldly gift. To explain about how each and every time it made her sick might have been a deal-breaker. Nobody wanted to see that, at least not voluntarily.

"Are you okay?"

The concern in Casey's voice surprised her. She didn't have to turn and look at the canvas to know what rested upon it. The face would be different. The reality of it would not. Wasn't her first trip around the block when it came to the ghost portraits, or at least that's what she called them. Others had harsher terms that she'd learned to tune out a very long time ago. Sticks and stones.

She stood with her shoulders straight and took a deep breath. Okay was a relative term. Physically, the nausea had already passed. Her spirit would take a bit longer to heal. "I will be. I need to clean this up." Her nose wrinkled.

"I can help." Casey tossed the blanket aside and stood up. Still dressed in jeans and a sweatshirt, she looked ready to leap and run at a moment's notice. She didn't blame her for being prepared to flee.

Tula shook her head. "I appreciate that, but I'll take care of it." The last thing she wanted was for Casey to clean up her vomit. Embarrassing enough that she'd witnessed it.

It took her ten minutes to scour the floor, rinse the bucket, and throw the towels into the washer. Neither one of them said a word as she used the orange-scented cleaner to wash away traces of her physical response to her return from the fugue state. It did an admirable job of wiping away all evidence from the floor, though not quite as good a job erasing it from the air. A diffuser with lavender oil helped. At least Casey didn't run screaming from the room. Small wins counted for a lot when the stakes were high.

Instead, Casey stood in front of the painting, now in full color view once she'd switched on the overhead light. Tula stopped in the doorway and watched her. From where she stood, she couldn't see Casey's face. No clue what she might be thinking or feeling, though she could make a few educated guesses.

It had happened, as she'd known deep in her heart it would. All day, she'd felt the ripples of unease. Evil infused the air, and no matter how bright the sun shone outside, each breath brought the taint into her lungs. It waited out there for the chosen victim to be in the right place, at the right time. For the beautiful woman who did nothing wrong yet paid a price not owed by her. That it happened so quickly after she'd asked Casey to act as witness did come as a bit of a shock. In a lot of ways, she wished she could have been wrong, that Casey could have slept on her sofa and not one damned thing would have happened. Better she think her crazy than an innocent woman lose her life.

"She's going to die." Casey's words were flat. Who could blame her, given what happened to her cousin?

Tula wasn't ready to give in to defeat quite yet. There were the as yet unknowns. "She may not be dead yet."

Casey turned intense eyes on her. "You paint the faces of dead women. I read your history. I've talked to the NYPD detectives. I've already seen your work." She pointed to the canvas.

While she'd encouraged Casey to do precisely that, the words still stung. She'd been happy here, sort of. As content as she ever expected to be in any case, and now her secrets were gaining traction in the race toward full disclosure. All it would take would be for her parents to get even a whiff of her location, and, bam, it would be over. They'd be on her doorstep in the proverbial New York minute. The thought of facing them, even after all these years, filled her with a child's terror. Her only hope if they located her would be enough of a head start to run fast and far. She'd done it once and, for two decades, enjoyed relative peace. She could do it again, except it would be different this time.

Before, she'd been a child. Yes, she'd been legally an adult on the day she bolted, but that didn't change the fact that she'd been sequestered away from the larger world her entire life. With few friends and no experience with a life where not every minute of every day was dictated to her by someone else, she'd been terrified. The terror, however, didn't deter her determination to disappear. Her sanity had hinged on it.

Now, her sanity tilted toward the jeopardy stage again, this time with a holstered, neutral witness. The one thing she hadn't considered when she'd suggested this course was the fact that, as a law-enforcement officer, Casey would be compelled to share her secrets. She'd wanted Casey to understand that she didn't have anything to do with the deaths, that she channeled only through her art the evil that walked among them. Now, it hit her hard that, by doing so, her life would be forever changed. Action and consequence. No getting around it.

"You must not have read all of my history." She wanted to make Casey understand, to get her on the same page.

"What do you mean?"

"If you found everything on me, if you talked to even one of the detectives I worked with before, you'd realize that these visions often come to me before the actual murder. It's how we stopped the two killers in New York. Law enforcement was able to reach two intended victims before they lost their lives. It may not be too late."

Casey squared her shoulders, pressed her lips together, and nodded. "All right then. We've got to get busy."

❖

Angel couldn't find Blue. When she left Tula's, he wasn't anywhere nearby. She paced for a long time, waiting, certain that sooner or later he'd walk up smiling and asking her how things went. Unease filled her as the hours clicked by, and it refused to let her rest.

At his favorite downed log on the lake's shoreline, she stopped. All she needed to do was sit here and wait. He'd join her before long.

Except he didn't. The quiet grew heavy and too much for her. Besides, staying here didn't make much sense. Blue wasn't in danger, though Tula might be. The whispers began to swirl on the night air, a chorus that didn't soothe the soul. One voice grew louder as she walked along the shoreline, like a siren's call to the sailors—music and singing that lured the unwary to a crashing death against the rocks.

The closer she got to Tula's, the more she tingled and tears stung her eyes. The world tilted, and she was powerless to change it. What looked like a clear path to stopping evil morphed into something she didn't recognize. All she could do was try to maintain her own balance.

Out of control were the only three words that resonated with her right now. Everything spun out of control. At a small park not far from Tula's, she stopped at one of the tables and sat down. Grasping her hands together, she dropped her head. Her shoulders began to shake, and she opened her mouth wide in a silent scream.

"Blue, I need you," she finally whispered between sobs. "I can't do this alone."

The moon rose high in the sky as she sat at the table, silence and loneliness her only companions. Her head tipped back, she watched its ascent. How long had it been since she stopped and gazed at the night sky? A lifetime or two. Once it would have made her smile. Tonight, it made her sad.

With the buttery light of the moon on her back, she finally rose and continued her walk toward Tula's. The night had all but slipped away, and soon the morning would push out all the shadows. Blue wasn't going to join her.

From quite a distance away, the lights in Tula's office spilled out onto the grass. She had expected as much. Her hope always rested upon what could be done with Tula's otherworldly talent, if those around her could believe enough to act, that is. She remained somewhat optimistic that the detective would be the one outsider to make the difference, that she would see and accept Tula's ability for the gift it was and act upon it. If she could do that, they could stop the killer. If she didn't, more would die.

She intended now to get close enough to gaze through the windows and ensure things progressed as they should. Before she could reach the edge of the grass that bordered her house, Angel stopped. The air had changed yet again, become thick and suffocating, painful. She put her hands on her knees as she leaned forward and took long, deep breaths. Calming.

A sound made her straighten and turn to her left. A big weeping willow tree grew on the border between Tula's and the next-door neighbor's property. In the shadows of the tree, a man stood staring into Tula's windows. It hit her with a jolt that the sound she'd heard had been laughter. He'd been—was—laughing, in near darkness, in the wee hours of the morning while staring into Tula's windows.

The air turned cold.

CHAPTER SIXTEEN

All right." Casey stared at the painting. "I can't come up with a good explanation for what I watched you do, and I can't dismiss it either. If this really is what you say, then we have to act as fast as possible."

"You know this is real." Tula pointed toward the canvas. "She's in danger, if…"

Casey turned her gaze to Tula's face. "If she's not already dead." A shadow crossed her face, and she put a hand on her shoulder. The slightest tremor rippled beneath her palm. "I'm following you. Just because you painted her face doesn't mean she's already been harmed. We may have time to stop him."

"I had hoped this would never happen again, that by coming here and starting over, things would be different."

Casey understood the concept of running away. Not that she'd ever considered doing it. While her family had problems, like any other family, this remained her home and her people. She'd be lost without them.

At the same time, she'd come up against many who'd taken the same route as Tula. Their lives were complicated, they'd done something really bad, or in a more basic way, they needed to escape a dangerous situation. Many valid reasons for running away and many criminal reasons for running away existed.

"It doesn't really work that way."

"You sound as though you have experience."

Casey shook her head. "Not at a personal level. It's been more on-the-job exposure. You know, people who thought running away and becoming someone else would change their lives. That everything would magically improve. From my perspective, it never happens that way. Their problems go with them, and that usually means that the trouble they tried to run away from brings them into my orbit."

"Like me."

For a moment, she studied her face. "No, not like you."

"I ran away. I tried to become someone else. The last few days have proved to me how I've failed."

"No, no. I don't think so." Casey might have come into this odd arrangement with a healthy dose of skepticism, but that had faded considerably as she'd watched Tula paint, her eyes closed and darkness all around her. If she'd been faking it, the woman possessed some serious acting skills. She didn't believe Tula could act her way out of a cardboard box. Everything she did and said rang true. "I think you came here for a safe haven, and that's entirely different from those who want to disappear for more nefarious reasons." She thought of the doctor over in Spokane who'd tried to escape a murder charge by assuming a new identity. Now, he'd failed.

The ghost of a smile flashed across Tula's face. "You sound like my friend Angel. She's always saying deep things like that to me too. Thank you. I really do appreciate it."

Casey's hand dropped away from Tula's shoulder. She still wasn't on board a hundred percent. More like sixty. "Let's take a picture of this and print it. I can start the work on finding out who she is." If this panned out, she might step it up to seventy-five.

"It's the middle of the night."

"And time is of the essence, right?"

Tula nodded. "Yes."

"Then I'm not waiting."

"Good."

❖

Tula really wanted to go with Casey to the police station. Surely she could help beyond just painting a face. A quite firm no-go with the detective, and she didn't leave any room for argument. A good look at Casey's expression warned not to push the issue. Despite the isolation she'd endured as a child, she'd been allowed time with the models she'd used as subjects in her paintings, all supervised by her parents, of course. Observing both the models and her parents had provided her the opportunity to learn to read subtle behavioral clues. In this case, the behavioral clues hadn't been subtle.

People always thought they could mask their true feelings, and in many ways they could. Like the fact that not a single one of the models cared for her parents. Her ability to see beyond the surface contributed to her artistic skill. What they hid from others glowed bright for her, and she'd possessed an uncanny ability to capture those concealed qualities in her work. It became that undefinable thing that helped set her work apart from that of other quite-good painters.

Despite her seclusion as a child, she'd been under no illusion about how people felt about her. The other artists hated her because of her success and because of that undefinable thing she possessed that they didn't. If they'd known the reality of her life, they'd have probably still hated her, but they'd have felt sorry for her too. Probably best no one knew about her personal tragedy, for she could deal with only so much emotion from others, good or bad. Too much would have overwhelmed her, and she hadn't needed anything else to deal with back then.

Who was she kidding? She didn't need it now either. Her formative years hadn't exactly prepared her to function in the real world. She'd managed the best she could and carved a life for herself. For the most part, it had turned out to be a happy one. Lonely, but she'd been dealing with loneliness since the day of her birth. She'd reached expert level.

Standing at the window, she watched Casey pull away from her house, the red taillights of her SUV disappearing around the corner. Until the moment the car turned the corner, she'd anticipated the sight of the reverse lights coming on, hoping Casey would pull into the driveway again and invite her to ride into the police station and help. Like most of the hopes in her life, it flew up in flames. The street remained deserted. No Casey at the door asking her to come with her.

Disappointed, she turned away from the window and walked to her room. Might as well try to get some rest, given she'd been up most of the night. Despite her best efforts to relax, sleep would not come to her. She buzzed as though she'd downed a pot of coffee and eaten a couple of chocolate bars. If history were to repeat itself, it would be a good long time before she slept again.

The doorbell brought her upright and running toward the front door. "Casey?" She flung open the door without checking the peephole first.

"I'm sorry," Angel stood on the porch, her hair swirling around her face as a morning breeze blew through it. Her blue eyes were bright, serious.

"Angel?" Something was different about her. Sad and what? Tula couldn't quite put a finger on it. "What are you doing out at this time of the morning?" Daylight was breaking, barely.

"I know this is crazy. I had a dream that you were hurt, and it compelled me to come check on you. I couldn't go back to sleep until I did. Come check on you, I mean."

Tula leaned out and glanced at the driveway. "You walked?" Granted, she lived in a good neighborhood. That didn't mean a woman alone should be out during the wee hours. Not a good idea even in this town. "Seriously, you shouldn't be out here alone."

"I'm fine. Besides, runners do it all the time. No different for someone walking, and I needed a big dose of fresh air after the dream. Are you okay?"

Her bright, blue eyes were intent on Tula's face in an almost unnerving way. Not at all, she thought. She said, "I'm good. Didn't get much sleep last night but not a big deal. It's not like I have to show up at a job site or anything. I'll grab a nap at some point." Why on earth was she rambling?

Angel glanced to the side, in the direction of Diane's house, and then back to her. "There's actually more."

The hairs on the back of her neck stood up. "What do you mean, there's more?"

"Something a little off." Angel's gaze cut again toward Diane's house.

She didn't have a good feeling about this. "Tell me."

"After my troubling dream, I walked along the lake to get here so I could check with you, and as I reached the edge of your property, I heard something. It turned out to be a man standing in your neighbor's yard under that big weeping-willow tree."

Angel had worried for nothing. Both her neighbor and her brother were odd enough to do anything, like stand outside under a tree at an unusual time. She didn't like Dante, thought him most likely the one who'd prowled through her house when she wasn't there, and would greatly prefer he went back to whatever rock he'd climbed out from under. Still, he didn't warrant her energy at the moment. "Well, Diane's brother has been staying with her, and I suspect it was him."

Angel nodded and glanced again at Diane's house. "It might well have been him. That isn't what bothered me."

Now her hands started to shake. Not good. Maybe she had dismissed the creepy Dante too quickly. "Okay. What was he doing?"

"Staring through your windows and laughing."

❖

Angel might have second-guessed her plan to come here if not for the disturbing sight in the yard. She'd witnessed much in her time and developed a well-defined sense of what was right and what was wrong. That man, standing under that tree and laughing, fell hard on the side of wrong. To walk away and not bring it to Tula's attention would have heaped wrong upon wrong. She'd had to wait for Casey to leave, and that delay had almost physically hurt. By the time Casey's car pulled out of the driveway, daylight had begun its ascent as it pushed away the darkness. With it came his retreat.

"Come in, come in." She held the door open wider.

Angel stepped inside and almost gasped. The air inside dropped on her like one of those popular weighted blankets. Only those blankets provided comfort. This did not.

"What's happened?" Angel studied Tula's face. Weariness, yes. Something else too.

"Nothing's happened." Tula's eyes narrowed as though she was trying to get to the root of Angel's question. "What do you mean?"

Angel shook her head. "I don't know exactly. It doesn't feel right in here. Something's off. Kind of like your neighbor's brother acting like a perverted Peeping Tom is way off."

"I'll admit that's pretty freaking weird. Diane is a borderline crazy, so I guess it's not a stretch to believe her brother is too, despite his high-profile career."

"Don't let him get close to you." The darkness that had surrounded him under that tree hadn't been a result of the shadows. He carried darkness with him, inside him. She knew his type.

Tula grimaced. "I had dinner with them both. Diane wasn't going to leave it be until I did."

"Don't go back again."

"Not planning on it. I got out of there as quick as humanly possible." Tula stopped and stared at her. The intense gaze made her a little uncomfortable. It never boded well to have intense scrutiny. It brought too many questions she couldn't answer. "Angel, you sound off. Sorry, that isn't very nice to say. It's just…you're different."

Tula wasn't wrong. Everything was different. Blue was missing. A creeper had been staring at Tula. A woman was out there alone and hurt. The waves of despair rolling off her were impossible to control, and she didn't even try. "Seeing that man in the shadows peeping in your windows rattled me." Not an inaccurate statement, though far from the entire truth. She'd never be able to share that.

"Come on. Let's see if he's still out there."

She couldn't tell her that he wasn't, because it would require an explanation for how long she'd stood outside waiting. Another of her secrets. What Tula didn't know wouldn't hurt her. Or at least when it came to her.

In the studio, Tula walked to the windows and stared out. "I don't see anything."

"He was standing there." Angel pointed to the big tree that bordered the two properties. Morning light glinted off the lake, and the trees swayed from a breeze.

"Not there now."

"Good."

"Angel, I'm fine. I really appreciate your checking on me. I promise, I'm okay. I'm not alone because I have a friend staying with me. Come on. I'll drive you home."

"No, no. I'll walk. It'll help to get out in the fresh air. I just wanted to make sure you were good after the dream." The repeated lie didn't bother her at all. Part of the job.

Tula squinted as she stared at Angel. "I don't like that idea. I'd feel much better if you'd let me drive you."

Angel smiled, hoping to reassure her. "I'm a big girl, Tula. Now that I know you're fine, I plan to go take a nap. I promise to keep my eyes open on the way home." Sounded good even if she technically didn't have a home to go back to.

She made for the front door and let herself out as fast as she could without being too obvious. As she walked away, she didn't look back, though she could sense Tula's presence on the porch. She kept her shoulders square and her pace steady. Her heart hurt as she walked, for everything was quiet now, the voices on the breeze gone. The silence didn't give her peace. It made her want to cry.

Too late.

CHAPTER SEVENTEEN

All the way to the station, Casey muttered. Absolutely un-frickin-believable. Yet, she believed it. Damn, damn, and damn. Her abuelita had struck again, proving once more that respecting one's elder often turned out to be a good thing. As Shakespeare wrote, "there are more things in heaven and earth, Horatio…" and her abuelita knew that saying intimately.

Casey understood that a wide-open mind yielded some amazing things. but what should she do with the information provided by said wide-open mind? She couldn't go into the office and hand it over to Mike, explaining that Tula painted a victim's face while in a fugue-like state that she just happened to witness firsthand. Despite being generally congenial to her, Mike would love nothing better than to amass enough ammunition to remove her shield, especially in this situation. She'd been told to stand down, and well, she hadn't quite followed that order. Mike would have a field day.

Handing this painting over would also put Tula at risk. Casey might still want more before she believed Tula innocent, but Mike would bolt like a steer out of the chute. He'd arrest Tula, get Casey suspended or, worse, fired, and then close the case. All in less than a day. Then he'd stand in front of the cameras and reporters to explain how he'd cleared a case of multiple murders. Whether or not he'd actually done that wouldn't matter.

Nor could she go to the sheriff. She'd been removed from the case, and to claim she'd simply taken the initiative wouldn't fly. They would say she had defied a direct order, and they wouldn't be wrong. She'd be screwed.

Nope. She was in this alone. Well, except for Tula. She pulled into an empty spot in the parking lot and turned off the car. Instead of getting out, she sat there, tapping the steering wheel. Then she went into the station, waving to the intake clerk before swiping her badge over the card reader at the door and making her way to her desk.

No one would question her sitting at her desk at this time of the morning. She'd been known to come in at all hours, night or day. Sleep wasn't always easy for her. Anxiety had been a constant companion since childhood, and it simply kicked in with no particular rhyme or reason. She'd watched it take down Papi more than once, and it had been one of the factors that led her brother to medicine. For her, managing her anxiety meant using work to alleviate the symptoms. She didn't need her brother's medicine, though it was nice to know she had a resource if her condition ever got away from her. Unlike Papi, she wasn't too proud to ask for help if it came down to that.

She picked up her phone and stared down at the picture on it. Before she'd left Tula's, she'd snapped a shot of the painting. An edge existed in the face, or at least that's what intuition seemed to be telling her. Something rang ever so slightly familiar. She'd evidently seen the woman before, and that's how she'd approach her search.

Outside her window, a marked cruiser pulled into the lot, swinging into the empty spot right next to her car. The uniformed officer that got out threw a small wave to the guard at the gate before walking out of sight. She'd be coming in through the north entrance, and Casey would have no more alone time. The day was beginning to ramp up. Might as well get to it. Sitting here pondering the hows and whys wouldn't help a whole lot. No time like the present.

❖

A knock at the front door startled Tula upright. She ran a hand over her eyes and then through her hair. How she'd managed to fall asleep after everything last night, coupled with Angel's surprise visit early this morning, she'd never know. Good thing she had. The buzz hadn't left her, and it didn't take a psychic to tell her what it meant.

"Come on in. I'll make coffee." She held the door open for a tired-looking Casey. An essentially sleepless night showed on her face, yet not enough to wipe away the attractiveness that drew her in. While Tula got the chance to grab some sleep, Casey had been at it for hours.

"You're an angel."

Casey followed her to the kitchen, where she spooned coffee into the French press. “Hope you like dark roast.”

“You’re a woman after my own heart.”

Those few words made her breath catch. She could deny it all she wanted, and it wouldn’t make a difference. This interesting woman with the black hair she wanted oh-so-badly to see down and around her face made her want to shed her secrets and come out into the light, sit together for months and share thoughts and dreams. This was a new one on her. She’d been more of a one-and-done in the past. A whole lot safer that way. That Casey knew many of her secrets already probably had something to do with the attraction, she rationalized, and it might not be real at all.

As she allowed the coffee to brew, she told herself to chill. This was business. As she set a steaming mug in front of her, the aroma of the freshly brewed coffee filled the air with a pleasing scent she loved. “I try. Now tell me what you found.”

Casey pulled some papers out of her jacket pocket and laid them on the table. “I kept thinking that I’d seen the woman before, and it took me a few hours of running through booking photos before I finally found her.” She took a sip of the coffee and sighed. “Thank you.”

Tula picked up the top sheet and stared at the picture. A terrible mug shot. Unmistakably the woman whose face was on the canvas in her closet. “You know who she is.”

“I do. Shelley Rodriguez. She’s been arrested three times on drug charges. Not unusual around here, as you’re probably aware. We have a thriving drug trade that keeps us on our toes. Shelley’s part of a family business that has spanned generations. Always liked her and thought if she’d been born into another family, she’d have taken a very different path in life. Sad, really. A lot of promise and zero support.”

Tula did know of the drug issue. What city or town didn’t have a thriving drug trade these days? An unescapable and quite sad sign of the times.

“Have you located her?” Hope surged. If Casey had gotten there in time, this woman could still be alive. God, she hoped so. All of this must be for something, or what was the point? The universe couldn’t be that cruel.

Casey closed her eyes and sighed. Her elbows on the table, she leaned her head into her hands. For a moment, she sat there not moving. She finally looked up, and in her eyes, Tula glimpsed pain. “We found her.”

The truth in those three words rang loud and clear in the kitchen. “She’s dead.”

“Yes.”

❖

Angel sat on the protruding boulder as tears streamed down her cheeks. Below her, law enforcement worked yet another murder scene. Lights were being set up in anticipation of the investigation to be performed there well past sunset, yellow tape stretched between stakes. A black tarp spread out on the ground hinted at the shape of the body concealed beneath it. Despite everything, evil had won yet again. She raised her head to the sky, clear and full of false promise.

“Why, God? Why give me this job and let me fail again and again? I don’t know what you want from me.”

No answer came. No words of great wisdom or understanding. Worst of all, no Blue to tell her it would be all right and that they’d stop this monster as they’d stopped monsters before. That they’d protect Tula and she’d live a long and happy life.

Nothing beyond silence met her pleas. Abandoned, with evil still heavy in the air, she wanted to curl up and close her eyes, forever. She knew better. A debt owed. A payment due. She had to soldier on because he wasn’t done.

The man she figured to be Casey’s partner walked around the murder scene with an air of authority. If not in control of the processing, he certainly gave the impression that he was the go-to guy. Around him glowed an aura tinged dirty gray. It fit her perception of the man, even from this distance. A result of childhood trauma? Maybe. The result of an ego incapable of handling challenge or change? More likely. She’d seen men like him before, with the same gray inside them. The first time, she’d thought she could help. She’d been wrong. She didn’t try again.

Now, she didn’t much care about the man or the drag on his soul. In fact, she wished him gone, for he did nothing to help what was happening here. He strutted like the wolf who leads the pack. Except in his case, instead of being a true leader, his presence here was all for show, while he expected everyone else to do the work. Wrapped up in his own self-importance, he noticed nothing around him. Not out here. Not anywhere else. Like being aware of the work that his partner managed to accomplish, even though she’d been told she could not be part of the investigation. Tula hadn't needed to share that fact with her. Like so many other things, she simply knew.

Angel continued to watch as he strutted around and pointed here and there, his back straight and his eyes covered with dark glasses. Undoubtedly, he believed they made him look smart and savvy—the ever-competent, and important, detective. How she wanted to run down and scream in his face. Anything to wipe away that smug look, to get him to see beyond the obvious and the easy. He wouldn't. People like him never did.

The tension left her as she softened her shoulders and wiped away the tears. The fire went out of her as fast as it had taken flame. A phrase she'd heard a long time ago came to mind: *the luster had worn off*. Was that what had happened for her? No luster. Whatever she'd had before, whatever influence she'd wielded appeared to be losing its power. Everything. Every damn thing was going wrong, and she was helpless.

No, no, no. She couldn't give up now. Too close, with too much at stake. Not just Tula's soul, but her own. What she needed to do came to her in that moment. She had to shift her focus harder and faster toward Tula. This couldn't go on as it had been. She couldn't go on as she had been. That stupid clock ticked in the background as loud as Big Ben, and she stifled the scream that built inside her.

Blue tried to warn her in his beautiful, gentle style. In so many ways she'd tried not to believe him, all because she didn't want to. She still didn't want to believe it, except, as always, Blue had been right. During the sum total of their time together, he'd never been wrong.

One truth he always told her: evil can't be reasoned with. She stood and silently vowed to see this ordeal through. No more sunsets with loved ones missing. No more sunrises with bodies in the sagebrush. This had to stop, and stop now. The fool in the sunglasses wasn't going to stand in her way. Resolve hardened in her heart. Blue might have left her, but his lessons had not. She would make this right.

CHAPTER EIGHTEEN

Casey believed honesty was the best policy with Tula. She deserved it. What she hadn't expected were the tears. Tula sank to the chair and began to sob. She reacted on instinct and put her arms around her. "I'm sorry. I shouldn't have been blunt like that. I could have shared that news in a better way."

Tula shook her head, not moving out of her arms. "It's not you, and I appreciate you being candid."

"Then tell me. Tell me what it is," she said against her soft, thick hair, breathing in the fresh scent of her while her arms tightened.

They stayed in the embrace for at least a full minute before Tula's sobs faded. Only then did Tula gently push away. Casey dropped her arms to her sides. She liked it better when they were touching. Shame on her. Not exactly professional, and damned if she really did care at the moment.

Since everything about the murders fell way outside normal, this did too. Bottom line, Tula drew her in. What she'd seen her do blew her mind. That she'd been right three out of three times, just here in Moses Lake, and not factoring in what had happened years ago, she'd be a fool not to take her seriously. She had decided on the way over here to suspend her disbelief and do whatever she could to catch the bastard killing women in her town. If that meant believing in a paintbrush-wielding artist with psychic abilities, that's what she'd do. Mike and the rest of the MLPD could call her crazy later, after a killer was put behind bars.

"I don't want this responsibility." Tula blew out a long breath as she ran her hands through her hair, the long, silver strands falling between her fingers like silk.

Casey longed to reach out and touch that soft hair again. She kept her hands in her pockets. "It's not on you. We'll find him."

"For whatever reason, the universe decided to spare my life, and this is the result. I hate it."

She focused on Tula's eyes, the pain reflected in them. "You're talking about the TBI?"

Tula's hand drifted to her head, and her fingers stroked her scalp. Casey had seen her do the same thing several times. "Yes. I should have died. Everything I've learned about that kind of injury tells me I should be dead or, at the very least, mentally impaired. That I survived intact is a miracle, and miracles didn't really happen in my life."

Casey had seen her fair share of brain injuries during her time in law enforcement. Tula wasn't wrong about how they affected the wounded. In too many instances, they had devastating results. She didn't say how very glad she was that Tula had survived. Maybe another time she'd share that sentiment. "Tell me more about what did happen."

Tears pooled in Tula's eyes again. "I've only ever told one other person the entire story."

Her shoulders tensed. "A boyfriend?"

Tula's laugh sounded light and beautiful. Silver bells on a cloudy day. "Oh my gosh, no. Never had one of those." Her eyes met Casey's. "Never will."

Casey studied her face. Was she hearing what she thought she was? "Care to elaborate on that one?" Curiosity pushed the words right straight across her lips and out into the open.

Tula smiled a little and shook her head. "Not at the moment, but maybe later. How about I tell you of my dear Matthew instead? He's really about the only friend I had growing up, and I was allowed to have him as a friend only because his mother owned the most prestigious art gallery in New York. Probably the whole United States, to be honest. My parents wanted to kiss up to her like you can't believe. Thus, Matthew and I were granted time together."

"That's messed up." Casey couldn't wrap her head around the reality of Tula's childhood. One friend? How lonely and sad. Casey might not have been the most popular kid in school, but she'd had plenty of friends and got along with everyone. What kind of people did that to a child? She wanted to pull Tula into another hug.

"More than you can possibly imagine. If not for Matthew, though, I wouldn't be here today. He helped save my life. He still helps me. He's the one and only person who knows all my secrets."

Casey did understand that. Everyone needed at least one person who loved them unconditionally and had their back no matter what. This Matthew was Tula's. "And he keeps them."

Tula smiled and nodded. "I knew you were a smart woman the moment I met you."

"So tell me. I promise to keep your secrets too." She sure as hell hoped that wasn't a lie.

❖

Tula didn't hesitate long. At this point…why should she? Her life appeared to be coming full circle, and she couldn't do a damn thing to stop it. Hiding here in her beautiful house that looked out over the lake, carving out a successful career that provided her a sliver of creative outlet, and having a few friends had allowed her years of normalcy she wouldn't have had otherwise. For that she would be grateful, and now she could see an end to it all because of a killer.

As much as she wanted to turn her back and ignore what was happening here, running away again wouldn't solve a darn thing. She might squeeze out a few quiet years, and then evil would undoubtedly show its face again. When it did, the nightmare would return as well. No off switch existed. Maybe it would have been better if her mother had killed her that day.

When Tula didn't speak for more than a few moments, Casey took her hands. Her touch was warm, comforting. "Was it your father?"

It took her a second before she realized what Casey asked. She shook her head. "That would be the logical conclusion. After all, isn't it more often the father than the mother?"

"It is."

"Not in my house. Oh, don't get me wrong. My father was…is…a bastard. He never cared about me, only what I could do for him and how I could support the lifestyle he wanted to live. It was my mother who liked to freely swing her fists. Unquestioned obedience, always, or I suffered the consequences. Looking back as an adult, I believe she enjoyed it."

A shadow passed over Casey's face. Tula remembered seeing the same look on Frances's face when she connected all the dots. "You were their meal ticket."

"Meal ticket, entry into high society, media darling. Through me, they got it all, and they loved it. Me, not so much."

"I'm sorry."

She shrugged one shoulder. "It was a difficult childhood, and all I wanted to do was paint. I loved art. It opened my world in so many ways, yet they robbed me of the joy that should have been mine. And then on that awful day when I stood up strong and defiant to my mother, she hurt me worse than ever before. After I survived it, and I still don't know how, everything changed. The talent I'd been born with remained strong and true, only now it had the little extra you witnessed last night."

"The victims."

She nodded. "It started shortly after I recovered. At first my parents were horrified and wanted to keep it hidden. Not the kind of art that commanded six-figure price tags. Then it turned out to be a major publicity coup. The price for my work skyrocketed. The little painting prodigy who could channel serial killers. They were ecstatic. The money rolled in, and my prison turned from uncomfortable to maximum security."

"Good God," Casey whispered.

"Except for Matthew. Did I mention, he's rather gifted himself? You know, he graduated from Harvard Law. First in his class." She smiled, thinking about her dear friend. He didn't know she'd been there that day, so proud of him. A gamble for sure to show up like that. One she'd been willing to make just to see him on that most important day.

"Impressive."

"He saved me in more ways than one. My parents weren't outright thieves. They worried too much about their own reputations to be criminals in that sense. Instead, they set up a trust and, of course, paid themselves as trustees. Healthy salaries, to be sure. They didn't know that Matthew had gotten copies of everything for me. We'd been making plans for quite a while. By the time I turned eighteen, the mechanisms were in place to filter the income out of the trust and into accounts that Matthew and I controlled."

"Sneaky."

"Desperate. I had to do something proactive, or I'd have died in those rooms. The amount of the trust was astonishing and allowed me time to become the person you see today. Tula Crane, a self-employed commercial artist, was born."

"You stopped painting."

"For the most part, yes. Couldn't risk someone recognizing my work. Savvy art folks are everywhere, even here in Moses Lake. It's crushed a bit of my soul to not hold the brushes in my hands."

"I'm so sorry."

Casey meant it. Tula could see it in her face and hear it in her words. Something about her reminded Tula of Matthew. "Freedom was worth it. The peace it's given me made the sacrifice tolerable." She couldn't say it made it good, because that would have been a lie.

"I'm sorry for what you went through but…"

Tula cocked her head. "But?" Not exactly the response she expected after what she'd shared.

Casey's smile warmed the whole room. "But I'm glad you're here."

❖

"He's back."

Angel whipped around and started to cry. "Where have you been?" Blue stood on the grass, his hands held high in a posture that screamed *ta-da*.

"I had to go for a while. You understand."

No need to ask him where. "You're leaving me."

"In time, yes."

"It's the time now, isn't it? I feel it to the depths of my soul."

He shook his head, his long hair swaying. "Not quite yet. Soon."

A sob built inside. "I don't want to be alone."

His smile was sweet. "You're never alone. Not before. Not now."

"I feel alone."

"Ah, my beautiful girl, you get too much in your own head, as they like to say these days. Always have. Listen to me. You can do this with or without me."

The thought made her heart hurt and her eyes sting. "I can't."

"You can and you will." The perpetual teacher and cheerleader.

Angel put her hands over her eyes, warm tears sliding between her fingers. Blue had to know how very wrong he was. She needed him more than she'd ever needed anyone. This path would be impossible to traverse without him. No, no, no. She couldn't do this alone.

"You will help her, and together you will stop him. And then, soon enough, you will go home."

Her eyes closed, she shook her head. "I don't think I'll ever see home again. I don't deserve to." She opened her eyes when Blue didn't respond. He was gone.

CHAPTER NINETEEN

Casey decided one thing about Tula—the woman made a mean cup of coffee. She'd taken her second glorious sip when she heard a knock on the front door, followed by the sound of footsteps. She stood and let her hand drift to her gun. While she might be officially off the investigation, her duties as an officer were perpetually on. She didn't go anywhere without her gun.

After she'd run home to shower, feed Diego, and tend to the cows, she'd returned to Tula's ready for another demonstration of her psychic powers. She'd slept on the studio sofa again, only this time, nothing occurred. Every little creak of the house jerked her awake in anticipation. Then she'd lie there listening until she drifted off again. Not exactly a restful night. On the upside, a few hours of interrupted sleep was better than not sleeping at all, and at least no new face appeared on a canvas that she had to worry about. All in all, the night and morning proved to be nice and quiet until the knock on the door.

"Damn." Tula's expression darkened.

"Friend or foe?"

Tula's expression shifted to what looked like anger, which provided a quick answer to her question.

"Shoot me next time I forget to lock the door." She started toward the front of the house, although she didn't get more than three steps before she stopped and blew out a long breath. "Damn it," she muttered quietly.

A scary looking thirty-something woman blew into the kitchen, her overprocessed hair piled up on her head in an explosion of spikes. It reminded Casey of one of those cartoons where someone was shot out of a cannon. In contrast, a man followed who was as put together as she was not.

"Hey, my favorite neighbor. This girl is outta coffee, and her snobby guest is hoping you might have some premium-roast goodness we can snag. My mild grocery-store version isn't cutting it for his highness."

Casey was tempted to say *drive down to Starbucks*, and she then decided it wasn't her place to redirect the intruders on their neighborly conversation. Besides, Tula's expression pretty much said that she'd handle it. Looked like it might be interesting too, a little like Tula felt the same way she did. Go to Starbucks.

Tula's smile was tight as she made introductions. "Casey, this is my neighbor, Diane, and her brother, Dante."

"Hey to you too." Diane glanced at Casey and gave her a perfunctory nod before her gaze zipped back to Tula. No real interest in her. Clearly Tula lay square in her crosshairs, Casey a mere inconsequential, if not inconvenient, bystander. Interesting.

Tula continued. "Diane and Dante, this is *Detective* Casey Wilson, from the Moses Lake Police Department."

Now, they were getting right down to it. The emphasis on her formal title caused more of a reaction than she expected, and it meant a lot, given it usually got one. In any event, the brother, Dante, distinctly reacted. In contrast, Diane kept her eyes on Tula and didn't appear fazed by her profession. Very telling.

"Nice to meet you, Detective." Diane didn't bother to turn and look at Casey. Wow, talk about focus, and she'd bet her paycheck this impromptu visit didn't have anything to do with needing coffee.

"You have plans for today? Dante and I are going out on the boat later and thought you might want to come along."

Getting warmer. The invitation proffered did not extend to Casey. Diane wanted only Tula, the oh-so-needed coffee seemingly forgotten. Though Diane did all the talking, Casey kept an eye on the handsome brother who, while he'd come in with the same determined stride as his sister, now leaned more toward the door as in retreat. Curious for a guy who supposedly came seeking a good cup of coffee and nothing more. What game was being played here?

Tula didn't respond to Diane. Instead, she turned to Dante, her body language screaming confrontation. More curious. "Why were you spying on me a couple of nights ago?"

He managed what she was convinced he thought to be a look of shock. Casey had seen the same expression enough times in interview rooms to recognize it for what it really was: false. He knew exactly what she was talking about. Casey, on the other hand, did not.

"Why would you think I was spying on you? It's not like I want to do a story about you. I mean, you're talented, and with my contacts, I can help you expand your business, but sneak around to watch you? Not likely."

The more he talked, the more Casey's opinion about him solidified: liar.

❖

What on earth had she done bad enough to deserve Diane and her brother? None of Tula's other nearby neighbors felt it necessary to continually interject themselves into her life. Diane was like a bad rash that just kept coming back. She'd been around her enough to know everything had an underlying motive, and this one seemed clear. She wanted to fix her up with Dante. Never once had she given Diane, or anyone else for that matter, the impression that she was open to matchmaking. Diane needed no invitation to play whatever role she wanted. What anyone else in the world around her wanted didn't matter to that woman.

"So, you're saying my friend was wrong? You weren't standing outside night before last looking into my windows? Or are you trying to say my friend is a liar?" Irritating enough they barged into a peaceful morning with Casey, but even worse was Diane's bait and switch about the coffee. It hit Tula wrong.

Dante shrugged in a way that reminded her of an arrogant teenage boy ever confident in his good looks and easy talk. The guy that slid out of any jam because he was too cute and charming to ever be bad. "No, your friend wasn't entirely wrong. In fact, I was standing outside sucking on a cig. She"—he nodded in Diane's direction—"takes offense at smoking in her pristine little house. It helps me when I'm fighting insomnia. I don't sleep well in other people's homes, even when it's my sister's."

"My windows? Staring in my windows? How exactly does spying on me help with your insomnia?" She wasn't buying a damn thing he said.

"Not spying. Not my kind of gig. Of course, I probably glanced your way. Who wouldn't if they saw lights on at that time of night? You're making a big deal out of something that isn't. Nothing more than curiosity."

If it weren't for one small detail Angel had shared with her, she might buy the smooth explanation. As it was, she still believed he was full of it. At the same time, she figured she'd made her point. "I'll be sure to keep my blinds closed from here on out, even if the windows look out over a secluded backyard." She didn't clarify that it was a private backyard where no one should be able to look in unless they were making a real effort.

"Enough with worrying about some misunderstanding about an innocent situation Dante has clearly explained. He had a cigarette outside and happened to glance in your window. No big deal. He won't do it again. Right, Dante?" Diane didn't wait for him to respond. "Come on, Tula. Spend this afternoon with us. It'll be big fun. You'll see."

Wrong. It was a big deal. And wrong again. It would not be big fun. "I thought you needed coffee?"

Bottom line, she refused to play Diane's games. She had more important things to deal with than Diane's driving desire to hook her up with Dante, ugh, or his supposed ability to help with growing her business. No help needed on either front. She also didn't buy a word of his earlier protestations. Straight up Peeping Tom, as far as she was concerned. She'd had enough of both of them.

"I do need better coffee but…"

"But, nothing. I'm not going with you anywhere today, and you can drive up to Starbucks for your better coffee. I've got things to do and don't have time for this. You know the way out."

Okay. That was super bitchy. Damned if she cared though. She wanted Diane and Dante to leave. Right now. Get out of her house. Better yet, get out of her life.

"Well." Diane's tone grew snippy. The real Diane showing her colors. "Whatever. Just trying to be neighborly. I guess you don't appreciate the kindness of friends."

"I have enough friends. I don't need any more." A lie, given she had only a couple. Also true in a way, because she didn't need any more friends. Her gaze slid to Casey. Maybe room for one more.

Then she returned her attention to Diane. Dante's retreat was already in motion as he headed toward the front door. She'd noticed how he'd gotten a little twitchy after she introduced Casey. Given his profession, his reaction set off alarm bells. If anyone should be comfortable around law enforcement, it would be a journalist.

"Let's go," Dante shot back to his sister.

Diane opened her mouth as if to offer further protest and then shook her head. Without another word, she followed Dante out, her back stiff and her step fast.

"Well, that was awkward," Casey commented. "Sounds like I missed something, so fill me in. Did you see him spying on you?"

Glad to hear that Casey caught it too, she said, "My friend, Angel, was taking an early morning walk along the lakeshore—she doesn't sleep much—and saw him. She stopped by after you left to let me know. I forgot to tell you."

"I'm glad you've got friends looking out for you."

So was she. "She's nothing like the pain in the ass you just met. That woman tries me, and her brother gives me the creeps. I really think he also went through my house when I wasn't here."

"What? Why didn't you tell me this before?"

"Nothing concrete to prove anyone was here or that it might have been him. Just a feeling."

Casey nodded. "I understand. Nice to know we're on the same page there with golden boy. He's not ringing true, if you catch my drift, and if you ever feel like he's breached your home again, you let me know right away. Deal?"

"Deal." Not a hard promise to make.

"I don't like him or his sister."

It all hit for her. She hadn't liked Dante from the moment they met. No particular reason except for the intangible vibe that made her want to step away, and she didn't care that he had a successful career that played off of his handsome face. "She's intent on throwing me together with him."

"Pretty good ick-factor there."

Tula met her eyes. "Or dick-factor, if you want to get real specific." Casey's laugh made her smile and wince. "I guess that wasn't very kind."

"Pretty accurate though. Definitely a dick. Don't worry about him. Give me your phone."

That surprised her. What? How did they move from Dante to her phone? She hesitated for only a moment and then handed it to her. After all, Casey was the police, and she must have a good reason, or she wouldn't ask. Casey punched in a number and handed it back.

"There. If you, or your friend, see him peeping again, you call me. I'll have a patrol car here in five minutes, or less. That shit is not okay."

A little thrill ran through her. Casey's personal cell number. In her phone. To use whenever. "Thanks." With the phone in her hand and Casey's cell number in her contacts, she did feel safer, and she now kind of hoped that Dante did peep again so she could use that number.

"Now, let's talk about the murdered women. We've got to figure out where the link is. Once we do, I'll use it to get the bastard who killed my cousin."

Tula's heart ached at the thought of what Casey and her family were going through. It was one thing to paint the faces of murdered women. It was another to have one of them be family. She couldn't imagine the pain. "I want to do anything I can to help. I hate this thing I can do, but since I can't shake it, I plan to use it to stop him."

"We keep saying him. An unconscious reaction on my part. How about you?"

Tula stopped to think. True enough, she used *him* when she spoke of the killer. Or even thought about him, for that matter. The reaction felt natural, organic, and that's why she believed it to be true. How to explain that to a cop? Given Casey had offered the idea of reaction first, maybe it wouldn't be as hard to explain as she thought.

"It's the same for me. Nothing specific and yet very strong. It's male energy that comes to me."

"You have good instincts."

"Born of the real need for self-protection." She'd had to learn fast once she ran or she'd have never made it. Some of those lessons were hard learned. She figured Casey had her own story to tell. "In your work, I have to guess you've developed a strong sense of people. The good and the bad. The truth tellers and the liars." The ones who share only a portion of the truth, she added only in her mind, like Dante.

The gaze Casey turned on her made her shiver.

❖

"I'm sorry to bother you again."

Tula smiled and opened the door for Angel. "Don't be silly. You're welcome here anytime, and after what's been happening around here, everyone is scared."

Angel stepped inside and almost stopped as a ripple on the air washed over her. A mixture of good and bad. Gave her a sliver of hope actually. The last time she'd been here, the air had been filled with more bad than good. The tide had turned or, at the least, evened out. She'd take even.

"Are you all right?"

"I'm fine. Why do you ask?"

"That man I saw staring into your windows. I worry about him bothering you again."

Tula studied her face. Angel could almost see the wheels turning in her head. As much as she wanted to make this casual stop-by sound reasonable, her explanation didn't quite ring true. Honestly, she did want to know how Tula had fared since they spoke last. A least half a dozen times, she'd wanted to run up onto her porch and knock on the door. She'd waited only because it would have raised more red flags, and that wasn't a good idea. Too risky. She'd also had to wait for Casey to leave. Once the detective had gotten into her car and driven away, Angel took the chance and stepped onto the porch.

She reasoned her appearance would be seen as appropriate, given women had to stick together during dangerous times. It wasn't an unreasonable belief. In fact, if she'd heeded that particular pearl of wisdom years ago, her life would have turned out to be quite different. Water under the bridge. While she hadn't bothered to pay attention to it back then, she could try to use it now. If it helped Tula, that was all that mattered.

Tula glanced in the direction of the neighbor's house. "I don't think he'll be a problem."

"I hope you're right. Seeing him out there like that was pretty creepy, and in light of the murders, I would feel better knowing you're being extra safe."

A shadow crossed Tula's face. "He came over earlier, and I'm pretty sure he got the hint that I didn't appreciate his nighttime activities. I was fairly blunt about it. I'll be surprised if he does it again."

"Good! But guys like him don't usually listen. I've met more than a few in my time."

Tula nodded. "True enough. Luckily, I have an ace in the hole. My new detective friend is planning to stay here again tonight, and I don't think he'll risk anything with Casey around. They didn't exactly hit it off when they met this morning."

Relief eased the tension in her shoulders. The fact that the detective continued to stick close helped a great deal. Power in numbers wasn't an abstract concept. It worked. "Good. I'm glad. I'll rest easier knowing you're not here alone."

Tula's eyes narrowed, and a small frown pulled at the corners of her mouth. "What about you? I don't like the idea of you being alone either. Why don't you stay here with me and Casey?"

The invitation made her heart happy. Her world for a long time had presented no opportunities for real friendship. For Tula to offer that to her made all of this even more special. It made everything that would come after much easier.

She smiled and shook her head. "Appreciate it, but really, I'll be fine. I have someone who stays with me." *Most of the time*, she added silently. "No need to worry about me."

"I'll worry about every woman in the Columbia Basin area until this creep is stopped. I'll worry even more about my friends."

Warmth spread through Angel. A long time since she'd felt the bonds of friendship. "Thank you. I'll be careful, if you'll do me a favor and be extra careful."

"Always."

Little did Tula realize Angel knew the whole truth behind that single word.

CHAPTER TWENTY

All right. Let's think this through." Casey paced the length of Tula's studio. She'd run home quickly again to do some chores and get more clothes before returning. A flying trip, and now she picked up right where they'd left off. "Is there a way to make this happen? Maybe earlier, so we have a better chance of tracking down the victim ahead of time?" She'd been thinking about this all day and, so far, hadn't been graced with an epiphany. It made sense in her head, and she hoped that between them they could come up with something.

Tula stood in front of her easel, staring at the blank white canvas. She'd put up the new one after Casey had taken the previous painting with her. What she hadn't shared with Tula was that she'd taken a picture of the painting and provided it to the team. The original remained in the back seat of her car. It wasn't time for Mike to get his hands on the actual painting. Not fair to him really and yet an undeniable truth. By at least providing him with a photo of it, she eased her conscience. Not that he knew it came from her, because she was off the case after all. Another mysterious manila envelope showing up on his desk. Good enough.

"No." Tula shook her head as her gaze stayed steady on the empty canvas, her fingers dancing over it lightly. "It doesn't work like that. I have no control over what comes to me or when."

Casey stopped pacing and put her hands on her hips. "I was afraid you'd say that. Again. I know, I know. You've already explained it to me, and despite appearances, I'm not really that dense. Here's the thing. I have an idea I seriously doubt you're going to like."

Now Tula turned to her. "Try me. At this point, I'm pretty open, especially if it might help."

Easier than Casey thought it would be. She'd expected her to resist anything other than what she'd been doing. "Okay. How do you feel about more company here at your house?"

Tula shrugged. "You mean besides you, pain-in-the-ass Diane and her brother, and Angel?"

This Angel intrigued her, and she'd like to meet the elusive friend. Not who she had in mind though. "Yeah, besides them. Would you be open to another visitor, say my grandmother?"

Tula's eyes narrowed. "Your grandmother?"

"Yeah. I think she can help."

"I suppose…" The look on Tula's face didn't match her words.

"I'll understand if you'd rather not. It's just that, like you, my grandmother has some special skills, and I think they could help us. You know, I didn't appreciate, or believe for the most part, how special her skills were until I met you. Actually, to be more precise, until I witnessed you doing that." She pointed to the canvas.

Interest bloomed in her eyes. "What do you mean special skills?"

How to explain her skepticism of her abuelita's talents? Worse, her disdain for what her abuelita quietly shared with her? To her shame, she'd blown her off as being a superstitious old lady, a first-generation American who grew up learning of the old ways from her mother and abuelita. After seeing what Tula could do, Casey believed that she'd judged her abuelita too harshly all these years. If nothing else came out of this, she vowed to find a way to make it up to her.

"She's a bit like you, only with a lot more experience. I really think she might be able to help."

Tula stared at her for a few moments before nodding. "All right. Let's do it."

"Great. I'll go get her." Before she could take more than a few steps, the doorbell rang.

Tula's face turned dark. "It better not be Diane again. I swear, I can't take a single minute more of that family."

"Oh, shit." It hit her hard. She'd been wrapped up in her plan to bring in her abuelita and had failed to share the bad news. "I forgot to tell you that my partner Mike was planning to come to talk with you."

"The pictures." Sharp lady.

She nodded. "Yes, the pictures."

"He won't understand."

"Not at all, which is why he doesn't have any of the originals. Only photos of them."

"I don't know what to tell him."

"The truth always works the best." He'd write her off as unreliable, and that actually worked for Casey. He'd want a suspect more dynamic. She knew how his mind worked.

"The truth got me a whole lot of doctors' appointments in the past."

"Probably will again, but this time, you've got me. We'll work this through together."

Tula blew out a breath. "Thanks. That's a hell of a lot more than I've ever had before. Let's go talk to your partner." She started toward the front of the house and then turned back around. "You've been taken off this case."

"I have."

"Aren't you going to be in trouble for being here with me?"

"Without a doubt."

Tula hadn't been wrong about Casey's position with her partner. When Casey opened the door, Mike's facial expression as well as his body language screamed outrage. Not a happy guy. After a few minutes of intense questioning, she figured happy guy wouldn't be an accurate description of him on most days. Hard to believe he and Casey were partners. They couldn't be more different. From what she'd seen of Casey thus far, working with the guy every day had to be painful.

Something about him also made her want to take a couple steps back. Off-putting would be a polite way to categorize his aura. Jerk would be another, though unlike Dante, whose energy was black. This guy's life force came across more as gray. In the long run, still draining. If she had to be around him every day like Casey did, she'd lose her mind. Better woman than she.

"Ms. Crane."

The snap in his voice returned her attention to his words. "Yes."

"Am I boring you?"

"Excuse me?"

"Your attention seems to be elsewhere."

"I'm sorry. You were saying?"

"I was *asking* you to explain painting the faces of murdered women. Why did you do that? And why did you mail the photographs rather than coming to us in person? You'd have to know that we'd ultimately track you down."

He'd never grasp the truth, even if he called New York and talked to those who'd been around her twenty years ago. They'd been skeptics too, at least in the beginning. It even took Frances a little time to buy in, and she'd ended up as Tula's biggest ally. Not a lot different here when she'd tried to explain the reality of what she could do. In the end, Casey had to see it to believe it. Only then did she start to edge toward belief. After listening to Mike for a good ten minutes, she didn't think Casey backing her up would hold much sway with this guy. Full of himself and proud of it.

"The faces come to me, and I paint what's in my head." Keep it simple and short, and right on the truth.

"Really?" He drew the word out.

She didn't bite. "I knew you'd be skeptical of my work, and thus I opted to mail the picture."

"Pictures," he clarified. "Guilty people do things like that."

Again, she refused to rise to his bait and said calmly, "Guilty people wouldn't have done anything. I've given you all the information you need to check me out, and trust me, I don't do that lightly. I live here and keep a low profile for a reason. Opening myself up will destroy my peaceful life."

He nodded with a smug expression. "Because you hurt these women."

"Because I didn't."

"Well, we'll just see, now, won't we?"

"Indeed." Other than her paintings, he had nothing on her. She knew it, and so did he.

"Don't leave town."

"Wouldn't dream of it."

He turned a dark gaze on Casey. "We'll talk later."

She watched from the doorway as he got into his car and pulled away. When she closed the door and turned to Casey, she shook her head. "He's an ass."

Casey shook her head. "You have no idea. In a lot of ways, he means well, but that asshole part of him just can't stay tamped down. Not for any length of time anyway."

"How on earth can you be partners with him? I'd be on medication if I had to deal with him every day."

"Some moments I've considered that route."

"How much trouble are you going to be in?"

She pursed her lips and sighed. "Probably a lot."

"I'm sorry."

"My problems don't matter. Finding this killer and stopping him from hurting anyone else—that's what matters. So, let's get back to my abuelita."

❖

Angel walked into the silent church and sat down in the last row. Since she'd last been in a house of God, more decades had passed by than she could count. Memories rushed back and not all of them pleasant. Kneeling on the hassock, she clasped her hands and rested her forehead against them. The lights were low and the pews empty. Tears coursed down her cheeks.

From far down the hallway, the sound of sobs sent her hurrying. She flung open the door and rushed inside. "Sister, what is it?" She dropped next to the crying woman, whose silk dress pooled around her as she lay on the floor, her slender shoulders shaking.

She pulled her sister into her arms and brushed the hair away from Celia's face. With her handkerchief, she blotted her tears and wiped her lips. The delicate yellow flowers embroidered on its edges turned red. With a gentle touch, she tipped Celia's face up. Bruises stained her pale cheeks. "Who did this to you?"

"No, no, no," Celia said through a fresh set of tears. The blood on her lips slowed to a trickle.

While she knew the answer to her question, she pushed her sister to say it out loud, to put the monster's name on the air for all to hear. She'd seen it in his eyes on that very first day, even if everyone else had been blinded to his true nature. Tall, rich, and handsome. Titled. That's all the others could see. The darkness in his soul didn't shine to anyone except her. She'd always been able to see evil.

"I will not let this go on." Rage built inside until she could no longer contain it.

Celia sat up, and it was all she could do not to gasp as her hair fell away from her battered face and neck. Her beautiful, loving sister, black and blue as though she were a woman of the night bloodied by a cruel customer who took pleasure in inflicting pain.

"You cannot help me. No one can." Her voice caught. The despair in her words broke her heart.

She stood, curling her hands into fists. "You are wrong. I can stop this. I will not allow him to hurt you ever again."

Celia reached up and took her hand. "Please, sister, let it be. You will only make it worse. I beg you. Let it be."

"Father must be made aware."

"NO."

"Celia, he cannot continue to do this. No man has the right to lay hands on you, even if he is your husband."

"Leave me, sister. Please leave me. I will heal. No one else need know my shame."

She wanted to argue and didn't. Celia's words were resolute, and she knew her well enough to understand that they'd talk no more. Celia's sense of pride and honor would never allow her to defy the man who'd promised to love and honor her. No love. No honor. Only violence. No more.

As requested, she left the room. That was the only part of her sister's request she complied with, as she went in search of their father. Celia might want to keep this a secret; she did not. She would protect her, and she did not care what the cost might be. That monster would never hurt her sister again.

Their father's steps echoed loud in the hallway as he marched toward Celia's chambers after she'd shared with him what she'd seen. His outrage matched hers, which lifted her heart. His blinders were on no longer. He flung open the door to Celia's chambers without knocking, not that he'd ever knock. Following on his heels, she bumped into him when he stopped on the threshold.

"No," he bellowed before he raced inside.

At first, she didn't understand. Not until he dropped to Celia's side and pulled out the knife she'd plunged into her own heart, the beautiful silk dress stained crimson with her blood.

Angel's tears flowed over her fingers and dripped onto the hassock. The painful ache in her heart was as strong now as the night her sister died. It never went away. It never would.

She'd often wondered if coming to church again would provide her with forgiveness, if she could confess her sins and be absolved. The confessional, mere steps away, beckoned to her as it had that long-ago morning when she'd fled to the church in search of sanctuary. She hadn't stepped inside the confessional then. She did not now. Nothing had changed in the intervening years despite her repeated attempts to redeem herself.

Wiping away the tears with the back of her hands, she stood and walked to the front of the church. She lifted her gaze to the stained-glass windows, so beautiful and meaningful. They were designed to fill the congregation with hope, and she wondered how many stood before them and offered their prayers of regret and remorse.

Squaring her shoulders, she let the prisms of colored light wash over her. Her chin came up. “I am not sorry.”

CHAPTER TWENTY-ONE

"I've been waiting for your call."

Casey shouldn't have been surprised by her abuelita, yet the first words she heard did. "How do you always do that?"

"I've been telling you since you were a baby that I am a witch."

"You are not a witch. You're more like a psychic."

Her abuelita laughed. "If that makes you feel more comfortable, you may call me a psychic. It's at least a step in the right direction. Now, tell me the details. I am aware that you need me."

"You're right, as always. I need your kind of help, and I think you can make a difference in this case. Can I pick you up in ten minutes?"

"But of course. Tell your friend to put on some coffee. I like it strong."

"My friend?"

"Yes, your lovely lady friend."

"Abuelita, seriously, you're freaking me out."

"Always happy to shake up your world, my darling girl."

"I'll tell her."

Twenty-five minutes later, Casey pulled back into Tula's driveway, her abuelita in the passenger's seat. Before she could get around to help her, she'd opened the door, gotten out, and taken three steps toward the house. Then she stopped and tilted her head. Wearing blue jeans and a blue shirt, her long dark hair shot through with strands of white hanging down her back in a single braid, she was barely five feet tall, but power rolled off her like a barreling freight train.

"What is it?"

Her eyes narrowed as she turned full circle. "Evil. It's thick here."

"Tula's not evil." Of that she was certain. Being around her the last several days, she'd made that judgment call and was solid with it. She'd been in the presence of evil before, and Tula wasn't it.

Her abuelita shook her head. "No, not the woman." She pointed at Tula, who stood on the front porch. "In the air." She waved her hands around her head. "Nearby."

Great, just freaking great. "Let's get inside and talk. Tula, this is my abuelita, Valentina. Abuelita, this is my friend Tula. The one I told you about."

"Welcome, Valentina. Please, come inside." Tula held the door open wide.

"Lovely to meet you, Tula." As soon as she crossed the threshold, she stopped again. "He's been inside here."

At the same time Casey and Tula both said, "What?"

Her abuelita began to walk from room to room. She didn't wait for an invitation from Tula. Not surprising, given she was always one to do whatever she deemed necessary, and no one generally argued, given that she nailed it more often than not.

Her abuelita ran her fingers along door frames and the tops of tables with a light, butterfly touch that sometimes didn't even make contact. Not in the physical sense anyway. She moved from the living room, to the bedrooms, and even stepped into the bathroom.

Her expression darkened. "He's been here. He walked around as he touched your things. His essence lingers."

Casey glanced at Tula. The concern in her face mirrored the alarm in her own. "What exactly do you mean?"

Tula nodded and crossed her arms. "I knew it."

"What you told me about?"

"Yes. The disturbance in the air a couple of days ago." Tula dropped her arms, her fingers curling and uncurling.

"Damn it. I wanted to believe it wasn't really anything other than a side effect from your paintings." If she had powers like her abuelita insisted she did, how did Casey miss it?

In the studio, Abuelita stopped before the easel and put both hands on the canvas. Her breathing slowed, and she blinked. "He stood right here and looked out these windows. Wait." She closed her eyes. "He looked in and out of these windows."

❖

The cold chill that washed over Tula almost made her throw up. She'd had a vague sense something wasn't right, and now it all hit home what caused it. He had been in her house, and the tiny woman with the dark eyes and long streaked hair confirmed it. "Can you see his face?" She leaned toward Dante, except she couldn't be sure whether that was because she just didn't like him or it had really been him.

Valentina shook her head as she pulled her hands from the canvas and turned to look at Tula. "No, my child. It doesn't come to me in that way. You see the faces. I feel their spirits."

Her hopes sank as quickly as they'd risen. The way Casey had described her grandmother, she'd pictured a powerhouse with mad skills of precognition, someone who'd be able to put a face to the monster. So far, nothing worked the way she thought it would, and to top it off, learning what had actually happened transformed her concern into terror.

"Only those I know have been inside my house. I don't want to believe any of them could be this killer." The small pool of visitors made it easy to sift through. She still wanted to believe her home secure and that her connection to the murder came only as close as her canvas.

Valentina took her face between her hands and stared into her eyes. "Child, the wicked do not wear a face that can be recognized. They like to hide behind a mask of being pretty or handsome or kind-looking. It can be a doctor, a preacher, a grave digger. As good exists in all walks of life, so too does evil."

The chills grew more intense. "Why can't I paint his face then? I can't save anyone if I'm always running ten steps behind."

"That's what I'm here to help you with. Together we can bring this to an end." Valentina pulled her into a surprisingly comforting hug. She wanted to stay in her arms.

Casey stood in the doorway watching and listening. "How about we reconvene in the kitchen. We've had a request for strong, dark coffee."

Tula managed a smile. "I can help you out there." She stepped out of the hug and headed to the kitchen.

Ten minutes later, she poured three cups from the French press. No generic drip for this lady. A special guest rated a great cup of coffee. She handed the first one to Valentina. "I hope this is okay."

Valentina took a sip and smiled. "Perfect. Now, first things, first. Tell me how this started for you."

For someone who'd managed to keep her true life buried for two decades, she'd sure been spilling lately. No more incognito. She supposed all good things must come to an end. Damned if that stupid saying wasn't turning into her truth. What worried her more than the fact that her previous notoriety would undoubtedly follow her here was the likelihood of her parents appearing. They would never give up trying to find and lure back their meal ticket, even if they still lived comfortably off the income from the money they had pilfered from her trust. Truthfully, she'd make money to keep them satisfied and away from her, and the child who still lived inside her screamed in terror.

With her cup of coffee in hand, she sat down across from Valentina. Staring into her face, she found Casey's resemblance to her impossible to miss. Beautiful dark eyes and a square chin. Gorgeous thick, glossy hair. The same strength she noticed in Casey glowed from both grandmother and granddaughter.

"Art lived inside me from my very first memory," she said, and her heart swelled at the recollection. One of the few good ones. "All my life, I've dreamed in colors. As a child, I thought everyone did…" By the time she finished the story of her journey to becoming Tula Crane, her coffee sat cold and forgotten on the kitchen table. "And that's how we ended up right here."

Valentina set her empty cup on the table and glanced over at Casey. Her expression remained serious. "We can help her."

"We?"

She patted Casey's arm. "If you think the gift passed you by, darling girl, you'd be wrong."

Well, things were getting interesting. Tula studied Casey's expression of surprise for a moment before asking, "What have you been withholding from me, Detective?"

"Not a damn thing. Abuelita, you know I've never had even a twinge of anything." She stood and started pacing the kitchen.

Valentina leaned back in her chair and watched her. "Oh, really? Remember Becka?"

Casey shook her head and made a face. "Nothing otherworldly about what happened with her. That was a case of luck. That's all."

"Who's Becka?" Tula had to know more. Not wanted, needed.

"Oh." Valentina tilted her head, her dark eyes shining with pride. "Only a pretty young girl that my darling little Casey saved from a trafficker. Another hour and she'd have been lost."

"Gut instinct combined with law-enforcement experience."

"You can tell yourself that all day long, and it won't change a single thing. How do you explain that no one else around that girl picked up on anything out of the ordinary? Only you. My brilliant, special girl."

Tula studied Casey's face and saw her in a different way. The glow she'd missed before came now to her artist's eye. Or perhaps it was her grandmother who brought it out. Either way, it was there. She no longer felt alone.

When Casey said nothing, Valentina pointed a finger at her. "You can't explain it because you don't want to. You are my blood, and in that blood runs magic. Deny it all you want. It won't make a difference. You are special."

On that note, Tula agreed with her. She'd felt something for Casey right from the beginning, although she'd been unable to define exactly what it was. Now she knew, and it drew her in even more. Not exactly what she'd been expecting when she'd dropped that photograph in the mail.

Casey ran her palms over her hair as she gazed into her grandmother's eyes. "I want to argue with you."

Valentina folded her hands on the table. "It would be an exercise in futility."

"You always win."

"I'm always right."

❖

Angel walked out of the church with her head held high and her shoulders squared. The forgiveness she'd always wondered about should she step inside the church again hadn't happened. Not that it came as a big surprise. Not that she cared.

Funny how one could live as long as she and be completely oblivious to something like that. It highlighted how she'd grown in the intervening years in ways she couldn't have imagined when this all started. Blue liked to tell her that she often missed the big picture, and once again, he'd been right. Until now, it had gone right over her head. The knowledge gave her power. It also made her sad. She wanted to share this insight with him, to tell him that she got it. Finally.

He'd be proud of her, and that meant a lot. She'd have been lost on this journey without him, but until right now, she hadn't truly understood him. She'd assumed he'd been one of those kind souls who always saw the best in people, who forgave them their worst sins and helped them be better people.

Now she understood the distinction between her beliefs and the truth. He was a good person, always had been and always would be, his path to heaven assured from the day of his birth. This had nothing to do with any of that. He'd clearly been brought to her to help her understand herself. The guilt, the shame, the fury—what she'd done that day all factored in. Year in and year out, she'd wished it could have been different, that she'd acted another way in that moment of intense emotion.

Only today, kneeling on the hassock and crying beneath the stained-glass window, did she finally understand what he'd been able to grasp all along. Why he'd walked by her side these many years. Not once did he complain or bemoan the unfairness of any of it. Not once did he blame her.

She stared up at the sky and blew out a long breath. In a way, she felt stupid for taking so long to see what had been in front of her the whole time. In another way, she was grateful that she finally understood. It was the end for her, and she could make peace with that reality. She would also do everything in her power to help Tula stop this devil. Once they accomplished that feat, her time would be up. She smiled as she looked at the sky.

"I understand. I finally understand." She put her hands in her pockets and walked away from the church. The smile vanished.

Chapter Twenty-two

"All right, so say I buy into the juju. What can you do…what can we do…to help Tula? We have to be able to be proactive rather than playing catch-up with this guy." Casey still didn't quite know what to think. She wanted to tell Abuelita that she was wrong about her possessing any supernatural-type abilities and couldn't quite summon the energy. Or the conviction. Damn it.

Casey knew she got what she was hinting at. She also understood that her abuelita had her own way to do things and would act in her own time. She wanted to push her because time was an issue. It would do no good to try, because tiny as she might be, she would be immovable.

Abuelita nodded, and a small smile that looked suspiciously like triumph pulled up the corners of her mouth. "Buckle up, ladies. We've got work to do, and the night is burning. I need a pen and paper to make a list. We're going to need some things."

"Are you sure?" Casey was beginning to second-guess her grand plan to bring her abuelita in. Not that she didn't believe what she'd told them so far. Abuelita wasn't usually wrong about these things. Wait. She was never wrong.

She put her hands on her hips, and that phantom smile disappeared as she stared up at Casey. "Do what I tell you. I'm not one of your suspects you get to question. Let's move."

Tula walked over and stood behind her abuelita. "Casey, she's right. I can feel it too. Something is changing, and pretty quickly. It's like it's becoming more desperate. It's thick and suffocating in the air. I'm surprised you can't sense it."

Casey couldn't argue with both of them. Something about the two women together sent a wave of energy through the kitchen, though not so much that they ganged up on her. More like a confluence of power when they stood shoulder to shoulder. "Okay. Tell me what you need." She was done trying to fight what she couldn't see or feel.

"Have to go back to my house," her abuelita said.

"What? I thought you wanted to help us." Talk about confusing the hell out of her.

Abuelita rolled her eyes. "Listen to me before you jump to conclusions. I'm not going back to my house. You are." She continued to tell her in detail what she wanted Casey to bring back to Tula's.

"Why don't you go with me, and that way you can be sure all the right things make it back here."

She shook her head. "No, my sweet girl. I'm not leaving Tula. We must stay here together."

Again, no sense in arguing. She'd lose in the end, so she might as well do as told. "All right. Go over it again for me, and this time I'll write it down." She pulled out a small notebook and pen from her jacket pocket.

List in hand, she raced across town to complete her assigned task. It didn't actually take her long to reach her abuelita's house, where she used the keypad she'd insisted on having installed a couple years earlier, along with a state-of-the-art security system, to enter through the back door. It always felt like home when she walked into the kitchen with the bright-blue walls and cheery yellow cabinets. Her abuelita possessed a flair for color that worked, though the skill had passed her by. If she tried to put these colors in her house, it would turn out to be an epic fail. A woman with her design skills needed to stick to the basics, like dark walnut cabinets and neutral paint. While boring, such a color scheme didn't scare anyone away either.

Exactly where she'd been told it would be, she located the locked box. For as much time as she'd spent in this house, she'd never seen it before, and she'd have remembered it. About six by twelve inches, with a beautiful carved top and a delicate locking latch, the mahogany box was old. Not as heavy as she expected, meaning its contents couldn't amount to much. According to her abuelita, important nonetheless.

Curiosity had her driving back to Tula's way faster than she should have, even for a police officer. It wasn't like this was an emergency or she was on duty, for that matter. After the uncomfortable interview with Tula earlier, she'd already preempted Mike and called in for a few days of annual leave. Given she'd been taken off the murders, and rightfully so, others could pick up her caseload for a day or two. She rarely took leave anyway, meaning they owed her. Mike would be royally pissed when he ran in to tattle on her, only to discover she'd taken herself way out of the queue. He hated it when anyone got ahead of him, and as far as she was concerned, she was just getting started. She'd been patient with his dinosaur ways, until now. He'd run out of time.

She didn't bother knocking when she got back to Tula's. She barged right through the front door. Figured it would go over better for her than it did for Diane. "Okay, Abuelita. Here it is." She handed her the pretty box. "What have you been hiding in there?"

Her abuelita smiled and winked. "All in good time, child. You needed to be ready before I share my secrets with you."

"Come on. You've always declared yourself to be a bruja blanca."

"A bruja what?" Tula looked from one face to another.

Casey pointed to her abuelita. "My abuelita has proclaimed for as long as I can remember that she is a white witch, or as they call them in Mexico, a bruja blanca."

"It is so." She held the box close to her chest.

"And, if I'm following your logic today, I'm one too. Isn't that what you've been trying to make a case for, Abuelita?"

She smiled and nodded. "As we shall soon see."

❖

Tula couldn't tamp down her fascination. Casey's grandmother came in a small package that held so much power she wasn't sure the walls of her house could contain it. Didn't require a big leap of imagination to believe her to be a white witch. Magic rolled off her, unseen and tangible all at the same time. Someday, she'd love to paint her just to see if she could capture some of the magic.

Without a whisper of hesitation, Tula understood that help had arrived in that tiny package. It would serve no purpose to deny her own grain of otherworldly power. It had raised its head too many times to be able to discard it as anything beyond what it was. So, it didn't require much more than a skip to believe in Valentina's gift. Casey might not see it. Tula did.

"What do we need to do?" She looked at Valentina and the mystery box she held tight.

She turned approving eyes on Tula. "We are going to draw out your magic, and we are going to stop this devil."

A great plan that she and Casey had been trying to leverage for several days without success. She wasn't sure how a little box could change the game. "How?"

Valentina looked to her granddaughter. "We will do it together. A trinity of power, if you will."

"Seriously, Abuelita. I know you think I have some kind of supernatural power, but I don't." Casey was shaking her head. "I have a gun and a badge, and that's where my superpowers end."

A small smile turned up the corners of her mouth as Valentina first looked at Casey and then Tula. "Did you believe in your powers at first?"

The question took Tula a little off guard. "Ah, no. I thought I was just painting a face I'd conjured up in my mind. I mean, I was pretty young at the time, and I did have a rather vivid imagination."

"Did you want to believe?"

All of a sudden, she could see where Valentina might be going. "No. In fact, it didn't make sense to me at all. I thought it was some kind of weird coincidence."

"But you came to believe because you had to."

She could still remember the moment when she understood. "I did."

Valentina handed the now-unlocked box to Casey. "Open it."

Casey took the box and opened the lid. Her eyes narrowed, and her lips pressed together. Tula peeked over her shoulder. "What the hell are these?"

"Hummingbird feathers."

"Excuse me? I did not just hear that." She snapped the box lid shut and stared at her grandmother. "Abuelita, you cannot have these. It's illegal to possess them, and you know that."

Valentina appeared unfazed. "Of course it is unlawful to have the feathers." She looked smug. "Unless you have a permit."

"What? A permit? Why on earth would you have a permit to own hummingbird feathers?"

"You shall see, my beautiful girl. First," she turned to Tula, "I need for you to cut a square of your shirt for me and then give it to Casey."

Tula was tempted to ask why, except her curiosity level had gone up about a thousand percent when she saw those feathers and even more when she heard that Valentina had a permit. First time she'd ever heard of someone getting a permit to own hummingbird feathers, or any feathers for that matter. She grabbed a pair of scissors and began to cut away a chunk of her shirt. She handed it to Valentina. "Now what?"

"Now it is Casey's turn."

Fascinated, Tula watched as Valentina instructed the confused Casey on what to do with the tiny feathers inside the box. First, she had her fold them inside the piece of Tula's shirt. The feathers weren't the only contents of the box, and next she told Casey to take lengths of bright thread in at least six different colors and wrap them around the cloth-encased feathers. When she finished, she held a colorful bundle about the size of a car key.

Casey held it out in the palm of her hand. "Now what?"

Valentia put her hand beneath Casey's and then looked at Tula. "Put your hand on top of Casey's."

For a moment she hesitated. That little bundle almost glowed in Casey's palm, or so it seemed. She blinked, and when she looked again, she saw simply feathers, cloth, and thread. Her imagination was running amok. She turned her hand over and let her palm meet with Casey's, the tiny bundle of cloth and feathers in between.

Everything went black.

❖

As Angel walked along the shoreline, a bolt of energy hit her and knocked her off her feet. She flew backward and landed on her back, her head thudding against the sand. For a few seconds, black dots blocked out the fading light of the day, and pain radiated throughout her.

When she opened her eyes, Blue stood over her. "Well, that kicked your butt."

She pushed up to her feet and brushed the sand out of her hair and off her clothes. "What in the world was that?"

He shook his head. "I don't know. One minute you were walking along the shoreline, and the next minute you were flat on your back. Something is going on around here, and it's more than your girl."

"She can't do that even with my help."

"No. Definitely not."

"Her friends."

"I think so, yes."

For the first time in a long time, something akin to true optimism took hold in Angel's heart. "I hope so. Maybe that's what we've needed all along. A boost from the powers we don't have the ability to tap into." She'd had a good feeling about the cop, and for a change, she hadn't been wrong.

"Come. Let's walk their way."

"Give me a moment. I need to center myself, gather some strength." Angel closed her eyes and clasped her hands together. After her visit to the church and the bolt of energy that had knocked her down, she wasn't ready to jump up and slay dragons.

As she listened to the sounds of the day heading toward its end, peace settled over her. Determination too. They would need both to bring this to a close. Closure, what a beautiful word. What a feeling to anticipate.

She opened her eyes and frowned. No Blue. She shouldn't be surprised, yet his absence hurt as though he had intentionally abandoned her. Too much time alone lately—something she wasn't used to and didn't want to be. Maybe if she walked to Tula's as he'd suggested, he would catch up. She hoped so.

The closer she got to Tula's, the darker the sky became. The air grew cooler, and the wind picked up, carrying the whispers.

"I hear you." Tears flowed down Angel's cheeks.

CHAPTER TWENTY-THREE

What the hell!" Casey caught Tula before she hit the ground, her own knees shaking with the effort not to let them both drop. Not that Tula was a big woman. Tiny by Casey's standard, but her dead weight was a challenge. "What did you do to her?" She gazed up at Abuelita.

She looked pleased, as if she'd been expecting this all along. "She's harnessing the energy we were able to call as a trio. Alone, it is more difficult. A trinity can do much, much more."

"Abuelita, I'm not a bruja." She managed to lower Tula gently to the floor, checking her neck for a pulse. Strong, steady. She wished she'd open her eyes.

Abuelita put a hand on Casey's head as she knelt next to the unconscious Tula. Despite her protestations about not having any supernatural powers, she'd started to feel them the moment she held the tiny feathers in her hand. By the time she'd finished the little bundle of feathers, cloth, and thread, she had begun to buzz. Damn her anyway. Casey had always just wanted to fit in, to be like all the other kids. She'd tried so hard, and for the most part, it had worked. Now her efforts unraveled at the speed of light. Thank you, family. Thank you, bruja blanca.

"Stop fighting."

"I don't want it." If she'd been a few decades younger, she'd have stomped her feet.

"It isn't a choice. It's a calling."

"Corny."

"Truth." Abuelita kissed the top of her head.

Whatever. Real mature. Good thing it had stayed inside her head.

"We need to help Tula." Redirect. It worked on interview subjects, so maybe it would work with her abuelita too.

"We just did."

Redirect: a miss. "By knocking her out? That's how we helped her?"

"We didn't knock her out. We boosted her access to another realm. Darling, you have to understand the subtle differences. It will come to you as you learn to harness your own powers."

"I'm not a bruja." She could keep saying it until the cows came home.

"Repeat it as many times as you want, and see if it makes any difference."

Casey decided to let the subject go for the moment. They could argue about it later, when they didn't have to worry about women being murdered. She turned her focus to Tula once more. Her pulse remained steady and her breathing even, as though she simply slept. Not in obvious danger other than being in a coma-like state. The cop in her had a really hard time not calling emergency services. She could use a well-trained EMT right about now. She reached for her phone only once and then slipped it right back into her pocket after her abuelita softly put her hand on top of hers and shook her head.

She stayed next to Tula, brushing the hair from her serene face. "I don't know about this other realm."

"Hold her hand. Feel her power, and then tell me you don't believe."

As much as she wanted to argue, it would be useless. She took the offered suggestion and reached out for Tula's hand. Warmth filled her the second they came into contact. Her eyes closed as she took a deep breath and let the feeling flow through her.

Slowly she opened her eyes and looked up. "You're right. She's fine, but she's somewhere else, seeing things we can't."

Abuelita nodded and sat in one of the kitchen chairs. "As I knew she would. Now, we wait."

"You just met her."

"A bruja can recognize a kindred soul. She is special."

"Right…" Too much woo-woo. True enough, she'd seen a lot already that didn't have a rational explanation. Holding Tula's hand and acknowledging the connection was about as far as she wanted to go for now.

"Why do you think you were drawn to her?" Her abuelita didn't appear inclined to let the topic go. It was as if she'd waited all of Casey's life for this moment, for her little granddaughter to become as special as she. She didn't think she could measure up, even if, and it was a big if, she turned out to be a bruja blanca.

"Because she inserted herself into a homicide investigation that included the murder of family." Seemed fairly basic to her and a pretty plausible explanation of why she'd come here in the first place. Mama told her to do whatever she had to for Rita, and that's what she'd been doing since.

"No, sweet child. You were drawn to her because of your own power. Don't"—she held up a hand when Casey opened her mouth to argue—"even try to go there. First, think about any other time in your career where you've stayed at the house of someone on the suspect list. Just one time."

Damn it. How did she manage to do this time and time again? It wasn't like she even talked about her work with her family, yet Abuelita always seemed to know everything. Like the fact that she'd never done anything like this before.

"I'm not a bruja blanca." Her protest sounded weak even to her.

❖

How did she end up on the bridge spanning the lake? The wind blew through Tula's hair, and she had to grab it with one hand to keep it out of her eyes. She'd been in her house with Casey and her grandmother, and now, here she stood, alone and confused. A little scared.

She squinted as she looked down the beach. It was Angel, kneeling in the sand, and though she couldn't be sure from so far away, it looked to her like she was sobbing into her hands. That wasn't like her friend. Angel was the epitome of optimism. She never failed to raise Tula's spirits whenever she felt down. In fact, like magic, she had a way of showing up when Tula's world darkened with despair. It wasn't fair that now Angel was in pain. She wanted to run to her and pull her into her arms.

By the time she made it from the bridge to the edge of the lake, Angel was gone. Must have continued farther along the beach. She continued to walk toward where she'd seen her. It was in the direction of home anyway.

She rubbed her head as she trekked along the edge of the lake. Was her old head injury playing havoc with her? Given the stress of the last few days, it wouldn't be that strange. Not that she really possessed much clinical knowledge of how TBIs worked, beyond what she'd looked up. It had been years since she'd noticed any lingering effects, recent blackouts aside. Clearly, the injury had popped back up in some form. This journey away from home that she couldn't remember making had to be an effect as well. She'd never lost time before. Except, of course, during the painting fugues.

In the distance, she saw another figure. It wasn't Angel. This time, it was a male. Tall, with dark hair and a confident stride. Too far away to make out the face. Her step quickened as a vague feeling of urgency swept through her. She needed to catch up.

The closer she got, the more she hurried. The hair on the back of her neck stood up, her fingers buzzing. Something was wrong here. Very wrong. As she grew closer, the figure became clearer. He carried what looked like a body over his shoulder. A woman's body. Though her step quickened, he maintained the same pace and the distance between them. She started to run.

Tula's eyes flew open, and she stared into Casey's face. "What just happened?"

"I think I brought you back."

"Back? I was out running along the shoreline. I almost had him."

"Him, who?"

"The killer." Tula sensed it from the moment she'd seen him. The man carrying the woman was the killer, and she'd rushed to get close enough to see his face.

"I knew it would work."

Both Tula and Casey looked at her grandmother. Valentina sat at the table while Casey and Tula crouched on the floor. The floor? She glanced down and wondered how she got there. "You knew it would let me see?"

She nodded. "I did."

"You saw the killer?" Casey stiffened all over. The cop just shifted into investigation mode.

Tula didn't like the fact that she'd disappoint them both. Their expectant faces told her they were ready for more than what she could share. "I saw his back. I saw him carrying a woman. No details. No faces. Nothing that puts us any closer."

Casey looked disappointed. Her grandmother did not. "Not to worry, little one. It is simply the start. The magic is all around you now, and this was merely the first glimpse. The magic will show you more as you are ready."

Valentina was wrong on that count. She'd been ready since the first painting. She was past ready now. Time clicked away really fast. That woman, slung over the retreating man's shoulder, was in danger. Not dead yet, but she would be soon if they didn't act fast. They didn't have time to nurture whatever magic they'd made together.

"We've got to turbo-charge this thing." She waved her hand to encompass all three of them.

Casey looked to her grandmother. "What should we do next? Tula's right. I don't think it will be very long before this asshole kills again. We can't wait around. We need to be proactive."

Valentina nodded. "Stay together, and the magic will call to you. Now, phone me an Uber. I need to go home."

"I thought you said we needed the trinity for this thing to gain force?" Tula would have asked the same question if Casey hadn't beat her to it.

"The three of us started it. You two are strong enough to finish it. You no longer need me. The magic is yours. Use it."

"I don't know." Casey looked doubtful.

Tula stood and reached out to Casey. Warmth spread through her when Casey took her hand. "We have nothing to lose by trying."

"See. Tula understands. Trust her, beautiful girl, and trust yourself. You can do this. Now, my Uber."

"I'll take you." Casey let go of her hand and started toward her grandmother.

"You will not. I said, stay together. Abuelita always knows best."

Despite the gravity of the situation, Tula smiled. She had been around this woman less than a day and loved her already. She cut her gaze to Casey. She had some rather warm feelings about her granddaughter too.

❖

The sky cleared, and the breeze once more turned warm. Angel's thoughts returned to her family. Whenever her mother experienced a chill she would say, "Someone just walked over my grave." Angel felt like that now.

Whatever had just passed over her now was important. That much she would bank on. She cut her gaze to Tula's house down the beach from where she stood. As she walked closer, her heart beat faster. Yes, that was a good thing.

A bit of something similar to relief washed over her. Tula's new friends were precisely what she needed. She could have used good friends way back. She'd been left to her own devices, and that ended up not turning out very well. Good intentions aside, she'd let everyone down in that moment.

"Stop."

She whirled and cried out. "Blue."

His smile lit up his eyes. Easy to understand how that face could make a woman fall for him. "Stop obsessing about the past."

"I can't help it. I worry that I won't be able to help her this time, and my failure could put her in danger."

"It wasn't your fault."

He wasn't talking about Tula. "I can't go there right now. This is far more important."

"You can't deal with this until you deal with the truth."

"We don't have time. You know it as well as I do. The end is coming, and if I can't help her with this, it could be the end for her too."

Blue put his hands on his hips. "I repeat, it was not your fault. You have to face that fact sooner or later. It is the only way and your only path home."

"Home, home, home. I'm sick of hearing about something I'll never see again."

"Are you really so full of yourself that you believe you know everything?"

Her head snapped up and she met his eyes. "You know something, don't you?"

"Time draws to a close for all of us sooner or later. Help her, and then help yourself."

"With the cop with her now, I can't do anything." She liked that Casey was with Tula, but it limited what she could accomplish.

"You will figure it out. You always do."

He didn't add that while she always figured out something to do in difficult situations, it wasn't always the right thing.

CHAPTER TWENTY-FOUR

Last night, Casey rejected Abuelita's request for an Uber and called her mother instead. Mama had shown up right away, no questions asked, and ferried her home. The family didn't question orders from the matriarch. Well, unless said matriarch ordered a rideshare, and then Casey, the cop, stepped in to provide her with one she was more comfortable with.

Afterward, Tula and she had talked for several hours. Nothing in-depth, no soul-baring revelations. Casual and light. A parody of what a normal evening would look like for a couple of friends hanging out. By the time they finally went to bed or, in Casey's case, to the sofa, she had a profound sense of disappointment. Despite Abuelita's assurance that together, she and Tula could create the kind of magic needed to stop the monster, nothing else occurred. As in zip.

It had taken her a long time to drift off to sleep. She missed Diego and the sound of his purr. Whenever she had trouble sleeping, it would lull her into relaxation. She'd worry about him being home alone, except the guy was pretty independent. Stan had promised to swing by on his way back from the hospital to check his food and water. She could be gone a week and miss him like crazy, while he'd look at her like she'd just left an hour earlier. She smiled thinking about him.

In the morning, a shower felt great and washed away the last cobwebs of a short night's crappy sleep. At least she smelled good and looked somewhat refreshed. She shouldn't scare Tula, in any event. She slipped into a clean pair of jeans and her favorite sweatshirt. Ready for another day of what? Waiting, she supposed.

Tula wasn't in the kitchen, although the scent of coffee, faint enough to let her know it had been made some time ago, told her she'd been up. She figured she had a good idea where to find her. It had been another night without incident. Casey hadn't awakened to find her before the easel with a paintbrush in her hand.

Casey stopped in the doorway and studied her for a moment. "Good morning."

"Good morning."

"So, what do we do now?" She'd had her hopes set on something, anything, happening after the display of power put on by her abuelita. The anticlimax had her struggling.

Tula had her back to Casey, staring out the studio windows to where the lawn, green and thick, stretched down to the beach. The morning sun rose bright from the east, and a strong wind blew, causing waves on the water. The sheets and blanket she'd left in a tangled mess when she'd gone to shower were now folded and piled on the end of the sofa. "We wait."

"That doesn't feel right." Casey wanted action, not sitting around waiting for something to happen and then reacting to it.

Tula turned and looked at her. She couldn't read her expression. "I can't turn it on and off."

Casey got what she meant, only things had changed since that first night when she'd witnessed her painting during a fugue-like state. Abuelita had altered the game. Before she scrapped it all and returned to plain old police work, she had an idea. "Let's try something."

Tula threw out her hands. "It didn't work with your grandmother. I still didn't see his face."

Casey understood the frustration she could hear in her voice.

"You saw the woman's face, right?"

"No. Not hers either. I didn't get close enough. All I could really make out was that a man carried a woman over his shoulder. She wasn't very big and had long hair. That's as much as I could see."

"Well, let's think this through then. I mean, I've got skills that we can use. Instead of sitting around waiting for something to happen, let's push this." The cop in her wanted to charge forward. Some of this might be out of her area of expertise. It didn't mean she couldn't still use her particular skill set.

Tula tilted her head as if considering the concept. "It is definitely worth a shot."

Casey held up her hand. "First, we need coffee."

"I'll make a fresh pot."

"No. I mean really good coffee. No insult intended."

Tula smiled, and the light came back into her face. "None taken."
Casey pulled her car keys out of her pocket. "I'll be right back."

❖

The minute Casey walked out the door, a chill washed over Tula. Had this emptiness been around before Casey stepped into her world? She walked through the living room, brushing her fingertips over the furniture. Yes, it had been empty around here before Casey showed up. Even more so before Valentina managed to unleash buckets of power.

Great. Someone brings murder back into her life, and she has a come-to-Jesus moment with herself. Reality sucked. It really did. Not that it should come as a surprise. Her whole life had been one big disappointment after another, except when it came to her art. That had always been her true joy and her escape. When she painted, she could lose herself in her own private world, where beauty reigned and no one could hurt her.

Except, of course, when it came to the faces of the dead women. Not quite the private world anyone would choose to willingly embrace. On another level, though, as much as it frightened her as a child, as a mature adult she could see how maybe the universe gave the gift to her for a reason. Out of tragedy could come goodness. Her life might have been a disaster, but her paintings helped put away killers. That end result didn't suck.

She only wished she had more control over any of it, and all of it would be even better. Story of her life. She'd never had control, even here in this world she'd created from nothing. Not in this lovely home on the lakeshore where she could watch the ducks paddle serenely across the water and drink coffee on her patio as the gentle breeze kissed her skin. Even here in the midst of all the beauty, control remained an illusion, with her always at the mercy of happenstance.

She smiled when she thought about Casey. She shouldn't smile, because as a cop, Casey presented a very real threat to her existence here. Two things gave her a bit of grace. First, that she'd witnessed the truth of what Tula could do, and second, her wonderful, open-minded grandmother. If not for those two things, she'd probably be sitting in a cell right now. Not that a cell wasn't still in her future. A smart woman wouldn't discount Casey's partner Mike. He'd most certainly be coming for her.

At the sound of the doorbell she spun, her heart racing. Damn it, probably that Mike again, and this time with handcuffs. Not now. They were getting closer, and she didn't want their momentum stalled. She also didn't want to face the man alone. Casey knew how to handle him. Tula, less so. She willed herself to remain calm and walked to the front door. Thank the gods. Not Mike.

"Angel. What's up?" The look on her friend's face worried her, as did the frequency of her recent visits. Angel usually came surrounded by light and love. Today, it was as if a black cloud had dropped on her. Also, she routinely stopped by once every few months, not once every few days. Something wasn't sitting right with Angel, which frightened her.

Her smile was weak. "Just checking in on you again. The sight of that guy out by the tree still freaks me out."

Tula winced. She'd admit she was on the same page about Dante. He had an air about him that bugged the hell out of her, and it was more than the aggressive personality he shared with his sister. That was most likely an asset in his chosen profession. Each time he'd been in her space, she'd been unable to resist the urge to put a lot of space between them. Not a normal reaction to people, even for someone who'd been as sheltered as she was. "I'm with you, though honestly, I don't think he's an issue. A pest, sure, but one I can send on his way, and I have to think he'll be gone soon. Or at least I hope he will. He does have a job on the other side of the country."

Angel raised an eyebrow. "One word for you my friend: telework."

Her heart sank. "Damn. I didn't even think about that. Well, let's hope they require on-site attendance immediately, and he goes home like right now."

"Stay away from him." Angel sounded more concerned than she'd ever heard her.

"Angel, seriously, are you all right? You don't seem yourself, and you're really pale." Angel was a lovely woman, with long hair and a classic face. She'd be perfect for a throwback painting of an aristocratic woman from centuries before. Her features were delicate and pure, her eyes soft and filled with secrets. Angel might think she could hide that last part from Tula, but she'd be wrong. Her artist's eye saw everything.

Angel's smile was a little brighter this time, perhaps a little more forced. Tula had touched a nerve. "I'm fine. Maybe a tad bit tired. Nothing for you to worry about. I'm more concerned about a freaky neighbor trying to harm you."

"Appreciate the concern. My friend is still here, and no one is going to get past Casey. Would you like a cup of coffee, some tea? Come on in and sit down for a while." It occurred to her that though they'd been friendly for quite a while, Angel never stopped long enough to sit at the kitchen table and have something to drink with her. An occasional brief conversation out on the patio, and that was about it. Why hadn't she noticed that before?

Angel backed toward the door and stepped out into the sunshine. "No. I'm good. Appreciate the offer. Another time. I've got to go this morning. You know, things to do and people to see." Angel almost ran down the front steps.

Tula didn't turn around and go back inside until Angel rounded the corner and disappeared from sight. "Strange," she muttered. She'd connected with Angel in the first place partially because of her rather odd personality. She reminded Tula of herself—not quite mainstream. The last couple of times Angel had stopped by, she'd seemed very different, less herself.

Might be her turn to visit Angel for a change. Since they'd met after bumping into each other on their respective walks along the shoreline, the pattern had been for Angel to stop by her house, they chatted, and then Angel went on her way. Occasionally, she sent a little business to Tula. Like the never-shared drinks, she'd also never been to Angel's house. All she'd ever said was that she lived down the lake a distance. Narrowed it right down on a big lake with a whole lot of homes. Some kind of friend she'd turned out to be. In her defense, she needed to keep a low profile, thus she stayed close to home.

When the killing of the women ended, she'd make an effort to return the friendship Angel had shown her by stopping by her house. They'd sit down together, drink some coffee, and sincerely connect. Yes, that's what she'd do, and it would be all better.

❖

Amplify. That was the only thing Angel could think of to do. The sound of the clock ticking in the back of her head sent her frustration soaring. She'd pulled all the tricks out of her bag, and so far nothing was working, at least not at the level it needed to. Tula had to push harder, and Angel had to help her do it.

Blue liked to tell her that she was a problem solver. He'd seen the quality in her the first day they met. As a child, she'd been the one to figure out the how and the why of everything. Because they were a rich and powerful family, she'd heard the whispers about her getting away with bad behavior because of her skill. They weren't entirely wrong or entirely right.

In the world she came from, a mere girl held no power. Every one of them learned that lesson quickly. Most settled in and went with the status quo, adapting to the limited life assigned to them by gender. Others, like her, fought it their whole lives. She'd like to believe that if she'd had more time, she could have really made a difference.

Blue had told her to make peace with the reality she'd created for herself. The order was tall. Maybe too tall. If she couldn't help Tula, how could she help herself? Her hope lay with the topaz she'd left on the table at Tula's. It took more out of her than she thought to accomplish what looked like a simple task. For her, not so simple, and she felt its effects now. It had to be worth the drain. As small as it was, the stone would serve as a conduit to concentrate the energy that maybe, just maybe, would provide the amplification needed to end the evil taking root here.

"You still have to forgive yourself."

She jumped. "Damn it, Blue. You've got to stop doing that."

He shrugged. "I'd think by now you'd feel me."

She'd think so too, yet that didn't seem to be the case. Part of her penance, she supposed. Her *gift* allowed her to feel those who needed her help, like Tula. When it came to herself, not even a twinge. Out here on her own, so to speak.

"I didn't back then, so why would I now?" Yes, that was bitchy. He deserved it. They were trying to help Tula stop a killer, trying to save lives. She didn't have time to go over ancient history a million more times. If she never had to think about it again, it would be too soon. Besides, he had to know as well as she that Angel wasn't inclined to forgive herself. What she'd done didn't deserve forgiveness. As they liked to say these days, it was a moot point.

"I think we need to keep an eye on the creep."

Blue let her go with the redirect. Every once in a while, he conceded. "Agreed. What did you say to Tula?"

"Less about our conversation and more about what I left her."

"And that would be?"

She pulled at the collar of her shirt, revealing her bare neck. "Time to let it go."

Blue's eyes widened. "You left her your sister's topaz."

She nodded. The one tangible thing she'd carried with her since that fateful night, it remained her constant reminder of what she'd done and what she'd lost. Had she been wrong? It had been with her because a day would come when its power would be needed. "I believe it will help to amplify her powers, and combined with the energy of the cop and her grandmother, it will enable Tula to bring this to an end."

He nodded, and his expression of surprise changed to one of approval. "See? I'm right."

She raised a single eyebrow. "About?"

"The timing of everything. Most of all, you."

She ignored the last part of his comment. "I have to help in any way I can."

He wasn't taking her up on the redirect this time. "You have to come full circle."

"Shut up."

He smiled and began walking along the shoreline, his shoulders square, his hands clasped behind his back, as if he didn't have a care in the world. His voice carried as he sang. "I come to the garden alone, while the dew is still on the roses, and the voice I hear, falling on my ear…" A beautiful person inside and out. Though his song and easy stroll spoke of a man without worry, looks could be very deceiving. Blue had always been a master at hiding his true feelings.

She had not.

CHAPTER TWENTY-FIVE

Tell me I'm not crazy." Casey sat in the line at Moonbeam Espresso talking to her sister, Eleana, while she waited for her ordered drinks. Fortunately, she'd caught Eleana between classes at Western Washington University, where she impressed students and faculty alike as a philosophy professor. Casey figured her to be the perfect person to talk to before she headed back to Tula's. She wouldn't get stuck on details, like reality.

"Geez, Casey, I'm actually impressed."

"Oh, you mean because I'm putting the job I worked so fucking hard to get in jeopardy?"

"Yes. That's actually part of it."

Not what she expected to hear. She'd figured Eleana would tell her to get her head squared away and not risk her profession. The doctor, the professor, the detective—all glowing testaments to their parents' belief in their children. None of them had wanted to disappoint the parental unit by not succeeding, though in her case, they had hoped she'd reach a little higher like her brother and sister. Still, they'd supported Casey, and she did her best to make them proud. She risked delivering disappointment now, and strangely enough, it seemed Eleana supported her in that particular endeavor. Lots of surprises lately.

"Okay. I appreciate your support. I don't understand it. Mama and Papi will be furious if I fuck this up."

"I hate to break it to you, sister, but your focus has always been a bit too narrow. What you've missed in the big picture is that Mama and Papi will love and back you no matter what."

A nice sentiment, even if she'd point-blank accused Casey

of tunnel vision. She could live with that. But what had Eleana left unspoken? "What aren't you saying?"

"You know I love you."

"Of course." She'd never been in doubt when it came to her siblings. Close as children, they remained that way as adults.

"Then understand I say this in love. You have always been two steps outside. Mama, Papi, Abuelita, and even Stan have kept a foot inside the circle, while you turned away."

That statement actually hurt a little. "Because I'm a lesbian."

"Oh, hell, no. No one cares about who you love, as long as that person is good and kind and loves you back. Besides, we knew it long before you did, so don't even try to play that card."

All right, she'd been put in her place on that score. Where then was Eleana going with this? "You're talking your philosophical theories now. Remember—sister, not student."

"Call it what you will, *sister*, but all of us have understood that there is more to this world than what you can see and touch. It's part of what has helped us on our personal journeys. You've been fighting it since you were a kid."

Nope. She wasn't buying in to this argument. "Stan is a doctor, a man of science. Don't tell me he puts stock in the bruja stuff."

"He is absolutely a damn fine doctor and a proponent of science. He's also a spiritual man. They're not mutually exclusive."

"Yeah. He still goes to mass."

"Stop getting stuck on petty details. I'm not talking religion. I'm talking about a belief in the spiritual world. That, my beautiful, hard-headed sister, is where you have missed the boat, and it sounds to me that right now you're about ready to take a step onto it at long last. Open your heart. Open your spirit, and see where it leads you. You may be very surprised. In fact, I'd bank on it."

Her sister's words lingered in her mind long after she got the two lattes and made it back to Tula's. She pulled into the driveway and jammed the car into park. Lattes forgotten, she leapt out of the car and sprinted to the front porch.

"What the hell are you doing here?"

❖

Tula had never been so happy to see someone show up at her house. When Casey raced to her side, she felt even happier, less alone.

Dante, hands in his pockets and smiling like he had not a care in the world, looked right into Casey's eyes. "I'm here to talk to Tula. You have a problem with that?"

Tula wanted to say she saw light in his eyes. She couldn't. They were cold and dark. Creepy. So much rushed back to her. Twenty years in the past felt like yesterday. The reporters, the cameras, the push to get to her and win the lead story for the evening news. Dante embodied all the coldness of those vultures. He probably thought his good looks and the fact his sister was her neighbor got him a free pass to barge into her world. Wrong on all counts.

"Yes," Casey snapped. "I have a big fucking problem with that." Her hand drifted to the gun at her waist. The movement caught her attention. Dante's too.

"Right." He drew out the single word as his gaze lingered on the gun. Slowly he brought his eyes back up to meet Casey's. "I come over, a friendly neighbor, and you go all alpha cop on me. Not very neighborly if you ask me. But wait, this isn't your neighborhood, now is it?"

Tula would have to be deaf and blind to miss his insinuation, and she took immediate offense, even though the insult was directed at Casey. "Uncalled for, Dante, and more than a little racist."

He shrugged and shifted a so-what look back to her. "Just pointing out the obvious."

She took Casey's hand, the trembling not from fear. "Why don't you go back and hang out with your sister? Better yet, why don't you just leave Moses Lake and go home? There's no big story for you here."

"Well, see, here's the thing. I kind of disagree with you. A big story is brewing around here, and I will be the guy to report it. Multiple murders aren't nothing, even if you don't think they're a big deal. This is the kind of thing they call a career-maker, and I'd be a fool to ignore the opportunity dropped right at my feet. Besides, I smell another story right here, and until I uncover it, I'm not going anywhere."

A chill slid down Tula's spine. "You're trying to create something that doesn't exist."

"Again, I disagree. I didn't get to the big show without having some serious skills at sniffing out the good ones. You have a secret, Tula Crane, and trust me when I say I'll figure it out before I go anywhere."

Casey moved to stand in front of her. "You've been asked to leave, and I suggest you do that, Mr. Big Show. This is private property, and the owner has requested that you step away."

The anger that rolled off Casey matched the fury ratcheting up in her own body. Dante intended to cause trouble. Like everything around her the last few days wasn't trouble enough. That she'd had to share the truth with Casey, and then her grandmother, had stressed her out plenty. The thought of someone like Dante with major, nationwide media connections and a creepy, unsavory vibe finding out her true identity sent panic soaring through her.

"Leave," she said. "Now."

Dante smiled, waved his fingers, and backed down her steps. "We'll talk again real soon, ladies." He winked at Casey, and Tula's stomach rolled.

They stood side by side until Dante was out of sight. "I hate that guy."

Tula couldn't help it. She laughed. "Ditto."

"I brought lattes." She inclined her head toward the car.

"I could use one right about now. With a shot of bourbon."

"It's only ten."

"Make that two shots of bourbon. It's cocktail time in London."

❖

Rage mixed with heartache sent her feet flying across the passageway floor. Her fingers held the knife with such force she wondered if her bones would snap. Physical pain did not matter. What happened to her did not matter.

The lessons the priests and nuns taught came to her now. The words of Leviticus 24:19-21 delivered in the classroom and from the pulpit rang in her head: "And if a man cause a blemish in his neighbour; as he hath done, so shall it be done to him; Breach for breach, eye for eye, tooth for tooth: as he hath caused a blemish in a man, so shall it be done to him again. And he that killeth a beast, he shall restore it: and he that killeth a man, he shall be put to death."

She flung open the chamber door. "Devil!" Her voice bounced off the walls.

With the knife held high, she rushed in and used every ounce of strength she possessed to plunge the blade into his heart as he turned his face to her. He fell to the ground, his hands covered in blood as he clutched the buried dagger, and his blue eyes met hers, confusion and pain turning them cloudy.

She stumbled backward, caught the hem of her gown with her shoe, and tumbled to the floor. Covering her face with her bloodied hands, she screamed. "No!"

Angel's eyes snapped open, and sobs shook her shoulders. She could never outrun the memory, no matter how far or how long she tried. The passage of years never erased the look in his eyes as he'd dropped to the floor, a crimson pool forming around his body. The metallic scent of his blood filled her now, just as it had done back then. Every detail burned into her memory with a clarity impossible to erase.

Her fingers strayed to her neck. One sin deserved another. Or, so she'd rationalized at the time. In the heat of the moment, it had all made sense. It had been just.

She covered her eyes and tried to shut out the memories. She would not go back. No point. Blue took a different spin on it and tried to bring her to his way of thinking. He'd been a better soul than she was right from the beginning, and his stand hadn't changed. He remained a good man and would be for eternity. Her? She tried to do the best she could and to make small amends whenever the opportunity arose. She fell short more often than not, and she'd learned to live with that fact. Still, she welcomed any step toward the light.

Now, she pushed away from the past and moved to focus not on herself, for her fate had been written in the stars a long time ago, but on Tula. She deserved nothing beyond goodness. She'd been an innocent, and if Angel could help put any of what had happened to her as a child right, she would finally have made a meaningful step toward making amends. That's the best she could hope for.

She wiped away the last of her tears and stood tall. Too many useless tears lately. The wind whispered again. Evil was waking. Hopefully, with her help, Tula's gift would bring his face into the light. If that happened, it would all be worth it.

CHAPTER TWENTY-SIX

The day dragged. The company didn't. Casey originally thought that being off the case and out on leave would drive her batty. Surprisingly, it hadn't, at least not yet, although technically, she'd kept both feet in it by staying at Tula's. Being here with her felt right, and it wasn't because her abuelita told her as much. As had her sister and, she suspected, her brother, if she were to call him. A family gang-up that sounded a bit like it had been years in the making.

How had she missed it? Her family paranormal clique, that is. To her mind, she'd been tuned in to them all. At least it felt that way when they were together. They weren't one of those warring clans who spent gatherings arguing and fighting. Theirs were filled with laughter and songs, hugs and kisses. Mama loved to sing and could play the piano like nobody's business. The woman should have been a professional musician. Yet she'd been too busy raising her children to be successful and well-adjusted members of society. Her audience turned out to be the family that clamored for her music every time they were near a piano.

It hadn't even rattled Mama when they'd had the talk. Casey had dreaded it and shouldn't have. Mama had smiled, patted her hand, and told her how she'd known forever that her little girl was different from her other children. Maybe that should have been her first clue that she wasn't always tuned in to her family. Casey believed she'd been hiding this big, dark secret, and the whole family already knew. They were just waiting for her to share in her own time.

Kind of like sharing that they were all on Abuelita's sheet of music with the family skills of a bruja blanca. They all believed, or so Eleana claimed, each embraced their own piece of magic. Everyone believed it, except Casey.

Until now.

Casey sat on the sofa and watched as Tula continued to stare at the blank canvas. Outside the studio windows, the sun began to drop behind the mountains to the west. Darkness was falling fast. They'd made zero progress.

"I wish something, anything, would come to me." Tula's frustration sounded in her words.

She got up and went to stand next to her, putting an arm around her shoulders. Tula didn't twitch or move away. "My abuelita swears it will. We're powerful together, and we'll stay together until this is done."

Tula turned and stared into her eyes. "I believe her." This time hope sounded in her voice.

Casey couldn't believe the way she was feeling. A little giddy, like the first time she'd experienced a crush. Guilt made her drop her arm and take a half step back. Not the time or the place for feelings like this. She needed to remind herself that someone out there was stalking and killing women, including her own cousin. She had to focus on what they could do to stop him, because thus far her esteemed partner, the guy leading the investigation, hadn't accomplished jack.

"I do too." She might have moved away, but she couldn't look away.

Tula touched her cheek. "I bet you have no idea how beautiful you are. Promise me when this is all over, you'll let me paint you."

Tula's fingertips against her skin sent tingles throughout her. So much for avoiding a crush. This was full-on attraction to her, regardless of the situation they were in. "Anytime." Did she really just say that? She had never aspired to be a portrait model, or even thought of it for that matter. It wasn't like she hung out with artists like Tula. Or thought of herself as beautiful. She even hated having her picture taken.

"I'll hold you to that." The smile Tula gave her did it. Casey kissed her. No sweet peck either. A full-on, heart-pumping kiss.

And then, Tula went limp in her arms.

❖

Tula came to with a flutter of her eyes and a jolt to her system. She stood in front of her canvas…again. This time Casey stood next to her. With slow, exaggerated movements, she put the paintbrush down on the table and then raced to the bathroom. She made it in time.

Five minutes later she returned, mouth rinsed and teeth brushed. "How long?"

"A little less than an hour."

She studied the face that now filled the formerly blank canvas. "Damn."

"Yeah. You were like a madwoman with oils and a paintbrush."

"Maybe you should have filmed me." It might have been interesting to see herself work. Maybe also horrifying.

"Too fascinated to even think about doing that, and I was afraid to move for fear of jolting you out of your trance."

"Sorry about before." She recalled the warm, wonderful kiss. At least she'd had a second or two to relish it before she'd blacked out. Leave it to her to take a caring moment and turn it into something weird. She had skills, that was for sure.

Casey looked at her and shrugged. "Can't say it's the first time I kissed someone and they weren't thrilled. Can say it's the first time I kissed someone and she blacked out on me."

"Sorry about the blackout, and you're wrong about the kiss."

"Wrong?" She had her hands behind her back. The closeness from before wasn't in the air any longer. The room was a little cooler, and it wasn't because it had gotten dark outside.

She put a hand on Casey's arm. The electricity was still there. "It was thrilling and very much needed in that moment. I'll try to stay with you next time."

The light returned to Casey's eyes. *Thank goodness*. "All right then. I'll hold you to it."

"I think your grandmother hit it perfectly." Not a change in subject. More an explanation, or at least an explanation as to why she'd blacked out seconds after Casey's lips met hers.

Another demonstration of how in tune they were with each other. Understanding came into Casey's eyes. "We're more powerful together."

"Yes. Until now I didn't realize it took connection rather than a mere sharing of space. I mean, the whole hummingbird-feather thing did sort of point it out. In my head, that was different. Apparently, it wasn't."

Casey nodded. "If I were a betting woman, I'd lay odds she knew that too and left us alone together to figure it out ourselves. She's sneaky like that. Why tell when something can be learned by experience?"

"I like her."

"She has that effect on people."

"She's powerful." Tula stared at the painting, convinced that their connection had kick-started the process and that maybe, just maybe, they'd be in time to help this victim.

"More than I ever realized. Now we have to figure out the identity of the woman you saw in your vision. This has to be her, don't you think?"

She shook her head. "No. It's not her."

"I don't understand."

Tula wasn't sure how to explain. The vision from before didn't figure into this face, and this most recent blackout had morphed into something different as well. Like all the rules changed after the joining of forces facilitated by that little bundle of hummingbird feathers. "Before, I've always come to with no memory of what made me paint the face."

"I'm not following. What are you trying to tell me?"

"This time, it's more like the vision I had after your grandmother was here. I could see him, I could see the woman, and I painted what I saw."

"Does it really matter if it was different? We have the woman's image, and we can track down who she is. That is what's important."

"It is, except..."

"Except what?" Frustration came through clearly in Casey's voice.

Tula thought back to what she'd observed during this latest round of fugue state, and her heart beat hard. Fear could do that to a person. "Here's where it gets freaky. We don't need to focus to figure out the identity of the woman."

Casey tilted her head and studied her. "Okay. You're losing me, and we don't have time to play the thousand-question game. We have to find this woman and get to her before the killer does. I, for one, don't want to trust Mike with this situation. He'd focus on you and come after you like a freight train while totally missing the importance of following up on her identity. We're on our own here. Let's get moving."

"That's not it. I agree about saving her and about your partner coming after me first. He doesn't leave me feeling warm and fuzzy. While he might be a good cop, he has blinders on. If everything you read is correct, my paintings were instrumental in stopping killers before."

"You nailed him, but let's not get sidetracked. What's holding you back? Why don't you want to track this woman down right now?"

"Because I know who the killer is."

❖

"He's got her."

Angel felt it too. "I know."

"Do you think the topaz will help her?"

"It has to." Angel was out of ideas. Out of magic. Not that she had any real magic. Working at redemption didn't quite qualify on that front. "I only wish I could have seen his face. He somehow knew we were watching."

"Sometimes a devil takes an unfair advantage."

"I grow weary of the unfairness." Angel wasn't exaggerating. Too many years of witnessing the uneven scales wore on her soul. She'd always been more of a balanced-scale kind of woman, even if she had to be the one to balance it. Or attempt to, in any event.

Blue gazed at the moon as it started to cast light into the night sky, cool and clear. The stars sparkled, a beautiful canopy on a night teeming with evil. "Are we still talking about Tula?"

Her head snapped up. "Yes. Of course, I'm talking about Tula." Lately, Blue had a one-track mind, and it didn't have anything to do with stopping this killer. If he really wanted to help her like he continually reiterated, he needed to focus on that problem and nothing else.

"Really?"

"Blue, honest to God, I'm not going there. Not now. Not tomorrow. Not ever." He had to let it go.

"Famous last words."

"You are such a pain in the ass."

"At least I'm something."

Tears welled in her eyes as her irritation fled. "You were always something, and that, my love, has been the problem all along."

CHAPTER TWENTY-SEVEN

Say that again." With one sentence, Tula had managed to throw a bucket of cold water all over the warm attraction building inside Casey. How long had she known? Her fingers curled, and she silently told herself to relax. Tension wasn't helpful.

"I know who the killer is." Tula held her gaze. If she felt guilty about withholding that tidbit of information, it didn't show.

"You saw his face? When? Why didn't you tell me? I thought you said you didn't see him." It all came out in a rush.

Tula waited for her finish. "I didn't see him before. The one and only time I glimpsed his face was during this latest frenzy." She pointed to the freshly painted canvas. "And even during this, I didn't see him full-on."

"Then how can you be sure of who you saw?"

"It was enough to figure it out. Some faces stick with you."

"Wait. You didn't get a chance to look into his face?" She'd been around enough witnesses to understand that firsthand identification was flawed at best. People simply did not pay attention to detail as much as they believed they did. As a painter, Tula might possess better-than-average skills. Even so, did she want to bank on that possibility in a critical situation like this?

"I got a good look at his profile."

Casey shook her head. "Tula, that would never hold up in court, and we sure as heck would never get an arrest warrant on an identification through a profile." Her initial hopes sank. They were back to tracking down a potential victim, and the clock was ticking too damn loud for comfort.

"Hold up. Under normal circumstances, I'd be right there with you."

Something about the tone of her voice brought back a little of the hope. She studied her face and liked what she saw. "Tell me."

"It's Dante."

"Say what? The jerk who strutted around here like he owned the place? Owned you?"

She nodded. "It was him."

"Are you one hundred percent certain?"

"A hundred and ten percent. Let's just say his face stuck with me, and not in a good way. I tend to remember people who make that kind of impression."

That made perfect sense. Casey did the same thing. Some people did not blend into the woodwork. That peacock definitely didn't blend. "Right there with you. I wish I could have seen it."

"You can. Give me half an hour." Tula headed toward the studio closet.

"You're going to paint him." She didn't know if they had the leeway for her to produce another painting.

This time she shook her head. "Nope. I'll draw him. When I'm not under, I can't paint like a savant, which means it would take way too long to produce something. I can, however, draw almost as well as I can paint, and a whole lot faster."

"Get to it then, and I'll try to figure out where we go from here."

She believed Tula, so she pushed the witness-unreliability issue to the background. Not her typical take on people, particularly people she'd just met. The standard rules didn't apply here. First, because her abuelita vouched for Tula, and if she said good soul, then good soul she was. Second, because her own intuition, which she still maintained didn't spring from bruja blanca genes, told her they were heading in the right direction. Tula could do something that defied explanation, and she believed in it enough to act.

That she'd seen and recognized Dante's profile while in one of her states also rang true. Tula's drawing would give her a chance to concur. While she'd seen this Dante for only a few minutes total, she'd developed an instant dislike, and she possessed an uncanny skill at remembering the folks who left a negative impression. Hazard of the job.

The problem wouldn't be to confirm what Tula saw. It came down to what to do about it. Mike would laugh her right off the force. Of course, that would be after he made damn sure the powers-that-be knew she'd been working on the case after being told to stand down. In that respect, he'd be technically correct. Rogue wasn't a good thing, even on occasions when it yielded superior results. He liked to work by the book when it benefitted him, and this would be one of those instances. If he could solve the case and get her demoted, resulting in an opportunity to gain a new, male partner, he'd be a happy man.

She had to go rogue this time, but how to keep it legal and prosecutable? Whatever they did, it had to hold up in court. She might be going off script, but she refused to step outside the law. If she did, she'd need to find another profession.

❖

Tula's hands shook as the drawing came to life. The profile stayed clear in her mind, as though she remained on the grass watching the man walk along the rise with the body of a woman slung over his shoulder. Moonlight hit the side of his face, and it elicited the same reaction now as the moment she'd seen it in her vision. Chills raced down her arms, and her heart picked up its rhythm. In the vision, she'd wanted to chase him and pull the woman away to safety. Like before, she'd been powerless to move closer, able only to watch. At least she'd gotten a look at him and a clear view of the woman's face. Not the same woman as in the other vision, for in that one, her hair had been light and long. This woman had short, dark hair, just as she'd painted.

The drawing done, she dropped the pencil and stood back. If she'd harbored any doubts about whom she'd glimpsed, they evaporated. As they did, she raced to the bathroom. After she emptied her stomach, she rinsed her face with cool water. Before when this had happened to her, it involved strangers. She'd been a mere conduit to convey important information. That and she'd been a child without the awareness of what it all really meant. That ship had sailed a long time ago, and now she understood the horror of it all.

And the man had been in her house, according to Casey's grandmother, more than once. Why? What game was this monster playing? She supposed her first reaction should be disbelief, and that it wasn't said a great deal. Maybe the same force that had her painting these faces also gave her confidence in her intuition. It hurtled her closer and closer to a truth that seemed just beyond her reach. It all raced toward her, and a collision neared.

Air, she needed air. The studio had grown stuffy. Or frightening. She couldn't quite distinguish the difference. Casey had left shortly after she'd started drawing, and if she'd said anything to Tula, she hadn't heard it. No idea where she'd gone or when she'd be back. Whenever she worked, she became so immersed, a tornado could blow through, and she'd be oblivious. Probably developed the skill to protect herself from her incessantly hovering, threatening mother.

Not that she blamed Casey for taking off. Tula didn't harbor any illusions about herself. Given her upbringing and then her seclusion as an adult, she wasn't exactly mainstream. In short, she'd describe herself as a bit of a weirdo. She couldn't fault Casey for needing some time away from her. That, and someone with her skill set had to find it difficult to work through the whole sort of psychic thing Tula did. No doubt, as a police officer, she'd had fair exposure to those claiming to be psychics who weren't, and that pretense had to get really old. She was, frankly, a little surprised that Casey continued to roll with it as well as she'd been doing and hadn't arrested her yet.

Outside, she tipped her head to the sky and breathed in the fresh air. The sound of ducks on the water made her smile. She'd purchased this house mainly because of them. The moment she'd walked out the door and heard them, she'd been entranced. At the time, she'd taken their presence as a sign she needed to be here. Tonight, moonlight shining on the water, they looked as though they were enjoying an evening aquatic party. How could one not want to live around such innocence and beauty?

The ducks had turned out to be a good sign too, until a few nights ago. Proved the old adage that a person couldn't run away from their problems. She'd effectively eluded her parents, but not herself. The baggage had come right here with her, waiting unpacked for almost two decades.

"Hey, neighbor."

The ice slid down her back again. "Diane." She didn't need to look over to see that Diane wasn't alone. Time for a break from the dynamic duo. A jail cell for at least one of them would do the trick.

"It's cocktail hour. Come on over here, and we'll make the evening a bit more relaxed. Dante makes a mean dirty martini."

She raised her head, and the ice grew colder when she met Dante's gaze. How had she not seen it before? Blinded by the annoyance that Diane always stirred up, she supposed. Darkness wrapped around his handsome face as though he always stood in the shadows. If she'd painted him, her artist's eye would have caught it immediately.

"I'm working tonight." Not a lie.

"You and your little friend?" The sneer in his words carried easily on the air.

Her jaw tightened. She kept her words light. "Yes, Detective Wilson and I are working this evening."

"Going into law enforcement now, are you? And here Diane's been raving about your artistic skills. The best graphics artist in the Pacific Northwest." Dante's stance was relaxed, his hands in his pockets.

"I'm assisting the detective with some artwork." She stared into his eyes that, even at this distance, were flat and black. Soulless.

He smiled. Not warm. Not friendly. Ugly on a face that cameras loved. "Come on, dear sister. The ladies are too busy for us mere mortals."

"Another time." What in the world had possessed her to say that? Another time would never arrive. All the years of performing as the perfect little artist for her parents made such a lie an impossible habit to shake, even when she suspected she stood twenty yards away from a killer. An even worse description whispered through her mind: serial killer.

"I'll pencil you in." Dante laughed as he turned and headed back into Diane's house. Even his stride oozed arrogance.

Diane's eyes narrowed as she studied Tula. "Kind of rude of you to always turn me down."

Dear Jesus, let it go. "I'm a busy woman."

"Not that busy. You forget how long I've lived next door."

"Give it a rest, Diane. I'm not in the mood, and I'm not obliged to take anyone up on visiting, even if they're my next-door neighbor." She guessed it took the right shove for the defiant edge in her to finally claw its way out. She liked it. Very empowering.

"And here I thought you'd be good for my brother. Called that one wrong, didn't I?" She turned and stomped away. Her words carried as she walked. "Some people are just born rude. I'm done with that bitch."

Thank God.

❖

Fury had driven her as she'd run down the corridor, the knife heavy in her hand. Worry that she would be too weak to use it never entered her mind. She'd been practicing with it for months. From the first time she'd seen the bruises marring her sister's perfect skin, she'd done what her sister could not. She had prepared.

It hadn't been fair. None of it. Life should not have to be unbearable for women like them, and yet it happened over and over. Why couldn't love come to them? The kind she read about in books—real and tender and forever. She had waited, hoping over and over to witness it and instead saw far too much of the violence and hatred. The fear.

For her, love would have been unlikely. She had made her own kind of peace with that fate. To be less than a full partner did not work for her, and she doubted any man existed who could or would be her equal, except for one, and she had held out a sliver of hope that one day he would take a stand on her behalf, love her as a woman and not a possession.

It had been different for her sister. Always the good and obedient daughter, she had done as she'd been told. She still did as she was told, only with a different master, and that was why she sprawled lifeless on her bedchamber floor.

Her father's fury varied from hers, and though she had been the one to bring him into it, she had also known they had different ideas of justice. He would have punished her sister's husband in a quiet way, one that hurt his pocket while it saved him face. Appearances were everything, even after something so heinous.

She had been preparing for the day when she would be required to hand out her brand of justice. That night all her work had been put to the test. No longer could she stay silent. No longer could she allow one she loved to be harmed. If no one else would stand openly for her sister, she would. Society's rules be damned.

He had stood with his back to her when she charged into the room. Tall with thick hair and broad shoulders, he could have easily overpowered her. Stealth and surprise were two of the weapons she had relied upon—and the blade in her hand. It all came down to a single moment, and all her work prepared her for it.

Her lifelong friendships with everyone, including those not welcome in the circles of her family, helped her understand exactly where to strike. Two of those friends had been happy to give her lessons on life and death, for they had both seen it firsthand. Pulled from their humble homes to serve, they had stood on the battlefields together. Their stories guided her, and righteous fury propelled her forward to stop a devil once and for all. God would be on her side—of that she harbored not a single doubt.

When he had heard her footsteps, he started to turn. He'd been too late. By the time his eyes met hers, and recognition hit, the blade was already buried in his flesh and the organ that sustained his life damaged beyond repair. She'd screamed as she stumbled back. Blue eyes had been filled with question as they locked onto hers.

She had killed the wrong man.

Angel's eyes snapped open, and tears slid down her cheeks. No matter how many times the scene played in her mind, the pain never diminished. Some errors could not be righted regardless of how hard and how long someone tried. Hers was one of those. She'd failed everyone, and that failure had colored her world forever.

Blue told her over and over to forgive herself. On that score, she felt him to be quite wrong. No one could forgive something that evil. She'd believed herself to be a good, kind person, and in that instant, her true self was revealed to herself and to those she cared about. Since then, she'd been on a mission to redeem that single horrid act. With Tula, she believed she'd made a difference, at least initially. She'd guided her away from the monsters who'd given her life and who'd also taken it from her. She'd kept an eye on her all these years, hoping to channel evil away from her kind soul.

Tula was everything she'd wished to be in life and everything she'd fallen short of. If she could save her once and for all, then she could finally rest. She had to believe in the possibility and that it would happen sooner rather than later. Weariness bore down on her heavier than ever. It was time for her journey to be over—one way or the other.

CHAPTER TWENTY-EIGHT

Casey looked up. "Shit." With her laser focus on the computer, she'd failed to realize how much time had passed. She got up from the unassigned workstation located in a far corner and set up for a potential new hire. Perfect place to do a little unauthorized searching because it was on the opposite side of the station from her own desk and, by extension, Mike's. He didn't need to know she was here, and given she was officially on leave, better to keep low. It worked too. Only a couple people even noticed her, and she'd given them a BS reason for being here. Never realized that she had a talent for lying. She'd have to make time to go to confession.

Time to wrap it up and get out of here before anyone did stop to question her presence. As it was, soon enough IT would see her login, and she'd have to explain it. For now, she'd run with what she'd found and deal with the fallout later.

She'd meant to spend only an hour or so looking up the talented and successful Dante Macy, and instead, hours had zipped past. No doubt Tula wondered what in the world happened to her. Probably considered her a flake.

She grabbed the pile of papers off a printer as she simultaneously punched Tula's number into her cell. "I'm so sorry," she said as soon as Tula picked up. "I got caught up in the hunt and lost track of time."

"Don't worry about it. It's that kind of day."

"I've got stuff to show you."

"I have things to share as well."

She stopped. Something in Tula's voice put her on alert. "What's happened?" If that asshole threatened Tula, she'd take him out. She moved even faster. It had not been a good idea to leave Tula alone. What in the hell had she been thinking?

"Nothing in particular happened."

"I don't believe you. I can hear it in your voice."

"Trust me. It's more about observations and intuition than action. Just come on back, and we'll talk."

She loosened her grip on the phone. "Okay, sorry. This situation has me on high alert."

"Right there with you."

"I'm leaving in five but have to make a quick trip home to check on my cat and feed the livestock." She hated to leave Tula alone even a minute more than necessary. She also owed it to Diego to swing home for at least a few. Not that he'd care one way or the other, but she'd feel better. It didn't hurt to feed the cattle herself too. She didn't want to impose on family and friends too much when it came to the herd. Besides, weird as it sounded, she enjoyed taking care of them. A cop and her cows. Had to be a sitcom in there somewhere.

"No worries. I'll see you when you get here."

Casey ended the call and stuffed her phone into her pocket. Before she left, she had to figure out the best way to loop Mike in without letting him realize it came from her or that she'd been using department resources for hours. It hit her in a flash. Smiling, she reached for a highlighter. From the stack of papers she'd grabbed off the printer, she pulled out two sheets and began to highlight text. When she finished, she made her way to Mike's desk and dropped them there. He'd notice as soon as he sat down. Knowing him, he'd read the highlighted text first and then start rolling. He wouldn't question where the information came from because he'd be intrigued and in a hurry to take credit for anything he found because of it. Enough for her. It had to be.

She made good on her promise to leave in five. Once back at her house, she gave Diego a big hug, which made him stiffen, and then filled his food and water. Litterbox cleaned and put back, she looked around, satisfied that he'd be fine even if she had to be gone for a couple of days. She jogged on her way out to the barn. She'd called the neighbor earlier, and he'd undoubtedly already been by to take care of the livestock. She wasn't wrong. Everything in the barn was in order.

By the time she was ready to head back to the car, Diego was lounging on his cat tree staring out the window. No trauma there. "I love you too," she said before leaving. He didn't look at her. She smiled as she closed and locked the door.

The drive over to Tula's house didn't take long. One thing about Moses Lake, rush hour traffic wasn't exactly daunting. Driving around

Seattle this time of day made her want to scream, and every time she had to do it, she wondered why anyone in their right mind would want to live there. Here, mildly annoying at best. She was happy with mildly annoying.

With the car in park, she let her gaze stray to the house next door. Lights glowed through the open blinds, providing a clear view of the inner room beyond. In her line of business, she never understood why people opened their homes to prying eyes. Never a good idea. Of course, as soon as she met the woman who owned the house, she'd known something about that family wasn't right, and her research backed up that observation.

While Dante had been the focus of her interest, she'd pulled everything she could find on both brother and sister. An interesting history emerged. Dante's brought up red flags on more than one front, despite his documented professional success. A few accusations of misconduct, all dismissed. A charge of assault, charges dropped. An ex-girlfriend with a restraining order. A misunderstanding, according to Dante's written statement. One had to dig deep to find any of it, and without the kind of resources she had at her disposal, impossible to find. Someone behind the scenes had gone to a great deal of effort to candy-coat the image of the handsome rising media star.

Diane wasn't absent her own red flags. Not quite as glaring as Dante's. Enough to give Casey pause. Like a stay at Eastern State Hospital when she was eighteen. It would take jumping through more hoops to get the details on that one, but given what Casey had seen so far, not much would surprise her about Diane or her brother. Something was definitely fucked up about this family, and she didn't like it. They were way too close to Tula and way too interested. She hoped they didn't have any insider information on Tula's true identity, although it made sense that they might have, given how invested they seemed to be in her.

Time to bring Tula into the loop on her neighbor. She also wanted to study the picture she'd drawn of the killer to see if that profile screamed Dante at her too. She leaned over and picked up the container of enchiladas sitting on the passenger seat. Her abuelita wouldn't tolerate anyone working on an empty stomach or, worse, working with a stomach filled with crappy food. She'd called and insisted that Casey swing by and pick up the container of homemade goodies. Her entire car smelled of the wonderful chicken enchiladas that never failed to win the day. Nobody cooked like her abuelita.

Her cell rang. Probably Tula, who hadn't looked out the window to see her sitting in the driveway and was wondering when she'd be back. She groaned at the display. Not Tula. "Isla, what in the hell do you want?"

"Why would you send cops to my house?" Her whine was as irritating as a screeching bird. The gorgeous woman's beauty was entirely superficial. All on the outside, not a drop on the inside.

"Why would you destroy my property?"

"You weren't calling me back."

Seriously? She stated her reason as if everyone would react that way. "Let me be clear, again. I'm never going to call you back. I'm never going to call you, period."

"You don't mean that because you can't deny we're soul mates."

"We're nothing. Leave me alone, or next time you'll see a restraining order. Don't call me again. Don't come to my house again, or I promise, and hear me well, Isla, you'll see the inside of a courtroom."

"But darling…"

She ended the call and made a mental note to block her number. She didn't need this kind of irritation right now. Oh hell, she didn't need it any time, not just now. At least here at Tula's she'd be safe from the possibility of Isla showing up. Small blessings and all that. She grabbed the food and got out of the car.

"Hey, you're back."

Dante's voice, tinged with a cockiness that put her nerves on edge, made her hand tighten on the pan of enchiladas. Dealing with Isla set her nerves on edge. Dante added insult to injury. "You're still here. Isn't Hollywood calling?"

"All in good time. First things first. You know how it is—things to do, people to see." He put an emphasis on *people*.

"Tell me, Dante. Exactly what things? What people?"

The sneer she'd come to associate with him shone through his words. "That an official question?"

She kept her own voice even. Not going to play into his bait. "Oh, no, not official. You'll know when it is. Let's just call it neighborly interest."

"Of course, and as we've already established, this isn't actually your neighborhood. That said, unofficially, I'm just hanging out with my sister for a bit. You know, unused leave time I have to eat up, along with a juicy story screaming for a journalist like me. You have a good night now, and say hello to Tula." If his words dripped any more sugar, she'd throw up.

Before she could respond, he turned and disappeared into the house. Her stomach rolled.

❖

Tula watched the exchange through the window and resisted the urge to open the door to scream at Dante. She'd had enough of that ass. His toxic presence was tainting her world, and she hated him for it. She hated him more for what he was doing to innocent people without anyone being able to stop him. She planned to change that.

Outside her window, Casey held her calm as she faced off with Dante. A true professional. She liked that about her—liked a lot about her. Enough that she'd be sad, in a way, when this was all over. Glad that a killer was stopped and would be unable to harm anyone else. Sad that Casey would go back to her life, and Tula, well, she'd more than likely move on, become someone else in another town far away from Moses Lake.

Suddenly a text message came in that made her breath catch. Three numbers: 9-1-1. Any other time, she'd swap out the sim card before making a call that the text message signaled. It didn't matter anymore. The jig was up. Hiding here wasn't an option any longer.

"Matthew, what's wrong?"

He sounded sad. "They've found you."

He didn't have to tell her who. "How?" She'd really hoped to have a little more time before being forced to deal with her parents.

"My mother called me and said they'd been contacted by someone on the NYPD after inquiries came from a detective in Moses Lake."

"Damn."

"What's going on out there?"

"Another killer."

"Oh, sweetheart. I'm so sorry."

Tears welled in her eyes. How she missed him. "It's okay, Matty. I have a friend."

"I'm glad. Is he keeping you safe?"

"Yes, she is."

"Oh, it's like that, is it?"

"No, not like that."

"But you're hoping."

"A girl can dream."

"I hope it works out for you. I really do, and she'd be a lucky woman to get you. But, seriously, are you safe? Shall I make you an exit strategy? I can get you out of there in twenty-four hours. Your parents haven't quite figured out where Moses Lake is, so I'm thinking you have a few days before they show up."

Tempting. And not. She looked out at Casey, who stared after the retreating Dante. No, not ready to throw in the towel quite yet for more reasons than one.

"I have to finish this."

"It's not your fight, and I don't care about the fucked-up visions that get sent to you. You don't owe anyone. Your life matters more than strangers'."

"I know I don't owe a debt. I also can't walk away if I can help. It wouldn't be right."

"You really believe you can help?"

"I know I can."

She could almost see him drop his head and run his hand through his thick, curly hair. "All right then. You do what you need to, and when you're ready, you know where I am."

"I love you."

"I love you more."

She put the phone back in her pocket and watched as Casey walked onto the porch and stepped into the house.

❖

"Damn, damn, damn." Angel pressed her hand against her mouth.

Blue looked out over the lake. Moonlight shone on the surface that tonight appeared smooth and glass-like. She loved peaceful, quiet nights like this, especially when he shared them with her. Except this one didn't feel like any other. Not peaceful or quiet below the surface. Quite the opposite.

"He's getting ready." Blue had his hands clasped behind his back.

"He is." She could feel it too.

"What are you going to do?"

She looked toward Tula's house, where lights once again shone from the studio windows. "I don't know that I can do anything else. I gave Tula back the sight. She's been brought together with others who can join with her, and I left her the topaz. I have no more rabbits in the hat."

"I disagree. You always know what to do. You protect those who can't protect themselves, and that's a rabbit you've been pulling out of your hat as long as I've known you."

She stared into his eyes. "Oh, I always have a plan. Except you and I both know that my best-laid plans can go sideways in a second, and the consequences are massive."

"One fail does not a legacy make."

If not a legacy, then what in world had it all been about? "It does in my book."

"Your book is not a best seller."

"Even after all this time, I don't understand you. You were there. You know exactly how wrong I can be, yet you try to bolster my confidence every chance you get. Why? Tell me once and for all why."

For a long moment, he stared at her. She tried to hold his gaze and wasn't able to. She looked away. "You're not ready."

She turned back to him. "Oh, for God's sake, if I'm not ready by now, when in the world will I be?"

He smiled, and his blue eyes seemed even more full of light. He'd been that way the first time she'd seen him—tall, handsome, and filled with life. A breath of fresh air when a storm swirled. Everyone loved him, men and women alike. He'd been true even back then. "Soon, my beautiful little Angel. Very soon."

"Crappy answer, and you know it." She refused to let him off the hook. He'd started the conversation, and he'd been on it hard for days now. He didn't get to pick and choose when to dole out bits of information.

"It's the right answer."

"Do you ever get tired of being cryptic or self-righteous?" Apparently, he did get to pick and choose.

"I do not."

That statement made her laugh because it was so him. Easy to see, even now, why everyone loved him so. "I want to hate you. I really do."

"No, you don't."

She sobered and shook her head slightly. "No, I don't."

"You love me."

"Always have."

"Always will."

"Yes. I always will."

"And I, you. Now, let's concentrate on Tula. We can heal ourselves after she's safe."

"Deal."

CHAPTER TWENTY-NINE

"Okay," Casey said as Tula handed her a glass of iced tea to go along with the fantastic dinner. "I didn't mean to take off on you earlier, especially without giving you much of an explanation."

"I did wonder where you'd gone. Sorry about not listening when you told me you were leaving. I get caught up in my work."

Casey grimaced. "On me as well. I can do the same thing. I get stuck in my own head and sort of block out everyone around me. Ask Mike. Pisses him off to no end when I get on a roll and ignore everything and everybody. He hates it when people don't drop everything to be schooled by him. You know, given he's so much more experienced than anyone else." She took a bite and almost sighed. She'd needed some good food.

Tula shook her head as she laid her fork on the empty plate. "If it's all the same with you, I'll take your word for it and skip the ask-Mike part. Don't get comforting vibes from that guy."

"He's a pain in the ass, but in all honesty, he's not a bad guy at heart. More a product of his generation than anything else."

"I'll take your word for it and call it good."

Casey laughed. "Probably not a bad plan. He can ruffle feathers without much real effort. Anyway, here's the thing. Your neighbors got under my skin, especially when you said you saw Dante in your vision."

"You believed me." Tula looked surprised.

"Of course." Casey didn't need to share that she'd been skeptical at first. Her bad.

"You say of course, but come on. You looked at me like I'd escaped from a mental ward when you first came here."

Tula wasn't wrong. That thread of thinking had been in her mind. Any rational person would have had the same impression. Time and events, and her abuelita, had shaken things up for Casey, and everything looked a little different now. A bigger world than she'd ever imagined, with a lot more possibilities.

She decided that she should 'fess up. "You're right. I did, and I apologize for that or making you feel bad. For the record, I don't think you're crazy, and you're sure not Eastern State Hospital material."

"I'm not crazy." Tula's eyes were watery.

Damn, she hadn't intended to hurt her. "You're so not. I can't really explain what you are, and frankly, I don't care. This thing you can do is amazing and important and really, really special." She should add that Tula was special as well though left that part unsaid. For now. "I want to use your gift, not pretend it doesn't exist. I want to help you help others. That's all that's important."

A single tear slid down her cheek. "Thank you."

Casey shook her head. "You don't understand."

"I understand that someone finally appreciates me, for me."

"I'm sure the NYPD appreciated you." Cops were pretty pragmatic for the most part. They also could keep an open mind when they needed to. She suspected that while they hadn't understood the young recluse who painted the faces of victims, they had been willing to set aside their preconceived notions in order to stop a killer and save lives. If that meant tapping into the magic of a minor, that's what they did.

Again Tula shrugged. "For the most part, I wouldn't know. I was kept in my prison and told to paint. My parents didn't really give a good goddamn about saving lives. They cared about the publicity. They cared about how the value of my art skyrocketed after they leveraged the psychic child artist."

Casey didn't stop to think. She moved to Tula and wrapped her arms around her. "I care. I care about you, and I care about saving lives. You are a beautiful woman, inside and out, and I'm so very sorry for what they did to you."

She half expected Tula to pull away. Didn't happen. Instead, Tula laid her head on Casey's shoulder and wrapped her arms around her neck. In the middle of something crazy, something wonderful was happening.

"Thank you."

Casey kissed the top of her head. "No thanks necessary. I know talent when I see it, and when my abuelita tells me to stick close, well, who am I to argue?"

"I like your grandmother."

Now Casey laughed. "She's a pushy old bat, but she's the best."

❖

Tula could feel power building in her body the moment Casey wrapped her in a warm embrace. Valentina hadn't been wrong about anything, especially not the magic they pulled in from the universe when they were together. The first time she stepped into the same space as Casey, she'd felt the shift in power, and it upped the ante. After Valentina entered the house, it skyrocketed. Something about these two women spoke to her spirit in a way she never could have imagined. In all the time she'd lived safely by keeping her world tight and small, it never occurred to her that she might find herself in the company of kindred spirits.

Now, with Casey so close, calm flowed through her. A brand-new feeling for her, and she wanted to stay here forever. Or at least for a few more minutes. She'd take whatever she could get.

"What is it?" Casey said against her hair. "What's wrong?"

So much for masking her emotions. Casey picked up on them in a second, which shouldn't come as a big surprise considering that part of her job entailed sensing the emotional vibes others put off. She could explain about the call from Matthew, although she wasn't as upset by it as she would have been a week ago. She'd essentially put it out of her mind once she'd ended the conversation. She'd deal with her parents when they showed, and no doubt there'd be a when.

No, her emotions were more immediate and more personal, even if little that merited concern. "Nothing really."

Casey held her out at arm's length, her eyes narrowing as she studied her face. She wasn't buying in. "It's okay. Tell me what the 'nothing really' is about. I can help."

She gave her a small smile. "You already have." Casey could have no idea how much. She'd changed her world, and that wasn't an understatement.

"Serve and protect is the name of my game. Now, just tell me. At this point, we don't have secrets."

Tula smiled, her gaze lingering on Casey's face. In it she saw strength mixed with kindness, a perfect combination for someone in her line of work and lethal when it came to resisting temptation. No matter what came after, she'd remember this time with Casey as something very special.

"You're going to think I'm pretty shallow."

"Not gonna happen."

Tula believed her and, more than that, realized she really did trust her. "I was thinking how safe I felt around you and your grandmother, and how I'd never had that type of security before."

"I'm glad you feel that way, and I hope you realize you can trust us. I know I came on strong at first, but can you blame me with the way you tried to sneak in the picture?" Her smile softened the words.

"No blame at all, and that's not what I mean."

"Explain it to me then."

"I'll try. You have to understand that I didn't grow up like most people. My skills as an artist came to light when I was really young, and my parents jumped on it like flies on rotting meat. I became less their child and more their money-generating prisoner. They weren't real good at the parenting thing before. They were worse after."

"You were abused." Casey's expression darkened.

This is why she never talked about it. She didn't want to be seen as a victim. "Yes."

"I wish someone had been there to help you."

"I do too, but they weren't, and I'm not dwelling on it. I was trying to get at how safe you make me feel. It's a new thing for me and one I'm very grateful for." Hard to convey what was in her heart without it sounding like a poor-me rant.

"Not fair."

Tula touched her shoulder. "I'm walking proof that life isn't fair. Never has been and never will be. Here's the thing. You make the best you can with the hand you're dealt. I've made my peace with that fact."

"You shouldn't have to."

"No, I shouldn't, yet that's my reality. I want you to know how much I appreciate what you and your grandmother have brought into my life. Yes, we just met, yet it's like we've known each other for a lifetime. In spite of everything happening, it's a breath of fresh air."

"Feels like that to me too. As though we've known each other forever."

Tula touched Casey's cheek. "Thank you. And now, let's stop this son of a bitch. Tell me what you found."

❖

"The air has changed." Angel tilted her head to the sky.

"You need to warn her."

"The cop is back." She'd noticed when Casey parked her car in Tula's driveway about an hour ago. She liked that she'd shown up because she didn't like Tula staying in the house alone. Darkness wrapped around her like the fog rolling in off the ocean. Thick, dark, and dangerous. "I can't stop by when she's there." Stating the obvious.

Blue pressed his lips together. "Let's give this some thought. How can we speed things up and bring him down?"

"I've been doing nothing except giving it thought. She's on the right track, the topaz is bumping up the power, and with the help from Casey, they're making ground."

Shaking his head, Blue paced, his hands behind his back. He'd always been a thinker, which had come in useful as they made their journey together. "Not enough ground and not quick enough. We know he's going to hurt someone again. We can't let him. He's taken too much from this community already."

"You're not going to get an argument from me. I'm thinking through every angle and option, trying to come up with something more to help. So far, I've got nothing except watching and waiting."

"You're sure you can't talk with Tula? Shoot her more of the visions?"

Angel shook her head. She didn't want to make either move. "Trying to go talk with her would put Tula in an uncomfortable situation. That's not fair to her."

Blue stopped pacing. "You're right. She wouldn't be able to explain a one-sided conversation to her cop friend."

"No, she wouldn't."

"Push a vision?"

"I have no more to give her. She's seen all there is to see, and somehow she's got to put it all together."

"Frustrating."

Angel dropped to the grass, put her head on her knees, and closed her eyes. She had to think. Surely, she could come up with another way to help Tula. "Maybe I can get her outside and at least share power with her for a few minutes. That might give her enough to push through."

When Blue didn't add anything, she brought her head up. A chill touched her skin. Gone again. She sighed and stood. Not his fault. This task fell to her, and while she appreciated being able to bounce thoughts off him, she had to do this alone. It had always been hers to accomplish, not his.

She walked along the shoreline and remembered home. A lake sat on the edge of the grounds there too. As a child she'd waded in the water, fished with her brother, and enjoyed rowing the small wooden boat with her sister. All good memories before everything went wrong.

At the lake's edge, she kneeled and reached out. She wanted to feel the cool water flow through her fingers, to splash it against her face and to allow it to refresh her body and soul. She pulled her hand back and stood. No sense even trying. It wouldn't work.

The moon rose as she walked toward Tula's. Somehow, some way, she'd bring her the power needed to stop the monster.

CHAPTER THIRTY

That creep has a history." Casey jumped right into the deep end of the pool.

Tula handed her a cup of coffee. "You want a shot in that?" She nodded toward a bottle of brandy on the counter. "I'm thinking tonight might call for a kick of something more than caffeine."

Casey shook her head. "Not that it doesn't sound great, but I don't want to risk anything clouding my head." Ultimately, she'd be forced to explain her actions with Tula when she'd been directed to remove herself from the investigation. When that moment arrived, the less she needed to explain, the better it would be.

"That bad?"

"Feels that way."

Tula nodded and sat in a kitchen chair. "Fill me in."

She took a sip and let it warm her. The brandy would have been nice. Plain old black coffee would have to do. "On the surface, he looks as good as his shiny, handsome face. Dig deeper, and the façade begins to crack. Keep going, and the cracks turn into craters. He didn't feel right to me so I kept on searching. That guy"—she tapped the drawing Tula had made of his profile while she'd been at the station—"attracts trouble wherever he goes."

"The way Diane talks, he's a big shot in the media. I'll admit, I investigated some on my own and found clips of him on network television. National stuff that backs up her bragging. He's good, I'll give him that."

"Oh, he is a media darling, all right. He's built quite a career. With his looks and smooth voice, people love him. Nobody checks beyond the surface, and if anything does seep out between the cracks, they don't believe it. I caught the seepage, and I did believe."

Tula sat across from her, turning her coffee cup in her hands. "Diane has been a pain in the ass since she moved in, but I've never picked up evil from her. She's unpleasant, yes. Maybe because I didn't care for her from the get-go, so I'd typically brush her off. I didn't allow enough time to really feel the vibes because I didn't want to be around her. It's possible the evil was coming off her all along, and I didn't connect it with what it was."

Casey nodded. "Makes sense, and I wanted the complete picture. I dug up everything I could on Dante and then took it a step farther—what made the guy. That means I looked at the family as well as Dante. Trust me when I say I found some darkness there too. His family isn't exactly Disney Channel material. For instance, when Diane was thirteen, she got expelled from a private school in Spokane for beating another student. She said the other girl gave her a look."

"Are you sure it was her?"

A friend in the Spokane Police Department emailed her a copy of the file, complete with a booking picture of the young Diane. Except for the outrageous hair color, she hadn't changed at all in the intervening years. Same wild hair, same face, same sneer. "No doubt at all."

"Wow. I guess you never know who your neighbors are, do you?" Tula let out a dry laugh. "I'm a good one to talk, aren't I? I'm the poster child for keeping secrets from my neighbors, my friends, my family."

Casey patted her hand. "Different circumstances. You and Diane have nothing in common. That family is messed up."

Tula raised an eyebrow. "Ah. So is mine."

A good point. One that needed a little clarification. "You're comparing apples and oranges. Their dysfunction was completely different. Diane beat other girls, and teenage Dante was accused of assaulting a young woman."

"He did what? And he still carved out a career that puts him on a national stage? How is that possible? More than that, how is it ethical?"

She'd been curious about that too until she'd read that file. "Young Dante flashed a smile and told a really good story. Charges were dismissed for lack of evidence. No one was willing to take it forward. I read the same story about him more than once. Oh, he did the crime but never did the time. We need to change that fact."

"What the hell kind of neighbor do I have?"

She sat back in her chair and thought about all she'd seen in her career and what she'd read about the Macy family. "Evil is an equal-opportunity employer. It lives on every street and in every neighborhood." She'd seen it everywhere, and while it hurt her to know that many truly terrible people hid in plain sight, she also believed the good people outnumbered the bad. She told Tula as much.

"I suppose you're right. Look at my own life. If you were to meet my parents, go to their home, you'd never in a million years believe them capable of the abuse visited on me, particularly as a small child. They are not good people, though for anyone looking in from the outside, oh, my, do they appear to be the epitome of doting parents."

"I've seen it before, yet each time you speak of what happened to you, I get really pissed off. I want to go cuff your parents, toss them in a cell, and throw away the key. That you turned out okay is a testament to your strength of character. I'm impressed."

Tula's gaze softened. "I appreciate that. At the time, you might have been a little young to make that happen, but I still appreciate the sentiment. It's part of what makes you such a good cop. Moses Lake is lucky to have you."

"I'm not too young now, and I have several pairs of handcuffs!"

"Well, you might get the chance yet. Your partner called NYPD, and after his call, the parents have been alerted to my location."

"I'll be ready to defend and serve."

"And I'll have your back anytime, anywhere."

She took Tula's hand. It was nice. "Has anybody ever told you how kind you are?"

"No."

Casey gasped. "Seriously?"

"You have to remember the isolation that's been my life. Being with you has allowed me to be the most open ever. Except for my friend, Matthew, you're the only one I've shared my sad story with."

Casey's heart did a little flip. Throughout her career she'd been good at instilling faith in people, thus they often shared with her when others failed. This was different—a lot more personal and important. "I'm glad you told me that."

Tula's thumb stroked her palm. "I am too."

She managed to get her thoughts back on track. "Okay, so about your creepy neighbors. Good old Dante has managed to get his life on an outward-facing, successful trajectory."

Tula's eyes narrowed. "That doesn't sound all that positive."

"It looks positive from the outside. Doesn't feel that way from the inside or from the coincidences that seem to follow him."

"Coincidences?"

"Yeah. That's the thing that really jumped out at me and why I planted enough information on Mike's desk to pique his interest. If he doesn't follow up on what I left him, he's an idiot."

❖

Tula's heart raced as she listened to Casey. What she told her echoed everything she'd been feeling since she recognized Dante's profile in the vision. Hinky was the single word that stuck with her from the first hello. He didn't read true, and that bothered her. Artists truly were sensitive. She'd been that way as long as she could remember, and rarely were her impressions wrong.

She hadn't been wrong about the Macys. She should have immediately refused the dinner invitation and not spent any time with Diane at all. She should have stuck to her guns and kept solid with the no she'd initially spit out for that awful dinner invitation. Instead, she'd given in. Looked like she'd agreed to have dinner with a killer, maybe a serial killer. Goose bumps rose on her arms.

"Doing nothing while we wait for your partner to pick up the slack doesn't work for me." Tula couldn't sit around, and from what she'd seen with Casey's partner, she didn't trust him to roll with the kind of speed required. Knowing what they did now, it wasn't right to wait for something more official to occur. Good people didn't do nothing.

Casey tapped the table. "I'm with you there. I have to figure out a way to keep an eye on Dante without letting him know we're on to his extracurricular activities."

"Do you think he's watching us? I mean, the thing about him peering through the windows was pretty creepy. Angel even stopped by a couple times to follow up because it had bothered her so much. That's not like her, which is pretty telling."

"I've been thinking about that too, and I don't think your friend was reading that situation wrong. Wish she'd have come by while I was here, so I could have coaxed a few more details out of her. We'll work with what we have. Is he watching a potential victim, or is he developing some kind of stalking obsession with you?"

Ice slid through her. "Way to send a chill right into my heart."

Casey's expression didn't soften. "I would like to think that's not the case, but we have to be realistic here. The way he looks at you *is* chilling, and I can't ignore that he has you in his sights. He's good for either one of those moves and has the potential to get really angry if things don't go his way. We have to figure out why he's creeping around you."

"Well, I know that Diane sees me as a potential member of the family, and to be honest, that idea makes me want to throw up for more than one reason. Actually, I should say she did see me as potential family material. She was pretty pissed off when I refused her offer of evening cocktails. Called me a bitch."

"Wrong on all counts. Not a bitch and not a potential member of that vile family. Maybe another family…"

Was she hearing what she thought she was? "A family that doesn't make me want to throw up?" Her gaze stayed on Casey's face.

She took her hand, and her grasp was warm, comforting. "Can I just say that particular scenario appeals to me."

The chills Tula felt right now were for a completely different reason. "Me as well."

Casey's eyes darkened, and a tiny smile turned up the corners of her mouth. "We'll take this road once we have this bastard in cuffs."

"Deal." She found it hard to breathe.

"Now, as much as I hate to bring the subject back to ick, we need to think about this mess." She released Tula's hand and tapped the drawing. "Maybe talk it through. First, your friend saw him standing next to the tree there in the back, and he was watching the house."

"She'd swear to it." Angel didn't exactly say it like that, but Tula felt confident she would. Angel wouldn't have made that many stops by her house if his peeping hadn't raised alarm bells for her.

"Then maybe we make it easier for him."

"You're not suggesting I ask him to come over here?" Tula couldn't support that plan. She didn't want him in her space ever again. As it was, she felt like she needed to scrub the place top to bottom just to get every trace of him out of her house. She didn't want so much as a skin cell lingering.

"No. Absolutely not." Her words were firm enough as to leave no doubt that Casey meant them. A relief on her part. Casey continued "You have a lovely little patio out there with a couple of padded chairs. You know, the kind made for relaxing under the moonlight. How about we have another cup of coffee and hang out there? Entice him back to his tree, and perhaps we can keep eyes on him from there without him being any the wiser."

Tula thought about the plan. "Detective, I believe you've hit upon a solid idea. Might be a little late for coffee, but we do want to stay awake and alert. Let me go make us a fresh pot."

The moon was almost full, spreading buttery light across the lawn and the lake beyond. Not a bad evening to sit out on the patio, though she'd pulled on a hoodie before taking a seat in one of the wrought-iron chairs she'd painted a cheerful blue. The pads were bright and pleasant as well. She liked to surround herself with colors and prints.

Ten minutes after they relocated to the patio to sip their coffee and talk about things like the construction up off I-90, Casey's idea came to fruition. A shadow shifted behind the weeping willow. Not a duck. Not a dog. Not a cat. Their target had taken the bait.

❖

Angel wasn't sure she liked how Tula and Casey sat out on the patio casually drinking coffee or tea or whatever they had in the mugs each of them held. Hopefully, nothing of the alcohol variety. They needed to maintain clear heads.

Beyond that, sitting on the patio with the moonlight as bright as an overhead light, they were too exposed. They had no way of knowing that he was prepped for violence yet again. The whispers that came to her on the night air warned her to beware, yet there they sat chatting away as if they had not a care in the world. This wasn't what she wanted to happen.

Only the heaviness of power that also came to her made her feel hopeful. Casey added to the power that Tula already possessed, and it showed. At least it did to her. Combined with what Angel tried to send her way, maybe they would be in time to stop him before he could kill again.

The sound of waves lapping against the shoreline made her turn. The turbulence on the lake tonight echoed her emotions. So much going on. So little control.

"No, you can't control what will happen next."

How in the world could he read her mind? "You enjoy this in-and-out thing, don't you? Mess with my head and then disappear, leaving me to figure everything out by myself."

She didn't turn around to look at Blue. He'd be standing there, as always, his thick hair hanging in his face, his hands in his pockets. Tall and handsome, with the confidence of a man born into privilege. At the same time, a man who didn't let legacy define him. Most loved him for the kindness he showed everyone regardless of their station. Some hated him because of it. She had loved him for all of it and still did.

Blue laughed. He didn't do that often, and she missed the sound. In the old days, he'd laughed a great deal. "I can't solve any of it for you. No sense in me standing around to accomplish nothing."

"You don't have to solve anything."

"No, I don't. You do."

Her patience waned. Too much resting on her shoulders to appreciate his lightness. She needed his support, not his flippant answers. "When did you become such a sage? You used to be fun."

His voice turned serious. She'd gotten his attention. "I've learned a bit along the way—what I can change and what I can't. You've been schooled in the same lessons, even if you choose to ignore them. You have one left to learn."

Angel sighed. Some days it was too much and she was too tired. "I don't care about lessons, any lessons. Too much. Too long. I want to close my eyes and never open them again."

He folded his hands. "Soon."

She shook her head. She'd heard it before. "You've been saying that for years."

His expression didn't change. "Years are just a blink."

"Whatever." She started to walk away. Not the time to get stuck on this particular stream of consciousness.

"Oh, you've been listening too closely to the kids these days. *Whatev!*" He did sound like a fourteen-year-old.

"Sometimes you can pick up very expressive language from the kids," she threw over her shoulder as she walked.

Her snitty comeback didn't faze him. He began to follow her. "True enough. Now, concentrate and figure this out. The clock is ticking."

Angel spun, and fury colored her words. "I know."

Blue stopped and smiled. "There you go. That's my girl."

CHAPTER THIRTY-ONE

Casey wondered about the unclear vision and brought it up quietly as they sat on the patio, covertly watching their observer. "Did you get a glimpse of the woman he carried?"

Tula grimaced as she looked over at her. "No, and that part bugs me. I mean, I've always been able to clearly see the victim's, or potential victim's, face, so it's weird that when the three of us joined forces, both his face and the woman's face were shrouded in shadows. All I could make out was that she's slim, with long, light-colored hair. I couldn't even see its color. Again, odd, because in the next vision I got not only the woman's face, but his profile. What kind of weirdness is the universe throwing at me?"

"How about joining forces again and seeing if we can amp up your vision?" Casey grasped at straws. She wanted to force something to happen before one or both of the women in Tula's visions were harmed. So far, she'd had no calls telling her that another body, let alone two, had been located. Good on that front. Still, if history was to repeat itself, both of the women were in danger. Unacceptable. So, if they needed to push, Casey was all in favor of trying something new.

"I don't understand. Are you wanting to go get your grandmother again? Go for the power of the trinity?"

Casey wasn't entirely clear of her own meaning. More a hunch based on Abuelita's comments. She held out her hand. If they'd amped up before when they touched, they should be able to do it again. Right? "The power of touch."

For a moment, Tula stared at her hand, and then with a nod barely visible in the light of the candle that sat on the table between them, she took her offered hand. Chills raced up Casey's spine. Darned if

Abuelita wasn't right. Again. For a tiny woman she sure did possess a ton of knowledge, and not the kind taught in a university. When this was all over, Casey planned to spend more time picking her brain. Maybe the idea of being a bruja blanca wasn't such a bad one after all.

"Do you think it will work?"

Casey held Tula's trembling hand a little tighter. "It can't hurt, and at this point, anything will help."

"He's still watching," she said on a breath.

"Perfect," Casey whispered.

She wanted him there in the shadows, thinking that they weren't aware of his presence, that he remained a covert watcher. At the same time, she didn't want to underestimate him. If she was right about him, and she was pretty sure she was, he'd been at this a long time. So far, she'd matched up eleven unsolved murders from Washington DC to Washington State. All of them coincided with his presence in the applicable cities.

Taken together with his childhood history and dysfunctional family, it all spelled trouble for the guy who looked shiny and bright on the outside and black as they come on the inside. No city or society needed a pretty-boy killer reminiscent of Ted Bundy. Her resolve hardened. She'd take him down.

She returned her attention to Tula. She loved the feel of her hand in hers while she also worried about the dark circles under her eyes and the trembling in her hand. "Close your eyes and rest. I know the last few days have taken a toll on you."

"I'm all right."

She was and she wasn't. "No question you're tough. Anybody with half a brain would be able to figure that out after two minutes with you. Doesn't mean you're not running on fumes. Let me keep watch and you recharge, even if it's just ten minutes. We'll wait him out."

Tula turned a tired smile on her. "I am definitely running on fumes, and you know what? I think this is helping." She held up their clasped hands.

"It doesn't hurt."

"No, it doesn't." Tula closed her eyes.

They sat that way for a least ten minutes before she felt Tula release her hand. Good. Tula needed some peace. Besides, it wasn't that unpleasant to sit out here together listening to the night sounds. Even more pleasant company. Except, of course, for the one standing in the darkness of the willow tree.

The coffee hit her bladder, and while she didn't want to get up and leave the sleeping Tula, nature had a more pressing idea. It should be okay. Five minutes tops and she'd be right back here. She jumped up and raced inside to the bathroom. Nature's call answered, she zipped back out to the patio.

Tula was gone.

❖

Tula came slowly into consciousness, wondering how she came to be in a swinging hammock. Foggy and unclear. Pleasant yet not. The familiar scent of the lake wafted into the air.

"Coming to, my little friend?"

She began to struggle as it hit her. She wasn't on her patio sitting in her chair and holding Casey's hand. She wasn't in a swing hammock. Her hair hung almost to the ground and her cheek bumped against his back as he almost ran down the shoreline with her slung over his shoulder. She wouldn't have thought him capable of this kind of physical exertion.

"Where are you taking me?" She tried to move her hands and realized they were restrained with handcuffs. Handcuffs!

"No sense in fighting me, princess. You're up against a real pro." He chuckled. No humor there.

As her mind cleared, it all started to connect like a spider building an intricate web. The victim she'd been unable to see clearly. Her face. Her hair color. In some sort of warped way, the universe hadn't deemed it appropriate for her to see herself. Every other face had been clear and paintable. No shadows except for one. She turned out to be the one.

As a child, she'd always believed she'd die at her mother's hand. The backhanded slaps, the trip and falls, the days spent locked in her room without food or water. Pain and misery had been her constant companion except for the hours she spent with a paintbrush and canvas. She'd believed that once her usefulness ended, the final beating would stop it all for her. It hit her now how she'd escaped that fate only to find herself at the hands of a madman. Some people didn't rate a break.

"Why?"

"Why not?" His breathing was heavy as he ran, her head bumping, bumping, bumping against his back. Her scar ached, and tears dripped from her eyes.

"What is wrong with you?" Her sadness at the end ahead of her was mingled with anger for allowing him the opening to kill her, for all the lives he'd taken and her failure at stopping him.

His laugh carried loud on the night air, cheerful and pleasant, as though they were out together for a romantic moonlight stroll. It didn't sound evil, just like he didn't smell evil. He wore some kind of cologne, light and pleasing. A serial killer with expensive cologne and a hearty laugh. It could only happen to her.

"Not a damn thing. My life is quite priceless."

"You're messed up." The end might be looming. She wasn't quite ready to give up, and ideas began to form. The handcuffs and the mental fogginess slowed her down. He'd either injected her with a drug or forced her to inhale something more vaporous. She remembered holding Casey's hand before she drifted off into sleep. It had been relaxing and comfortable sitting next to a fascinating woman who made her feel safe, and Lord knows, she'd needed some rest.

He answered her unasked question. "Yes. I gave you a little help."

"Help?" If she understood what was affecting her, she might be able to figure out how to fight it before she got to how to take him out. He'd pushed her a step too far.

"Clearly, you've forgotten what my sister does for a living. Chemicals are her life, and she gets me what I need to do my special work." He sounded full of pride, probably both for the way he got his sister to help him and for what he loved to do.

She almost threw up. "Diane is part of this?" She'd found the woman a huge pain in the ass and, after what Casey had uncovered, not a nice person. Murder, or helping a murderer, had never occurred to her. The Macys got worse with each passing minute.

"You know how it is. The family that kills together, stays together." He laughed so hard, he stumbled and almost dropped her. He recovered and kept going at pace that continued to astonish her.

"But she lives here." In a lot of ways, it didn't make sense for them to kill in such a spree when she lived and worked in the same community. However, that argument didn't hold a lot of water, considering other killers had done the same thing quite successfully for years before being stopped.

"Right now she lives here. She didn't tell you about her promotion? Oh, I suppose not, given how you hurt her feelings. Well, here's the thing. She'll be relocating to LA next month. That left Moses Lake as the perfect hunting grounds. You kill, drop, and leave. You didn't think I was really here on assignment, did you?"

"That's sick. You're sick."

"Don't knock it until you've tried it. I find it rather intoxicating. Better than a good fuck any day of the week. Poor Diane, though. She had high hopes for you. She thought you'd be perfect for me."

"Not in a million years."

"I have to argue the point with you, darling. You *are* perfect for me. Just not as a girlfriend or a wife. I have another plan for you. More fun, if you get where I'm coming from." His chuckle chilled her.

She closed her eyes and focused her energy. Here she was draped over the shoulder of a madman, hands cuffed and mind muddled. Powerless and yet not. She could do one thing—call for help. She'd been gifted with a power she didn't want. She'd been forced into fighting evil when she longed to do nothing but paint. She'd asked for none of it, and none of it was fair. She'd done it though, and she continued to carry on. Since all things deserved balance, right now was the time for that power to give back to her. She closed her eyes, clasped her hands, and concentrated.

Casey, come and help me.

❖

Tula's silent scream came to Angel as though she'd shouted it through a megaphone. The killer had her. Her heart sank. She had failed her, and now she was going to die. How could God do this to Tula? To her? She'd done everything asked of her and more. It wasn't fair.

"No, she's not." Blue read her mind again.

"He's got her, Blue. I don't have anything left to do. Nothing to give that will save her."

"He does have her and she's in danger, as is another woman, if he's not stopped. That doesn't mean you can't still help her. Can't still save her."

"How?" She'd used every trick she had. Burned up every ounce of energy breaking through barriers.

He put his hands on his hips and stared at her. "You charged in, defended your sister, and refused to let a monster's violence be unaccounted for. It made a difference in more lives than one."

"I failed then too." She remembered all too well how it had gone down. Yes, her sister's husband had been held accountable for what he'd put into motion. His reputation destroyed, he fled the country. Too cowardly to end his own life, he'd run away, but not far and not for long. His sins caught up with him in a drunken brawl. His fists had connected, but not with a woman that time, and the vengeance she'd failed to deliver came to him anyway. His death brought her little solace.

"No, you didn't. You made a mistake. You didn't fail then, and you're not going to fail now. Think this through!"

She had never heard him be that forceful, and his emphasis did get her attention. Gentle and encouraging had always been his way, even in a time when men were men. He got results, and perhaps that's why he'd been at her side all this time. "I can't do this." Yes, she was whining, and she knew it. Weariness and failure could do that to a person. She didn't want to be strong anymore.

"Damn it, you can. Now stop and think. You do what you have to do to make this right. Don't you dare give up."

"Easy for you to say." Tears stung her eyes. Oh, yes, whiny little bitch. She owned it because she had a right. She'd earned "whiny little bitch" a thousand times over.

"Do you, for one minute, think any of this has been easy for me?"

All right. That stopped her cold. Not once in all their time together had he talked to her like this. "No." She usually didn't consider how it had been for him. She got too caught up in her own misery. She'd modify her description to self-centered, whiny little bitch.

"Then stop crying like a delicate flower you've never been and help that woman. Your time is up."

"I don't know what to do." This time she screamed.

He screamed back. "Yes, you do."

She put her hands over her eyes. He was wrong. What else could she do? Her abilities were limited at best, and she'd used every piece of power she had. Blue didn't understand. He wasn't the one on the front lines. He wasn't the one who lost his soul.

She opened her mouth to argue more, and then she stopped. Damn it. She did know. Once again, he was right. "It will be the end of me."

He nodded and calmly said, "It will."

Peace settled over her. "I have to do it. I owe it to her. I owe it to you."

"You do."

This time she nodded and then began to walk from the shoreline across the grass toward the patio where Casey stood staring at the chair where Tula had been sitting. Her steps were silent on the grass, and Casey obviously didn't hear her until she spoke.

"I can help you."

Casey didn't turn, and Angel sighed. She didn't hear her words either. She'd hoped it would be easier.

"You have to try harder," Blue said from behind her.

Her resolve started to waver. It wouldn't work. "She's never going to hear me."

"She will."

She had to do more than just push through the barrier between life and death. "She doesn't believe."

"Make her believe."

She stepped onto the patio and closer to Casey. Taking a deep breath, she took Casey's hand. The first time she tried, nothing happened. She took another, deeper breath and tried again. Somehow, she had to make herself believe she could do it, believe she could step through the barrier and show herself to Casey.

She grabbed Casey's hand. This time the connection was solid, and Casey's eyes widened as she too obviously felt the contact.

She spun and stared at Angel. "Who are you, and where the fuck did you come from?"

Keeping her concentration on their connection, Angel answered. "I'm a friend. Please, you need to help Tula. He's got her, and he's going to hurt her if you don't stop him."

"No shit, Sherlock."

The sarcasm didn't shock her. "You have to save her. You're the only one who can."

"I don't know how."

Angel almost smiled. Damn Blue. She would be walking a mile in his shoes. "You do. Hold tighter."

She couldn't do much, but what she could do might just make the difference.

Chapter Thirty-two

Fucking crazy. One minute Casey stood alone on the patio wondering how Tula could disappear in a flash, and the next second some woman appears out of nowhere. And she did mean nowhere. Panicked as she might be, crazy she wasn't, except everything about this was nuts.

Her knees almost buckled as she tightened her grip on the mystery woman's hand. Like her connection with Tula, this woman had an otherworldly vibe, especially since she'd materialized out of nowhere. Though Casey managed to stay on her feet despite the energy surging through her body, her vision blurred. For a split second, she thought she understood what Tula had been going through. Then everything went dark.

When her vision returned, the mystery woman stood near the edge of the patio watching her. "What the hell just happened?"

"It's all I can do. I have nothing else left to give."

"You made me see all that?"

She shook her head. "I helped you harness what you already held inside you. It wouldn't have worked if you weren't already blessed. You wouldn't have even seen me."

"What in the world are you talking about?" She could see her as clear as a bell. Yeah, she'd sneaked up on her. Not difficult considering she'd been concentrating on figuring out where Tula went. Could have happened to anyone. Still, she wondered exactly where she'd come from. "Who are you, and why are you here?" It was a little late for a casual drop-in visit.

"A friend."

"I don't know you."

"Let's just say I've been watching over Tula for a very long time."

Casey didn't buy it. The woman looked to be in her early twenties or maybe even her late teens. Not a chance in hell she'd been hanging out with Tula for any length of time. Or perhaps they had different definitions of a very long time. "Define long time."

She inclined her head, and her long hair fell forward. When she met Casey's eyes again, hers looked old. "Since she was a child."

Apparently, she had *stupid* written in big red letters across her forehead. "Bullshit. What kind of game are you playing?"

"Please trust me and take what you've seen to save her. I can't do anything more. My time is up."

Casey started to call her out once more, and then she stopped. The woman had gone shimmery, as in she could see right through her. All of a sudden, a tall, handsome man stood next to her, holding her hand. Gone were the blue jeans and the yellow flowered shirt she'd been wearing when she'd first appeared. Now she wore a beautiful gown with a massive skirt, her long hair piled on her head in a style centuries out of date, a sparkling necklace hanging around her neck. An actress playing the part of an aristocrat in a period piece. The man also looked as though he had just stepped off the stage. Too freaking weird. She blinked, and they were gone. Casey stood alone on the patio. "What in the actual fuck?"

For a second, she stood rooted to the patio, but only for a second, and then she dismissed the insanity that just happened and raced through the house. No time to worry about whether she was losing her mind and seeing people that didn't exist. Her gut told her to act on what she'd seen in those moments of darkness when the woman held her hand. Strange woman. Strange ghost. Or could it be? Strange Angel? Holy crap. She might just be losing her grip on reality, but what a freaking ride.

She dug out her car keys and her cell at the same time. "I need your help."

Mike didn't take a breath. "Of course you do. I'm the guy, and everybody knows it. Surprised it took you this long to come to the table of Mike."

"Mike, for once would you please dial it down and listen." She didn't hold out a lot of hope. It was worth a try anyway.

For once, he actually did as she asked. The night was full of wonders that defied explanation. She filled him in on what she'd discovered about Dante, about the files she'd left on his desk, and where she was headed next.

For a moment, the call went silent, and then he said slowly, "This sounds like a lot of bullshit."

No kidding. She'd been on that page at first. Seemed like a million years ago. "I know exactly how it sounds. I'm asking you to trust me and go out on a limb. If I'm right about this, he's all yours. I'll stand behind you, smile, and clap as the governor gives you a big award for stopping a serial killer. The credit will be yours alone. You have my word." She had zero interest in the career-making aspect of this. All she cared about was saving Tula.

"You're serious, aren't you?"

"Never been more serious. We don't have time to do this by the book. If we don't get there soon, he's going to kill Tula, and that's a fact."

"Because you saw it in a vision?" The skepticism returned. Had she lost him?

"I did, and we can figure out how to spin it later. We'll find a way to make it so you followed up on a lead you developed. I promise. First, we have to stop him." She waited, holding her breath and praying that he'd step out of character and act without running into a brick wall of his own making first.

"All right, I'm on my way, but Wilson, if you're yanking my chain, I'll crush you. Your career as a detective will be done. You feel me?"

She could take a breath. "I feel you. Now move. Please."

She ended the call, shoved the phone into her pocket, and raced to her car.

❖

Her back screamed as he dumped her onto the ground. The ride in the trunk of his car hadn't been long, thank the good Lord, because she felt every bump and turn. She'd be bruised from head to toe. As he dropped her, a large stone slammed into her back, and the spikes of pain that assailed her made the discomfort of the trunk ride pale.

When her eyes adjusted to the dark, she realized she hadn't slammed into a rock. It was a headstone—very hard and very cold. She squinted and looked around. A cemetery. The others had been taken out to the Potholes. He'd brought her to a silent city. A message?

"Why?" She wiggled into a sitting position, her back against the headstone.

He laughed. "Why not? This seemed appropriate. I mean, the real

Tula Crane died years ago. Am I wrong? Mona Lisa. This Tula Crane might as well meet her end in a cemetery, since Mona Lisa didn't get a proper burial." He laughed again, almost a giggle.

Her stomach rolled. "You know who I am? Who I was?"

He composed himself and stood tall. The dim glow of the few pole lights scattered throughout the cemetery flattered him. He didn't look like a monster. "Of course I do. I'm amazed you've failed to realize how above-average I am. I can smell a story from a mile away, and you, my dear, are a story I'll be telling on the six o'clock news. The first time I saw you, I knew something wasn't quite right. A little digging, and lo and behold, what did I find? Pretty Mona Lisa Mendori, child prodigy worth millions. Said prodigy disappeared when she turned eighteen, along with the bulk of her wealth, leaving poor mommy and daddy scrambling to find their meal ticket. Am I getting this right?"

She wouldn't give him the satisfaction. "Why bring me here now? Why not kill me like you did the others?"

"All in my own sweet time, my pretty. Some business to attend to first." He made an exaggerated bow, a man playing to his captive audience.

"This is insane." In the back of her mind, she continued to scream for Casey. If their connection was as deep as she hoped, she'd come.

"A matter of perspective. You call it insane. I call it living a full life, and with a little help from you, my life is about to get even fuller. Ah, here's my little helper." He clapped his hands. "This is going to get really good. Who knew Moses Lake would turn out this spectacular?"

"Hey, Tula. How's it going?" Diane's laugh was as ugly as her brother's.

"Help me." Worth a shot.

Diane sneered. "Oh, please. Why on earth would I want to do that? You've always been a real bitch to me, and I only tolerated it because I knew my precious little brother would take care of you sooner or later."

"You tried to fix me up with him."

"A momentary lapse. For a few minutes I thought you might be good material to join team Macy. A loner who kept to herself. Better than that, kept her lips shut. You came across as a real good prospect, until you didn't, and then, well"—she waved a hand in the air—"here we are."

"You're helping him."

"Of course I am, stupid. He's my baby brother, and we've always been tight, if you get my drift." She leaned over and kissed him full on the lips. She straightened and looked down at Tula. "Now, bitch, I've got my laptop here so you can make a transfer and sign a document. Nice and easy."

She could guess where they were going with this. The second she did it, her life would be worthless, and she wasn't ready to give in just yet. "I'm not doing anything for you."

"Did I tell you I found your pal, Matthew?"

Her head snapped up. "What?" Her heart started to race, the urge to hurl great. If he hurt her one true friend, the person who'd protected her when no one else would, even if Dante killed her, she'd make his life miserable. She'd haunt him until his last fucking day.

"Yeah, so here's the deal. You transfer your money to the account I punch in for you and then sign the document Diane drafted. In case you're wondering, it will grant her the rights to your artwork. You do all that, and you have my word I won't kill your buddy." He made a crisscross motion over his chest. "Capiche?"

Her mind whirled. They couldn't do this to her. They would though. She could hear it in their words, even if the darkness that shielded their eyes from her would surely reflect the blackness of their souls. She'd stopped some awful people in New York. These two made them look like amateurs.

She had to stall. Casey needed time to find her. "Don't hurt Matthew. He hasn't done anything to anybody."

"Oh, baby girl, you're missing the whole point. I would think by now, given you've figured out my hobby, that I don't give a shit. Fun is fun. I am a man of honor, though, and I've given you my word that I won't kill him if you do what I say. Do it, and he lives. Refuse and well—" He shrugged and laughed.

❖

Tears rolled down Angel's cheeks as she stood behind a tall headstone twenty yards from where Tula rested against another one. She wanted to pull her into her arms, protect her with her life. Except she didn't have a life to protect her with. She'd given that up hundreds of years ago.

"You've done what you can," Blue said from behind her.

"I tried." Her heart hurt. She'd hoped that last surge of energy that allowed Casey to see her would change the course of the night. As she looked at Tula, handcuffed and pale, all her hopes crashed.

"You did good." Blue's optimism did nothing for her.

"It wasn't enough. No one has come." Not completely true. The monster had a sidekick, and she'd come streaking his way. The brother-sister duo, wrong on every level, came as a shock. She hadn't realized until this moment that the evil she'd sensed came as a package.

"Go to her."

"I have nothing. She won't even see me." She'd used what little she had left with Casey. She barely hung on now. Looking down at the gown she'd been wearing that night, she noticed the blood stains were dark spots on what once had been magnificent fabric envied by her friends. Her strength was gone, and everything had shifted back to where it all started, stains and all.

"She will know you're here."

She didn't agree. Without even a hint of magic left, she couldn't influence a single thing. "I'm stripped of everything. It won't help."

Blue took her hand. She closed her eyes and breathed in, out. That she could feel him after all this time spoke of the end. She curled her fingers around his and didn't think she'd ever let him go. Not again.

"Listen to me,' he said. "She'll know you're here because, through it all, you've loved her and protected her. Those gifts are more important than the powers or magic or whatever it is God gave you."

"It won't work." Her heart hurt that she'd failed yet again.

"Love transcends everything."

"I don't think so." If that were true, neither of them would be here now. Love would have saved them. It hadn't.

He was refusing to give in. "Don't be a brat. I know so. If it didn't, I wouldn't be here. Love has kept us together all this time."

The words she hadn't been able to bring herself to say before tumbled out in a rush of anguish-filled confession. "I killed you." Sobs shook her shoulders. "How can you say that love transcends? I loved you, and I killed you."

"You did." He kissed the top of her head. "I love you anyway. I always have."

"How? I ruined everything. How can you still love me?"

"I never stopped, and whether you believe or not, your heart is good. It was then and it is now. You tried only to protect your sister, not hurt me. Sometimes things happen that we don't intend. That doesn't make us bad. It makes us human."

"I killed you. I killed you. I killed you." His forgiveness hurt almost as much as her pain at destroying the life of the only man she'd ever loved.

"Yet we've traveled this journey together side by side, year after year."

"I don't understand any of it."

He took her face between his hands. How many centuries had she waited to feel his flesh against hers? "You do. You're not looking hard enough."

Even in life, he'd been the one to see the big picture. He'd pushed her to be everything she could, and in that moment when she'd plunged the knife into him believing him to be her sister's abuser, her whole world had crashed. People didn't recover from that kind of mistake. She'd known it then, and her belief never wavered about the action she'd taken next. It had been the right thing to do.

"I have to make this right for her. She can't die because I'm less than I should be."

"That's what this has all been about, year after year, century after century, and you're almost there, my love."

She stared into his eyes and started to protest yet again. Then, she saw something in his eyes that changed everything. She believed. Leaning into him, she kissed his lips, remembering the sweetness of the love she'd denied them both. "I understand."

As she walked toward Tula, she squared her shoulders. At the headstone Tula leaned against, she sat down and put her hand on hers. At first nothing happened, and she was afraid she'd been right—nothing more could be done. She'd moved beyond the veil that separated the living and the dead. No longer could she step between worlds, even if to show herself only to Tula. It had been a blessing to be at her side for so long, and now she'd have to let their union go.

Then Tula tilted her head in her direction while her fingers curled around Angel's. A slight pressure made her smile. Weak and fading, she had one last burst of energy to share, and it worked. Even if she failed to save Tula's life, she'd not leave this world alone.

"I'm here," she said, even though neither Tula nor her captives could see or hear her. "I've always been here. Your guardian angel."

Tula's slight nod made her cry all over again.

CHAPTER THIRTY-THREE

The only place that fit what Casey had seen while the strange woman held her hand was the Pioneer Memorial Gardens Cemetery, northeast of town. Founded in the early years of the twentieth century, it was the resting place of some of her family members. More than once, she'd gone with her abuelita and mother on Memorial Day to put flowers on their headstones and tell stories of their lives. While she appreciated honoring her ancestors, she never really liked cemeteries. And she sure as hell didn't like this one right now.

She drove through the dark roads a lot faster than was wise, or probably safe, and put her uncomfortable feelings about cemeteries aside. Getting to Tula before something horrible happened was way more important than her issue with cities of the dead. She and a good psychologist could deal with that later, after Tula was safe and sound.

The streets were quiet, damn it. She'd hoped Mike would make good on his earlier agreement to follow up on the information she'd shared and come with the cavalry. The silence all around told her something different. No Mike. No backup. He'd blown her off. Again. Big shock. She was on her own in this.

Nearing the cemetery, she turned off her headlights and coasted to a stop at the far edge of the defined property. From here she could see a tiny light moving around, someone walking with either a flashlight or headlamp. It resembled the same kind of movement around a nighttime campout. Thank you, stranger, for giving her a moment of sight. If not for that strange woman, she'd have never thought to come here.

Quietly, she got out of the car and went to her trunk. Better safe than sorry, she took her vest out and strapped it on. Because she didn't want Dante to hear or see her, she parked as far from them as she could while maintaining a visual. If surprise remained on her side, she'd have a better chance of overtaking him. She'd lost her cousin to this killer. She damn well wouldn't lose Tula.

With her gun in hand, she began to make her way toward the light, keeping low and tight to the headstones. Some were near the ground, while others were more elaborate and taller. She liked the tall ones—easier to stay out of sight—not that he would be paying attention to anything other than Tula.

The closer she got, the more a new fear began to kick in. She berated herself for not picking up on it earlier. More than one light bobbed around. He wasn't alone. From here, she could also now see that two cars were parked nearby. Two cars, two lights, two figures. One taller. One shorter. A man and a woman. It didn't require a very long leap to figure out the woman's identity. It also wouldn't be the first time she'd come across siblings who made crime the family business. Would be the first time she'd come across a brother-and-sister serial-killer duo. This had *New York Times* true-crime best seller written all over it, and Mike had bailed on her. He was going to be pissed.

Keeping to the shadows and by cover of the headstones, she made her way close enough to both hear and see Dante and Diane. Oddly, Diane held a laptop, while Dante tossed around a silver handgun. Couldn't quite determine the make and model of the gun from here, but it did track with the coroner's report on the other victims. His weapon of choice was a small-caliber handgun. No doubt the ballistics from the gun in his hand would match the wounds on the other victims here in Moses Lake and more across the country. Her stomach rolled as she fastened her gaze on the weapon that had taken her cousin's life. It took every bit of her self-control not to charge him and shoot a bullet from his own gun into his dead, black heart.

Rather than rushing in, she opted to pause and listen. Quite a conversation was taking place, and that didn't feel like standard operating procedure for a killer. Correction, serial killer. Did they really spend this much time talking to their victims? Not from what her training had told her. Then again, she'd never come face-to-face with one before, so she how would she know?

They kept talking about money and a document, and she finally figured out they wanted Tula to transfer her accounts to them, followed by signing away the rights to her art. Bastards. Nothing much worse than a couple of smart killers. They'd get their jollies from murdering Tula and then reap the rewards of her estate.

Her mind whirled as she tried to come up with a plan to stop them and, at the same time, get Tula to safety. A tall order to fill on her own. *Damn you, Mike*. How nice would it be if he could back her up once? Just once. Was that too much to ask?

Her gaze was drawn to Tula, and what she saw almost made her heart stop. "No, no, no," she whispered. "Stay put."

She hoped her urgent energy made its way to Tula. Despite the darkness, she could make out the subtle shift of her body. Tula was preparing to make a move. What scared her was that while Tula was an incredible artist, she wasn't a fighter. Even though she'd survived childhood abuse, this situation could turn deadly in a moment. Casey wanted more than anything for Tula to stay where she was and let her take down the two killers.

"Please, don't do it."

Her hope that their connection would transmit her energy and her words fell flat, failing on all fronts. In horror, she watched as Tula, hands restrained behind her back, rose and threw herself toward Diane. Casey didn't wait to see how Tula's move played out. She had to act and launched an attack from behind the headstone. At the same time she hurtled toward Dante, the sound of sirens shattered the silence. Nothing had ever sounded better.

❖

"NO!" Tula launched herself up to charge Diane. She hit her with the top of her head, right in the middle of her stomach, and the surprise collision sent them both flying. Adrenaline roared through her, and she readied herself for an onslaught from Diane. Handcuffed or not, she'd battle with everything she had. She would go down fighting, but the return fire didn't happen.

When she'd surprised Diane with the charge, the laptop she'd held flew through the air to land with a thud on the ground, followed by a louder thud as Diane also hit the ground. Tula rolled quickly and sprang upright, spreading her feet in a steady stance. When Diane came at her, she'd be in position to hit her again. Except Diane didn't move from where she lay on the ground. The headlamp she'd been wearing had come off and lay a short distance away, its beam stretching across the grass.

Her body buzzing, Tula shifted from foot to foot. "Come on," she muttered. "Let's finish this." Still nothing. What the hell was wrong with her? She'd strutted in like the cocky bitch she'd come to know, and now she stayed on the ground like a submissive dog? "Get up," she roared. "Get your ass up."

It took a second for it to register that when Diane had gone down, she'd hit her skull on one of the headstones. She stopped moving and studied her prey, out of arm's reach, of course. Pumped as she might be, she wasn't stupid enough to risk Diane playing possum. The stillness of her body didn't appear faked. Good. Served her right.

She leaned in for a better look. Through the darkness, Tula couldn't make out if Diane had been knocked out or was actually dead. Either way worked for her. In fact, as awful as it sounded, she'd prefer the latter.

It had hit her as she'd sat propped up by the headstone that regardless of what Dante said, he lied. His promises were as hollow as he was. He'd hurt Matthew without blinking an eye, just for the thrill of it. It had been an easy decision. Before she'd give them a single dime or sign over the rights to her works, she'd die. Rather have her toxic parents inherit the rights than to allow people as evil as Dante and Diane to possess them. Her mind had begun to buzz with thoughts on how to thwart their best-laid plans.

And then when she'd felt the unseen presence take her hand, she'd realized she wasn't alone and that she had to stand up for herself, handcuffed or not. The universe once more had sent her a message. It hadn't been time to give up back in New York, and it wasn't time to give up now. She was a survivor, and that had never changed. Survivors didn't lie down and die. They fought back. She took that mysterious, otherworldly encouragement and launched right into Diane. They started the war, and she'd end it.

After the few seconds it took to assess the situation with Diane, she thought about Dante. He was next. Out of the corner of her eye she caught movement. Ready to charge again, she spun, and then she stopped. Ten feet away, Casey had tackled Dante, the gun he'd been waving around whizzing through the air and landing somewhere in the darkness. Yes! Casey had heard her. Her relief made tears pool in her eyes. In an instant, fear replaced relief when she heard Casey's scream and Dante's wild laugh. Both were on the ground struggling. She wanted to help and screamed herself as she pulled against the handcuffs, stumbling and falling to the ground in her effort to free herself from the restraints. Pain radiated through her shoulder as she hit hard.

"Take that, you cunt." Dante roared as he rolled away from Casey, coming to his feet only inches from Tula. The blade of the knife he held glinted in the light of his headlamp that amazingly still sat on his head. The drip of blood fueled her fury.

She screamed again. "NO!" She twisted her body and brought her legs around with a burst of power, sweeping him off his feet. He tumbled backward with a satisfying crash. With speed aided by another burst of adrenaline, she rolled to her knees and powered up to her feet. She prepared to charge Dante again when the sound of running feet made her turn. She stopped and stared. The tears came.

"Nobody move." Casey's partner, Mike, a gun in one hand, a powerful light in the other, roared. She wasn't sure she'd ever been so relieved to see a cop.

"Fuck you!" Dante screamed. "Fuck all of you."

"Shut up." Mike turned his light on Dante, whose face was crimson with fury. No trace of the handsome media darling now. The real Dante had finally revealed his face. Ugly on the inside. Ugly on the outside.

She stepped over to where Casey lay curled in a fetal position on the ground. "She's hurt." She dropped next to her. She wasn't moving. "We need help now."

Mike was busy cuffing Dante and shouting directions to the uniformed officers that had run in with him. She heard something about emergency services. She leaned down and touched her cheek to Casey's. "Hang on," she whispered. "Don't leave me." She feared they wouldn't get here quick enough.

"They're on the way," Mike told her as he kneeled beside her. She sat up as he took handcuff keys from his pocket and released her hands. The gentleness he displayed didn't track with the man she'd met before.

"Thank you."

"We'll need to talk."

"I know."

"Stay with her." He nodded to Casey. "She's a good kid."

She touched Casey's cool face. "She is." Tula pulled her shirt over her head and used it to put pressure on the bleeding knife wound. She didn't care that she sat wearing only a sports bra in the darkness in the middle of a cemetery surrounded by a dozen police officers. Casey needed her, and that's all that mattered. Leaning close, she whispered next to Casey's ear. "Don't you dare die on me. Don't you dare."

❖

Angel didn't move when Tula launched at the killer. She'd done everything she could, and now it all rested with the two women. Tula and Casey. At first, she thought it was over and she'd been wrong. Story of her life and her death. While Tula managed to knock the woman down and out, the man pulled a wicked-looking knife. He used it to severely wound Casey. Possibly fatally wound her. She'd been powerless to do anything to stop him.

The sirens announced the arrival of help, and tears streamed down her face. Blue had been right. She'd pushed through, and it made a difference. Her burst of energy earlier helped Casey see this place, and that's all that was needed to bring her here. Joining hands with Tula, and tapping in to the very last reserves of her power, had given Tula the confidence to surge forward and fight for her life. All of it kept the killer and his oh-so-helpful sister off guard until help arrived. Even the unbelieving partner suspended his disbelief long enough to give it the old college try. All the pieces of the puzzle came together at the right place and time.

Now, that same partner handcuffed a writhing Dante, who screamed like a madman. No, that wasn't quite right. Not like a madman. He *was* a madman. The screams of "do you know who I am" were universally ignored, which made her smile. How the arrogant fell. Two uniformed officers grabbed him and dragged him to a waiting patrol car. The click of the back seat door closing was a sweet, sweet sound. She closed her eyes and savored it for just a moment.

She smiled when another officer checked on the unmoving Diane and, apparently satisfied she wasn't dead, rolled her over and put handcuffs on her as well. Only then did she groan, though she remained on the ground. The collision between her head and the headstone had been a hard one, and she'd have one hell of headache. A well-deserved headache. Karma in its most basic form.

Tula remained at Casey's side. She held her shirt against the knife wound, her bare shoulders and midsection pale in the darkness illuminated by the lights of the milling officers. She couldn't make out Tula's low, urgent words. Had she faded too far from this world to hear them? It didn't really matter, for she didn't need to. To watch her try to save the life of someone she cared for took her back to another night and another bloody wound.

Angel grabbed him as his knees buckled and he fell to the stone floor. Blood poured from the deep, accurate strike. She screamed as she held him. "No."

Blue looked into her eyes, his unspoken question reflected there. She rested her forehead against his for just a moment.

"I'm sorry. I thought you were Walter."

She tore her underskirt and wadded the fabric to press against the wound she'd created. The blood turned it crimson in her hands. Fast. Too fast.

"He hurt her," Blue whispered. "Again. I'm sorry. I tried to make him stop."

Her tears fell onto his hair. "He almost killed her, and I wanted to kill him. You looked just like him from behind. Oh, my God, I'm sorry."

Not totally true. If her vision hadn't been clouded by rage, she'd have noticed the subtle differences between Bertwald—Blue, as she liked to call him—and Walter, his older and always violent brother. They were nothing alike beyond their light hair and blue eyes. One was gentle, kind, and smart. The other, power-hungry and quick-tempered. It was the latter she'd come to hurt. To kill.

Instead, as he bled out in her arms, she held the one she'd loved since laying eyes on him when she was twelve years old. She'd killed all right. The wrong man.

As he took a final breath, she screamed again. The sound of feet running down the corridor pushed her to action. Once more she grasped the blade she'd intended to use on Walter and plunged it deep into her own flesh.

"Are you ready to let it go?"

She smiled, even though what had happened around her didn't warrant one. No. Her smile came from a different place. An understanding place. "I *am* sorry, you know."

"I've always known that."

"If I could take it back, I would. Not just what I did to you but what I wanted to do to Walter."

"Now you see it."

She nodded, her gaze still on Casey and Tula, although medical help had arrived, and Casey was being readied to leave by ambulance. Tula stayed close even as the EMTs pushed her back. Both were going to be all right. Angel's job was done.

"Yes."

"It's time to go home now."

"She's going to be okay."

"She is. You saved her and countless other lives."

"Redemption."

"Forgiveness."

Angel stood and stretched out her hand, the touch of his filling her with peace and joy. All this time, he'd been by her side and yet far away, touch denied her until the end. She'd never questioned the loss, believing it to be the price for her act of vengeance. The loneliness had been endless, broken only by the moments of interaction with those she'd been left behind to help, like Tula, and the brief conversations with Blue. At least she'd had that.

At first, she'd been lost and confused. Her notion of what the afterlife would be like didn't match what had occurred. Instead of hell, she'd been bound to the earth she'd tried so hard to leave. Eventually, she'd come to understand that her destiny existed with the living, even if she couldn't join them. A shot at redemption. She didn't know why and often wanted to give up, to let the devil take her soul. She believed she deserved it.

Each time it happened, when an innocent needed help, Blue would appear. As in life, he encouraged and supported her. He gave of his love freely and unconditionally. He should have hated her for what she'd taken from him, condemned her to the hell she'd earned. That he didn't often filled her with shame for allowing emotion to drive her into such an evil act. She'd loved him so much but couldn't be with him, and that's what had ended it all on that dark night. She'd spent centuries trying to make up for what she'd done. Year after year. Century after century.

Tula had been her last, a beautiful child with goodness, light, and magic in her soul. She'd been the most special one, and saving her had always felt different. More important. Maybe that's why she'd worried so much about failing. She turned and looked at Blue, and it hit her. She couldn't be responsible for losing one as special as Blue.

His touch told her she'd done enough. "I have to say good-bye."

He nodded and let go of her hand. For a second, she faltered, stretched her fingers out toward him. "Go. I'll be right here when you're ready."

"You promise?"

"Have I ever lied to you?"

She shook her head and turned back toward Tula. She walked

closer to the cluster of emergency personnel. "Mona Lisa." She wasn't sure enough of her remained to be able to reach through the veil.

Tula turned slowly and nodded. "Angel. I knew you were here."

It took great concentration to stay. "I did what I could."

"What are you?"

"Your friend."

"You're more than that."

"It doesn't matter what I am. You're safe now, and I have to go."

"Will I see you again?"

She shook her head. "Be well, Mona Lisa. Live life. Love well. Be happy. She will make you happy."

Blue came once more to her side and took her hand. The peace she'd never thought would come to her washed through her, golden and warm. She tightened her hand on Blue's as she turned her gaze to the night sky and the stars that beckoned.

CHAPTER THIRTY-FOUR

"Who were you talking to?" Casey might be half out of it with searing pain in her side making her gasp for breath, but she could swear that Tula had stood next to where she lay on the ground having a conversation with no one. By the time the EMTs had Casey loaded and headed toward the ambulance, Tula had gone quiet, though her gaze drifted out into the night as if watching someone walk away.

Tula took her hand and moved with her as the emergency personnel rolled her into the ambulance. "I'll try to explain later."

"I didn't see anybody. Another vision?" Seemed unlikely. She'd appeared to be wide awake and aware of everything, including Mike and his timely appearance. She owed him an apology for doubting him, even if she didn't say it out loud.

The touch of Tula's hand brushing the hair off her face soothed her. That and whatever the EMTs had put in that IV. The searing pain that made blackness come in and out eased enough to keep her alert. Or, if not alert, at least aware of what was happening around her. It pissed her off that she'd allowed Dante to injure her. She was better than that. At least Tula appeared to be unhurt, and really, that's what mattered.

Tula kissed her forehead. "Later. Right now, best thing for you is to rest and let these fine folks take care of you."

"Did I hear Mike's voice?" She could swear she'd heard him just outside the ambulance. She wanted to yell at him to get back out there and make sure Diane and Dante were locked up in handcuffs and shackles, give them no chance to get away.

"Yeah. You heard me." Mike's face appeared in her field of vision.

"Dante and Diane…"

He put a hand on her arm. "Relax. I got this. Both of them are on their way to a jail cell. Well, Dante is getting his butt thrown in one as we speak. The sister took a pretty good smack to the head, so she'll be locked to a hospital bed for at least a few hours."

"Watch her." She had visions of Diane talking her way out of the hospital. That couldn't happen.

"I got this," he said again.

She met his eyes. "You came."

He tilted his head to the side. "I took a shot on you having good intel."

"You believed me."

His words got gruff. "Yeah, yeah. I believed you. I mean, you're not always wrong." He smiled.

Yeah, she owed him an apology. Later. "You got him." Relief let her relax as the drugs administered by the EMTs did their job. She was feeling pretty good all of a sudden.

"I got the fucker and his sister. Talk about a dangerous, freaky family."

"I left you a lot more on your desk." She didn't know if he'd even been to the office since she'd dropped off the paperwork for him to see.

"I came straight here after your call. I'll follow up on it when I get in. Don't worry about it. We'll have these two locked down tight, and by the time we get their asses in court, they'll be wishing they'd never laid eyes on Moses Lake."

"Good."

"I'll take care of this. You go get healed up." He stepped back outside the ambulance, one hand on the door. Outside, the flash of colored lights cut the darkness.

"Mike."

"Yeah."

"Thank you."

He grumbled something as he turned and walked back into the mass of officers and arriving crime-scene techs. Casey let her eyes drift shut. Damn, that stuff they gave her was good.

"I'm riding with her," Tula declared.

She liked the sound of Tula's voice when she was assertive.

Nobody argued, and Casey relaxed into the drugs and the company, drifting into sleep…or something like it. The next time she opened her eyes, she lay in a hospital bed, the room lights low. She blinked to focus and then turned her head. Tula was sound asleep in a chair next to her bed. A blanket had been placed over her. She could get used to such a sight. Not waking up in a hospital, exactly, but waking up to see Tula. Yeah, she could get used to that.

"About time you opened your eyes, slacker." Stan stood at the end of her bed.

"Oh, so you're my doc now?" God, it was good to see him.

"Hell, no. I got you somebody even better than me." He smiled, and she could see the relief in his face. Her brother had been worried.

"I'm okay?" She was almost afraid to ask.

He nodded and stuck his hands into the pockets of his white coat. "You will be. You're going to be out of commission for a while, so better make peace with that fact in a hurry. You also better gear up, because Mama and Abuelita are going to be hovering around you like a swarm of bees."

Any other time that threat might fill her with fear. At the moment, it sounded wonderful. "I can take it."

He smiled. "You can. And, for the record, thanks for not getting killed."

❖

Tula walked out to the patio and handed Casey a glass of iced tea. The last three weeks had been busy, a whirlwind of activity that blew her quiet life in Moses Lake all to hell. Everyone now knew the story of little Mona Lisa and her escape from her controlling and abusive parents. The child-turned-woman who could paint the faces of those who were either murdered or marked for murder. That her work helped save some, including the woman in her last painting, made the story even better, for those who wanted to report on it anyway. She wanted to hide.

News crews swarmed for the first week after the arrests of Dante and Diane. For Diane, the hospital stay was short, and she currently sat in a jail cell like her brother. Dante had turned into the same big news he used to love to report on. He almost glowed with the attention. Throw in a sister who aided and abetted, and the networks were downright giddy with the ratings. Sickening and frightening. Law enforcement were still untangling his crimes all over the country and how Diane had helped him from time to time. His crimes had been consistent. Hers, off and on. Not that it mattered a great deal, given both of them would be in prison for life. She hoped they suffered.

Then there were her mother and father. Just as Matthew predicted, they'd made a flying trip out West as soon as they got the word about her location. Then came the pleading, the apologies, the "I always loved you" declarations. Add to those the come-back-where-you-belong pleas and their promises of a safe and beautiful life. How she'd craved their love as a child, to feel wanted and cherished, safe and protected. She'd prayed for it all, and none of it had happened.

Her life was a different story these days. Mona Lisa had died the moment she boarded a train traveling west. She wasn't that person anymore, if she ever really had been. Couldn't be now even if she wanted to be. She'd changed in ways that went completely to her soul, and most important, she liked Tula Crane. It's who she was.

With Casey at her side, she faced down the parents with no tense confrontation or harsh words. Just truth. She'd spent twenty years afraid of them, terrorized by the idea that they'd find her and drag her back to New York, incarcerate her once again in that studio. She had wasted so many years on useless fear. The reality came to her as she watched them walk up the brick path leading to her front door. In the years since she'd run, they'd grown old, and the ugliness in their souls showed on their pale, lined faces. They were flawed human beings who never should have been allowed to have children. Though they didn't have the same brand of evil as Dante and Diane, they were as accountable for their terrible actions as if their crimes were the same. It all boiled down to two points. She'd survived them and would continue to live her life without them in it. All that had been and continued to be hers would be returned to her: her paintings, her royalties, her sales. With Matthew's help, she would make it so.

People liked to preach forgiveness and give what they considered to be good counsel. They encouraged her to keep the two of them in her life because, after all, they were her parents. Each time she heard their preaching, she touched her head and thought about that girl hurt and dying on the cold studio floor. Then the memory brought a small smile, for she understood now how Angel came to be part of her world. She had survived that head injury only because of her guardian angel. She could forgive her parents for being bad people, but she wouldn't forget what they'd done to her or decide that she must reconcile with them. Everyone was responsible for their own actions and the consequences that came with them. They were gone, and if she ever had to see them again, it would most likely be from behind a counsel table in a courtroom. Worked for her.

"Don't dwell." Casey watched her intently. She had a way of discerning those times when Tula got snagged by disturbing thoughts. Maybe the magic unleashed by her abuelita and that shared by Angel in those few minutes when she'd appeared to Casey had made her psychic abilities manifest themselves. Casey had been special from the beginning. Now, she was even more special, and Tula liked it. A lot.

"I'm not." Not technically a lie. She wasn't dwelling, exactly. She'd call it more thinking things through. Sounded good anyway.

"Liar. Liar." Casey smiled, taking the edge off her words. "And, yes, you're dwelling on your parents. Don't let them get in your head. You're free from them and from ever having to hide again. They're gone, and we're here together on this beautiful morning. I mean, what more could we ask for?"

"New neighbors."

Casey laughed and then groaned, holding her still-healing side. "Stop."

"Too soon?"

"God, I love you."

Tula turned and stared. "Really?"

Casey grew serious. "If someone had told me that a woman would barge into a murder case, prove to me that paranormal forces were in action, and then make me fall in love with her inside of a month, I'd have personally escorted them to Eastern State Hospital. Yet here we are."

Tula kneeled beside her chair, took Casey's hand, and held it to her cheek. "Here we are." She kissed her.

About the Author

Sheri Lewis Wohl lives in NE Washington State, where she's surrounded by mountains, rivers, and forests. It's a perfect backdrop for her stories of danger, romance, and all things paranormal. When not writing, Sheri enjoys cycling, running, and training and working with her German shepherds, Zoey and Deuce.

Books Available From Bold Strokes Books

The Artist by Sheri Lewis Wohl. Detective Casey Wilson and reclusive artist Tula Crane are drawn together in a web of passion, intrigue, and art that might just hold the key to stopping a killer. (978-1-63679-150-0)

Cherry on Top by Georgia Beers. A chance meeting leaves Cherry and Ellis longing for a different life, but when Ellis's search for truth crashes into Cherry's insta-filter world, do they have any hope at all of a happily ever after? (978-1-63679-158-6)

Love and Other Rare Birds by Angie Williams. Ornithologist Dr. Jamie Martin and park ranger Rowan Fleming are searching the Alaskan wilderness for a bird thought to be extinct, and they're about to discover opposites really do attract. (978-1-63679-108-1)

Parallel Paradise by Mayapee Chowdhury. When their love affair is put to the test by the homophobia of their family, community, and culture, Bindi and Rimli will need to fight for a chance at love. (978-1-63679-203-3)

Perfectly Matched by Toni Logan. A beautiful Cupid named Hannah, a runaway arrow, and just seventy-two hours to fix a mishap that could be the best mistake she has ever made. (978-1-63679-120-3)

Slow Burn by Missouri Vaun. A wounded wildland firefighter from California and a struggling artist find solace and love in a small southern town. (978-1-63679-098-5)

The Inconvenient Heiress by Jane Walsh. An unlikely heiress and a spinster evade the Marriage Mart only to discover true love together. (978-1-63679-173-9)

Closed-Door Policy by Erin Zak. Going back to college is never easy, but Caroline Stevens is prepared to work hard and change her life for the better. What she's not prepared for is Dr. Atlanta Morris, her gorgeous new professor. (978-1-63679-181-4)

Homeworld by Gun Brooke. Headed by Captain Holly Crowe, the spaceship Velocity's crew journeys toward their alien ancestors' homeworld, and what they find is completely unexpected—and they're not safe. (978-1-63679-177-7)

Outland by Kristin Keppler & Allisa Bahney. Danielle Clark and Katelyn Turner can't seem to stay away from one another even as the war for the wastelands tests their loyalty to each other and to their people. (978-1-63679-154-8)

Royal Exposé by Jenny Frame. When they're grouped together for a class assignment, Poppy's enthusiasm for life and love may just save Casey's soul, but will she ever forgive Casey for using her to expose royal secrets? (978-1-63679-165-4)

Secret Sanctuary by Nance Sparks. US Deputy Marshal Alex Trenton specializes in protecting those awaiting trial, but when danger threatens the woman she's falling for, Alex is in for the fight of her life. (978-1-63679-148-7)

Stranded Hearts by Kris Bryant, Amanda Radley & Emily Smith. In these novellas from award-winning authors, fate intervenes on behalf of love when characters are unexpectedly stuck together. With too much time and an irresistible attraction, anything could happen. (978-1-63679-182-1)

The Last Lavender Sister by Melissa Brayden. Aster Lavender sells her gourmet doughnuts and keeps a low profile; she never plans on the town's temporary veterinarian swooping in and making her feel like anything but a wallflower. (978-1-63679-130-2)

The Probability of Love by Dena Blake. As Blair and Rachel keep ending up in the same place despite the odds, can a one-night stand turn into forever? Or will the bet Blair never intended to make ruin their happily ever after? (978-1-63679-188-3)

Worth a Fortune by Sam Ledel. After placing a want ad for a personal secretary, a New York heiress is surprised when the woman who got away is the one interested in the position. (978-1-63679-175-3)